Under Two Flags

A Novel of World War I

Janis Robinson Daly

Black Rose Writing | Texas

©2026 by Janis Robinson Daly
All rights reserved. No part of this book may be reproduced, stored in a retrieval system or transmitted in any form or by any means without the prior written permission of the publishers, except by a reviewer who may quote brief passages in a review to be printed in a newspaper, magazine or journal.

The author grants the final approval for this literary material.

First printing

This is a work of fiction inspired by real events, people, and places. While the story draws from the memoir, *With Old Glory in Berlin*, which presented personal experiences of Josephine Therese Marzynski, it is a fictionalized account. Some names, characters, events, and locations have been changed or reimagined for dramatic purposes. Dialogue and scenes have been created or altered to enhance the narrative.
No part of this book may be used or reproduced in any manner for the purpose of training artificial intelligence technologies or systems.

ISBN: 978-1-68513-732-8
LIBRARY OF CONGRESS CONTROL NUMBER:
PUBLISHED BY BLACK ROSE WRITING
www.blackrosewriting.com

Printed in the United States of America
Suggested Retail Price (SRP) $20.95

Under Two Flags is printed in Sabon LT Std

*As a planet-friendly publisher, Black Rose Writing does its best to eliminate unnecessary waste to reduce paper usage and energy costs, while never compromising the reading experience. As a result, the final word count vs. page count may not meet common expectations.

Cover design by Jess Marony, AuthorBytes
Cover photograph from Josephine Marzynski's 1917 passport photo

For my grandfather, Eliot Harlow Robinson, Sr.
(1884-1942)

A lawyer, artist, composer, playwright, architect, choir leader, tennis player, golfer, swimmer, yachtsman, ball player, editor, novelist.

And ghostwriter of Josephine Therese Marzynski's memoir, *With Old Glory in Berlin* (Page Publishing, 1918).

PRAISE FOR
UNDER TWO FLAGS

"*Under Two Flags* brings a fresh angle to the well-trodden world of biographical war fiction, telling the intriguing true story of a young woman struggling to co-exist between two nations at war. Aspiring opera singer Josephine leaves her family behind in Boston to study music at a Berlin conservatory...but World War I is raging, and as tensions rise between her host nation and her homeland, she realizes she may be forced to choose between career and survival. Janis Robinson Daly sensitively explores war, patriotism, and ambition in this well-researched tale!"
–Kate Quinn, *New York Times* and *USA Today* bestselling author of *The Alice Network*

"Janis Robinson Daly has done it again with *Under Two Flags*–created an unforgettable story with a fascinating and courageous female character center stage. I loved discovering the worlds of WWI and opera through the wonderful historical detail. The lovely prose brought me to the front row for every note. Brava, Janis!"
–Martha Hall Kelly, New York Times bestselling author of *The Martha's Vineyard Beach and Book Club* and *The Lilac Girls*

"With impeccable research and lyrical prose, Janis Daly illuminates the extraordinary true story of a young Boston woman who travels to Berlin in 1916 to study opera, and chooses courage over comfort when the world erupts in war. *Under Two Flags* is a richly detailed, emotionally resonant, and beautifully told historical fiction novel. Inspired by a memoir ghostwritten by Daly's own grandfather, this moving novel transports readers to wartime Berlin, where a gifted young American musician must navigate suspicion, sacrifice, and the transformative power of music. Both a celebration of women's resilience and a poignant meditation on belonging, Daly's story shines from the first note to the last."
–Eliza Knight, USA Today bestselling author of *Confessions of a Grammar Queen*

"A young Jewish woman with ambition and resolve leaves Boston to study opera in Berlin in 1916 in Janis Robinson Daly's novel, *Under Two Flags*. Although she's not ignorant of the war, Josephine Marzynski is determined to "never stop trying to grab my dreams and make them happen." However, her idealism and candor are soon challenged, and Josephine must adjust to life in a city defined by suspicion, duplicity, and fear. A fascinating, immersive work of historical fiction with tension that crackles from page one and a protagonist whose courage, passion, and independence of spirit shine throughout, *Under Two Flags* is a beautifully researched and written reminder of some of the less obvious costs of war and a love letter to music. I loved it.
–Penny Haw, author of *The Invincible Miss Cust and Follow Me to Africa*

"What would compel a Jewish girl from Boston to travel to Berlin in 1916 to study opera? What would stop her? In this fictional retelling of the little-known story of Josephine Marzynski's epic quest for fame, echoes of history mix with intrigue, deception, betrayal, passion, and resilience in this captivating novel from award-winning author Janis Robinson Daly."
–Ashley E. Sweeney, author of *The Irish Girl*

"Perfectly captures a young woman's drive for pursuing music."
–Jessica Bloch-Moisand, Voice Faculty, Expanded Education at New England Conservatory and Interim Artistic Director Mass Opera '24-'25

"As a mezzo soprano's voice can lift a libretto to transcendent heights, Daly, with her beautiful prose, impeccable research, and multi-layered characters, transforms the reader. A story of resilience, identity, and the redemptive power of music draws you into the darkest hours of WWI yet makes you yearn for a seat at the opera."
–Linda Rosen, author of *Abandoning the Script*

"In the style of Ariel Lawhon's *The Frozen River*, Janis Robinson Daly transforms a little-known firsthand account into a gripping tale of courage, survival, and the resilience of a young woman trapped in Berlin during World War I."
–Cam Torrens, bestselling author of the *Tyler Zahn* mystery/suspense novels

Under Two Flags
A Novel of World War I

TABLE OF CONTENTS

OVERTURE

ACT I

Scene I	*Achtung! Spionen Gefahr* (Attention! Beware Of Spies)
Scene II	Entering the Heart of Prussia
Scene III	Looking Backwards
Scene IV	Grabbing a Dream
Scene V	Going Over
Scene VI	First Impressions
Scene VII	An Iron Shield is Raised
Scene VIII	The City of Berlin
Scene IX	The People of Berlin
Scene X	*Klindworth-Scharwenka Konservatorium der Musik*
Scene XI	Ready for New Beginnings
Scene XII	Two Friends, One Foe.
Scene XIII	Rations
Scene XIV	Other Necessities Dwindle
Scene XV	A Question, An Answer.
Scene XVI	Pomp and Propaganda
Scene XVII	Rumors, Rumblings, and Reality
Scene XVIII	Closing the Door
Scene XIX	Stand by Me
Scene XX	A Proclamation: War

INTERMISSION

ACT II

Scene I	Friends and Enemies
Scene II	Fourth of July with the Red, White, and Black
Scene III	Travel within Borders
Scene IV	Frivolity and Fight

Scene V	The Fate of the Understudy
Scene VI	Darkening Shadows
Scene VII	She Who Guards Her Tongue
Scene VIII	Passports, Papers, and Parcels
Scene IX	Swan Song
Scene X	One Goal, Five Fingers.
Scene XI	Lost in Scandinavia
Scene XII	Despair and Delay
Scene XIII	Use Your Words
Scene XIV	Westward Bound
Scene XV	Sweet Land of Liberty

FINALE

AUTHOR'S NOTES

ACKNOWLEDGMENTS

READER DISCUSSION QUESTIONS

OVERTURE

January 1918
Boston, Massachusetts

I will use my words to recast perceptions. By doing so, a deep sense of responsibility falls upon my twenty-year-old shoulders. Many have said my experience of living in Berlin for thirteen months possesses the power to influence and impart a renewed support of sending American troops across the sea. My story will help Americans understand the motivations of an aggressor nation and the silent cries of its passive civilians. Their unspoken words plead to end the battles which have claimed so many. Ypres and Verdun. The Somme. Jutland. Hunger. Sacrifice. Despair.

I look up from my handwritten scrawl, which now covers eight sheets. Muted glows from bulbs under green glass shades of brass banker's lamps light every long, oak table. Massive bookcases surround me in the reading room of the Boston Public Library. History, knowledge, and opinions invite visitors to pull a reference book from a shelf and settle into a sturdy wooden chair. Fingers of every shape, size, and color open these books. Turning the pages gives readers opportunities for quiet contemplation.

As I shuffle my sheets and tap them into an orderly stack, a man in a neat, gray-checked wool overcoat and a gray felt fedora stops at my table. He tugs, one finger at a time, at his black kid leather gloves.

"Miss Marzynski?" he asks in a register accustomed to making hushed inquiries within the walls of a library.

I nod, stand, and extend my hand. "Yes. You must be Mr. Robinson?"

He takes my hand, a glint dancing in his brown eyes behind wire-rimmed spectacles, and gestures to the exit. "Eliot Robinson, with Page Publishing. Will you join me across the street at the Copley Plaza? I've reserved a table for the afternoon in their café. The lunch crowd will have cleared. We can talk freely. The manager has agreed to allow you to dine with me, despite their men-only rule. He's promised to keep the coffee hot and our cups filled."

When I left Norway five weeks ago, I decided I would tell my extraordinary tale and let others form their own conclusions. My proximity to the conflict armed me with invaluable insights and rare glimpses into the psyche of a nation at war. Like a boxer who predicts the next blow by watching his opponent's eyes rather than his fists, so too must nations understand the minds of their enemies to stand a chance of victory.

My firsthand account, given through the lens of Berliners, will offer a light through the darkness. Mr. Robinson will help write my memoir as an American woman studying opera in Berlin, November 1916 to December 1917. By doing so, we will arm Americans with the power of knowledge to face the pivotal days ahead.

"Thank you, Mr. Robinson. But please, call me Josephine."

ACT I

SCENE I

Achtung! Spionen Gefahr
(Attention! Beware Of Spies)

October 1916
Warnemünde, Germany

Tacked to a pier piling, a sign screamed in black capital letters: ACHTUNG! SPIONEN GEFAHR. At this point in my journey, after speaking German nonstop with Jack Meyers, my cousin and travel chaperone, I could decipher *Spionen* (spies) *Gefahr* (beware). Germany greeted us with suspicion, its teeth bared, poised to bite.

Jack and I staggered off the small boat at Warnemünde, Germany, the port city and entry point for those disembarking from Gjedser Odde, Denmark. My boots hit the splintered planks of the wharf. A tide of bodies from the boat swallowed us into a swarm. Before we could board the train to Berlin, we needed to pass through Germany's entrance inspection. Pale faces tightened with tension as we shuffled forward. A suffocating wave of air buzzed with anxious whispers. Ahead, a barnlike building loomed, reminiscent of an American frontier fort, its wooden beams rough-hewn and imposing. This time and place, however, were no more like an outpost on the Oregon Trail than the ruins of ancient Rome.

Once inside, our shoulders bunched against one another in the waiting room. Sweat and unease mingled in the thick air. Soldiers in their feldgrau uniforms moved about with precision. The high collars of their tunics aligned with a straight column of eight buttons down the front. Bayoneted rifles swung from their hips. Their presence seemed gray and foreboding, like their uniforms, while their unblinking eyes scanned our crowd. My stomach churned, a mixture of the remnants of seasickness and fear. Uncertainty gnawed at me, each moment stretching into an eternity. As we waited, the room seemed to shrink, as if the building itself sought to crush us before we set foot on German soil. We stood there, prisoners of our own dread of what awaited us.

A door creaked open. A single sentry motioned us into a larger room, though no more welcoming than the last. I forced my legs to move. My white-knuckled fingers gripped the handles of my luggage. My German emigrant mother had clutched the same weathered suitcase tight to her chest. Twenty-four years later, in the suitcase I carried a letter addressed to her dearest childhood friends in Berlin, Helga Hochberg and Klaus Müller, now Herr and Frau Müller, and harmless sheet music, nestled between my clothing and toiletries.

Inside, an officer sat behind an elevated desk. His expression told me nothing. Over his left shoulder, the German flag declared its place in the world—solid horizontal black and red bars bracketing a middle one of white. Black like the darkest night. Red like the bloodiest battlefield. White like snow, masking the horror of icy deaths.

Against the far wall, a score of soldiers stood rigid. Four lines of five across. Their chests puffed out despite the thinness of their frames. Middle-aged and frail, yes—but still dangerous order-followers of the Prussian army. Examine and search. Their eyes fell upon us, calculating chances to question and detain. Tucked safely in my bag, my passport revealed my truth. I was an

American, a Jewish girl of German and Polish descent. My reason for entering Germany was innocent. Yet, any of those soldiers might decide otherwise as posters instructed them, *Spionen gefahr*.

I wondered and worried, however, if to an untrained eye, would sheet music appear as encrypted messages? My pulse quickened. If pressed, could I convince the inspectors that I, a young woman from Boston, had traveled to Germany to study at the *Klindworth-Scharwenka Konservatorium der Musik*? That I left the security of an American home. That a passion embedded in my soul moved me to risk traveling across a treacherous sea. That I wanted to learn from the best in the world. Could I stand before them and admit the best were German?

A soldier shifted his gaze, his eyes narrowing ever so slightly. "*Öffnen, öffnen*," the sentry at the doorway said, his voice sharp as the crack of a whip. At his command, the soldiers paired off with each of us. The one with the narrow, slitted eyes moved toward me. Stubby and thick-necked, he kicked my valise, sending it sprawling onto the floor. With the toe of his black, polished boot, he tapped at the clasps.

"*Öffnen.*" The command was clear. Open my bag for inspection. Hands shaking, I fumbled to flip up the top, revealing the neat piles I had repacked before leaving the boat. He nudged them with his toe as if they were dead leaves, raked into piles and ready for burning. I felt a bristle sliding up my back when he sunk his grubby hands into my personal articles. A low chuckle rumbled from his throat as he picked up my extra brassiere. Flames of embarrassment surged up my neck and into my cheeks. He punched a fist into one of the lace-trimmed cups. "*Große Brüste*," he said with a smirk. Crude and cruel laughter burst from the other soldiers next to us. Little did they know I was fluent in German, enough to understand his vulgar reference to my chest size. Yet, I would not offer any signs of discomfort for his satisfaction. Instead, I cleared my throat with the softest *ahem*. And winked at him.

At the sound of the guffaws, Jack glanced over at the commotion to catch sight of my brassiere dangling from the soldier's hand. As a student of voice, I watched lips closely. I had no difficulty interpreting his lips' movement to form the words, "Behave yourself, Josephine."

I shook my head and mouthed, "I'm a good girl." Only a wink. A statement that I could be their ally, not their enemy.

The man holding my brassiere, old enough to be my father, if Papa were still alive, dropped it back to the top of the pile. He slammed the lid down and marked the outside of the blue leather with a quick, careless slash of white chalk. The sentry ushered the crowd toward two doors at the back of the room, gesturing for the soldiers to separate us. Men to the right. Women to the left. A matron, wearing the same woolen tunic jacket as the soldiers but over a skirt, spoke to our group of six women. Her broken English carried a calming tone. "Inside."

What else could she look through? Bear claws and eagle talons had already assaulted every piece of luggage. With a nod toward us, women ranging in ages from eighteen (myself) to the late forties, the matron pointed to the buttons, belts, hooks and eyes which kept our clothing secure against our bodies.

"*Ausziehen*. All off."

"Ohhh…" The woman next to me grabbed my forearm. I turned to her. Mrs. Richter, whom I had dined with on several occasions during our voyage, wore a deep purple velvet suit. With a semi-fitted coat fastened with matching buttons and loops, it flared above her knees. She looked like a wizened plum.

"Josephine, you don't think she expects us to remove our clothing? Here, in front of everyone?" she said.

"Mrs. Richter, I believe that is precisely what she means. And I think we had best do what she asks with haste."

I shrugged out of my brown tweed suit jacket and cream silk blouse. Unbuttoning my A-line skirt, I let it drop to pool on the floor. No one noticed I tucked my skirt's broad, banded hem underneath the folds of the fabric. I rolled down my stockings to the tops of my boots. The cold air prickled my bare shins. I stood waiting in my slip, ready as the matron's first…inspection? Victim? Only time would tell.

She pulled my chestnut tresses loose from the neat low bun at my neck. Her fingers raked through the strands with jerks. She raised her arms to a parallel line with the floor. I mimicked her actions. Cold, rough fingers slid across every inch of my body. Her touch seemed to burn treads of humiliation into my skin until I thought I must look like a well-used tire, rolling its way to a junkyard.

As I reached for my skirt, she slapped my hand down. Next to her, the acrid odor of smelling salts rose above the rim of a small metal bucket. Without a word, she retrieved a rag from the depths of a briny liquid. She swiped the rag across my arms, lifted my slip, and proceeded over my back and torso. The cold liquid stung. Jack had warned me of this procedure, even though I knew no invisible ink adhered to my body. Regardless, the alcohol-soaked cloth erased a slice of my dignity. The matron, satisfied that my body held no secrets, moved on to Mrs. Richter.

I ran my fingers along the hem of my skirt. The stitching remained secure. My careful folding of the red, white, and blue silk into a thin strip had worked. Ignoring Jack's insistence that I leave it on the boat, I had sewn my American flag into the skirt's fold the night before we docked at Warnemünde.

"I don't consider it good form to wave a red cloth in a bull pasture," Jack had said. "The U. S. selling munitions to the allies has rankled the Germans. If you're to spend the next two years in Berlin, learn now that in their eyes, you'll always be a Yankee and a *spionen*."

He had turned my face toward him with a gentle press against my chin. "Please, Jo, do not prod this raging bull and give him any reason to question your stay in Germany. Keep a low profile, and stay out of trouble. Your father would have told you the same."

With his instructions guiding me, I entered Germany ready to face the naked truth with my eyes open and my country's symbol of freedom brushing against my ankles.

SCENE II

Entering the Heart of Prussia

October 1916
Berlin, Germany

"Look, Josephine! Berlin!"

Like any great city in modern times, a lighted skyline revealed the unmistakable sign of a sprawling metropolis. The train approached the mighty Anhalter Bahnhof station, exposing Berlin's edges. Rigid silhouettes. Straight, monotonous lines. So different from New York and Boston, I thought, where buildings' heights and breadths varied as much as the populous who lived and worked inside them. As I stared ahead, the weight of the quiet, oppressive conformity of our final destination pressed upon us.

My cousin's bass voice punctured my introspective haze. I couldn't shake the edgy hesitation that had settled in since leaving Warnemünde. A winter chill had seeped through the train's walls. Outside, unseen threats mixed with the cloud cover's inky shadows. Tingles of the unknown skittered up and down my spine. If only I could have peered into the future, I might have understood the source of my unease. But a clairvoyant I am not. I could only feel it—a gnawing apprehension.

Too late for second-guessing. I had chosen to travel to an austere foreign land. A country at war. I patted my hat into position and looked through the window at the precipice before me.

"Jack," I said. "They don't darken the streets? London and Paris enforce total blackouts every night."

"No need. The Germans don't fear an attack. There's no danger in Berlin."

Jack's confidence and excitement tempered my anxious thoughts. The train's steel wheels screeched to an eventual stop. Jack seized his bags and rushed to the door. He appeared oblivious to his excess baggage—namely me. I hefted my valises, one in each hand, eager to meet the Müllers, my hosts in Berlin. I would disembark as a stranger into a strange land and into the home of strangers.

My unease disappeared the moment I heard a man's voice call out in German, "Jack! Jack! Over here."

It all happened in an instant. One moment, I stood alone on the station platform. The next, the owner of the voice grabbed my right hand and pumped it up and down as if searching for water from a deep well. Jack stepped in and made the formal introductions of Herr and Frau Müller, Klaus and Helga, to me, Fräulein Josephine Therese Marzynski, daughter of their childhood friend, Ricka Meyers.

A short, round man with gray hair, Herr Müller radiated good-natured warmth. Despite growing up in Germany, he looked every bit as if he had just stepped off a train at Boston's South Station at the end of a workday. His emerald eyes twinkled before he swiped at a hint of misty emotion with his handkerchief. It would not take long for me to learn that my host's heart held deep sympathy.

Beside him stood a woman, tall and sturdy, matching him in height. Purpose and kindness lined her face. Dark hair, with light streaks of silver, peeked out from under a neat wool hat. Her erect posture and wide smile spoke of capability and energy. She shared her husband's warmth but added a quiet strength of her own.

Frau Müller eyed me up and down, from my lace-up, dusty boots to my dark blue hat, trimmed with a cream braid around the crown and edge of a broad brim.

"Oh, my goodness. It's as if our dearest Ricka has returned to us." Frau Müller disregarded her husband's German sense of proprietary and drew me into an embrace as if pulling her friend close again. Taking a step back, she continued her analysis.

"Look at you. An absolute spitting image of your beautiful mother. Same rich chestnut hair and those beautiful blue eyes. Even your complexion is fair. Did she ever tell you how I wished my ruddy, pocked face was as smooth and radiant as hers? I tried her homemade face cream recipe countless times but never got the right combination of ingredients. My concoction formed into a solid lump or a soupy mess. Maybe you know the correct amounts?"

I knew exactly what she was referring to. Once a month, my mother sat at our kitchen table, her slender fingers kneading together one part beeswax, four parts almond oil, and three parts rosewater in a large ceramic mixing bowl. The thought triggered a pang of homesickness.

Herr Müller patted his wife's arm. "Plenty of time to talk recipes, Helga. You resemble your mother, Fräulein Marzynski, that's for sure. But so much taller than our friend, Ricka. She barely came to our shoulders. When she stood between Helga and me, she used to tilt back her head, toss her hair, and let loose laughing at the comedic trio we made. We looked like a 'W.' I used to say we were Ricka's *wachhabenders*—her sentries on either side of her. We will be your *wachabenders* too."

Within minutes of arriving, I had found a guardian in Herr Müller. As time passed, he would become much more.

"You must have gotten your height from your father, the Pole. Such a tragic loss for your mother, you, your sister, and brothers."

His hand squeezed mine in silent sympathy and looked over my shoulder. "Helga, do you think the bed you prepared will be long enough?"

Tired as I was, the absurd image of a child's crib flashed through my mind. His remark turned the moment light, bringing laughter to us all.

♪

Outside the taxicab window, a formation of German infantrymen paraded toward the station. Based on recent news stories, I assumed they were headed for the Western front, near the Somme River in France. By the next dawn, these men would find themselves six hundred miles away, lined up against barbed wire and laid down in muddy trenches. Mere replacements for the thousands upon thousands of casualties since that battle began three months ago in July.

Under harsh streetlights, their faces looked etched with dread. Mirrored expressions stared back at them from mothers, wives, and sweethearts, who filled the street's curbs. Many of the women wept with open abandon. Tears streaked their pale and worn faces. Their hands grabbed for one more touch, one more moment. Like a contagion, their sorrow hit me with unexpected force. My chest constricted as I thought of their fates. The rawness of it all—the farewell, the uncertainty—overwhelmed me. My eyes brimmed over, and I, too, cried for their despair. In that moment, I understood war wasn't a news story on a printed page but a brutal, immediate reality.

I imagined Frau Müller had seen similar sights to this during the past two years. Yet I expected one might never get used to the intimacy and distress of those scenes. Wrapping an arm around my shoulders, she said, "There, there, my dear." I felt her reach for my hand as a mother would take a child's as they crossed a busy intersection.

We traveled out of the city through an area that reminded me of Brookline, a gracious city next to Boston with manicured landscaping and dignified brick Tudor homes. Less than twenty-five minutes later, we arrived at a handsome stucco building on a broad street. Two young women in black dresses with white aprons and caps, servants I assumed, greeted us with smiles and curtsies at the front door.

"Anna, Greta," Frau Müller said. "Meet our young American friend, Fräulein Josephine Marzynski." The girls stared at me with curious eyes and immediately began chattering between themselves in hushed tones. This didn't help calm my nerves, but Frau Müller's casual remarks told me she trusted them. In my wearied state, they sounded and looked like chirping chickadees. I managed a quiet *"Danke"* as they reached for my bags.

Herr Müller led us into a high-ceilinged living room. I dropped onto a brocade settee. My eyelids drooped with my body. Yet the Müllers continued their excited chatter, bombarding me with questions about my family and life in America. Even Jack found it difficult to interject and steer Herr Müller toward a business discussion about the results of his trip to the States. Every few minutes, Herr Müller exclaimed, "Poor dear Josephine! She looks so tired."

And Frau Müller would counter, "Not at all, she looks splendid!" before resuming her questions.

A reprieve arose when Anna brought me a plate of *flammkuchen* and a cup of strong black tea. I devoured the crispy flatbread covered with cheese and onion bites. I found no chunks of ham scattered across the bread. Did the Müller household keep kosher, as my mother did? Or had the rumors of rationing meant ham had become scarce? I honestly didn't care. My hunger after a day of traveling consumed me.

It wasn't until close to midnight that the conversation wound down, and Anna showed me to my room. I sighed with relief to find a single bed, not a child's crib, and long enough to pour myself into fresh-scented, starched sheets. As I undressed, I noticed several small red spots on my torso. Alarmed that I might have brought an illness into the house, I called to Anna as she headed down the stairs to bring Frau Müller to my room. She calmed my worries but added with a grimace, "Oh, *liebling*, those nasty soldiers on the train pack *flohs* into every bag and pocket. They've bitten you."

A *floh* or flea, I learned, was what the English tommies called a "cootie."

Frau Müller instructed Anna to take my valises and the clothes I had shed to launder first thing in the morning. Her mention of the German soldiers startled my weary brain. "Thank you, Anna," I said. "But I can manage these few items myself in the sink." I took the skirt and blouse I had worn that day from her arms. I, not the German girl, would care for the skirt which hid the red, white, and blue within its bottom hem.

Although my body screamed to drift into a deep slumber, I sat on the edge of the bed and pulled out my quick stitches. As the hem opened, I withdrew my flag from its hiding place. Now, where to put it? The Müllers didn't worry me. They had sent for me, an American, to live under their roof and in their care. But what of Anna and Greta? As the many posters had told me, *Spionen Gefahr!* Could I trust these two young German women whom I had just met? Would a blatant display of American patriotism cause them to question my intent for visiting? I would tell Anna that she needn't bother with my bedsheets. I would attend to them on laundry day.

Smoothing the flag out flat, I slipped it inside the lace-trimmed pillowcase. I laid my head upon the pillow, knowing my sleeping breaths would whisper against a piece of my homeland. Yet, those breaths didn't come easily. My mind buzzed with all I had experienced today mixed with homesick thoughts. The nursery rhyme by Robert Louis Stevenson, which my mother still cooed to my brothers, David and Julian, quieted my mind.

...But every night I go abroad
Afar into the land of Nod.
All by myself, I have to go,
With none to tell me what to do...
And many frightening sights abroad...

What frightening sights might I see all by myself in the days and months ahead? Finally, my mind went dark on the night of October thirty-first, nineteen hundred sixteen. I now lived in Berlin.

SCENE III

Looking Backwards

In the pages that follow, I will not tell you my complete life story. But, since the threads of my past interweave with my time in Berlin, I shall explain why a young woman from Boston rested her head upon a hidden American flag in the middle of a nation engaged in war.

My roots lie in eastern Europe. Papa, Leopold Marzynski, emigrated from Poland to America as a young man in 1886, where he found work on the wharves of Boston. An observant man, he recognized the limitless demand for rope to tie up ships and rig the masts of the sailing vessels that plied Boston's busy harbor. Within seven years, he opened a cordage shop which served the many ships, received his naturalization papers to become a United States citizen, and met Ricka Meyers.

Mother did not emigrate to America as willingly as my father did. Her parents gave their unmarried eighteen-year-old daughter no choice. A father decided the fate of his family, especially wives and daughters. If he determined America offered a German Jew more economic opportunities and less anti-Semitism, then the Meyers would buy tickets, pack bags, and uproot their only daughter's life.

For my mother, emigration meant losses, not gains. I don't think she ever forgave my grandfather for what he forced her to leave behind—her older brother, Heinrich, and his young family, her closest friends Klaus Müller and Helga Hochberg, and studying voice at the *Klindworth-Scharwenka Konservatorium der Musik*.

By the time the Meyers left Germany in 1893, Heinrich had settled in the outskirts of Berlin with his wife and toddler son, Jack. Uncle Heinrich taught at a local school until tuberculosis stole him away in 1910. Upon hearing of Uncle Heinrich's passing, Klaus Müller offered to help the family. He would hire then seventeen-year-old Jack into a sales position at the growing pharmaceutical company where he had climbed the ladder to the upper reaches of management.

Inseparable from the age of five, Klaus Müller, Helga Hochberg, and Ricka Meyers had formed a kinship as strong as blood ties. The trio had shared school days and playtime, fears and dreams, until the day my mother trailed behind her parents onto a train headed toward the Baltic Sea and a new life ahead in Boston. As my mother told the story, my grandmother kept reminding her that she would make new friends in America. But my mother refused to accept that anyone could replace Klaus and Helga. When my sister Lillian and I chatted about our school friends, Mother would sit us down and ask ceaseless questions about them. She measured the depth of any friendship against the one she had with Klaus and Helga. She ended our chats with a sigh, sharing how much she missed her friends. "I envy them. Married now and joined forevermore as two. Perhaps if I had stayed, Helga and I would have vied for the role of Frau Müller. Maybe my leaving was for the best."

Those regrets and musings disappeared whenever she received a Berlin postmarked envelope. A radiant beam spread across her face as her eyes flew over the page. And again, with a second, third, fourth reading of news from the Müllers. Often, we would find her, letter in hand, filling the air with notes from Beethoven's "Ode to Joy." Her choice of that composition didn't surprise me. Rather, at a young age, I learned how music could speak. As I listened to her private hums, I thought of her exalted friendship and her dreams of studying music again someday.

With the same sense of loss of missing her friends, Mother also lamented her involuntary withdrawal from the *Konservatorium* at the directive of her father. With three years of study complete, her training as a lyric soprano gave her purpose. Germany's grand opera houses awaited Ricka Meyers to take the stage with her graceful and expressive voice. Her dark, chestnut hair flowed over her shoulders. With hands clasped at her waist and in a controlled manner, she projected the trills and leaps of sound out to the audience. A gift for them all.

Although my grandfather promised my mother could study her music in America, she never did. Pages of sheet music, sorted by composer and tied with baker's string, lay in the bottom of her dresser drawer like wrapped and hidden Hanukkah presents.

♪

By 1895, my father had taken the profits from his first cordage shop and opened a fur goods store. As word of his success grew, Leopold Marzynski caught the eye of young women and the attention of their fathers, eager to find a well-suited match for their daughters. Despite the matchmaking attempts of many Boston *shadchans* hired by other Jewish families, my parents met at Temple, fell in love, and married within six months. No tragic opera story for them. That would come later. They settled in the Meeting House Hill section of Dorchester, a desirable neighborhood of Boston. My siblings followed my birth in December 1897 in orderly succession. Lillian in 1900, David in 1906, and young Julian in 1910.

As the fur goods store prospered, Papa moved us to Roxbury, an area that city residents called a suburb with tree-lined streets, well-tended gardens, and lush lawns. The Marzynskis joined a growing population of Jews who looked to the future, leaving behind immigrant-dense Boston neighborhoods.

On warm summer nights, when daylight lingered after dinner, my father would pluck a leaf from the maple tree that shaded the front of our expansive three-bedroom home. He'd hold it to the sky and declare to us children, "See how this American leaf flutters in the wind? Yet, it's strong, defying the wind to float with freedom."

He spoke these words in English, affirming his assimilation. Inside our home, we spoke German for my mother's sake. Turning to the tree, he would run his hand up and down the rough grooves of the tawny bark. To us, he would say, "Always stand tall and proud like this tree. You too are rooted in this land. You won't ever forget you're a Jew or your heritage from Germany and Poland. But you are also Americans. You belong here, where you can live as a new Marzynski. Free to pursue a just life. Dare to dream."

He'd pause and point our gazes to follow the tree's branches reaching for the sky, even on days when dark storm clouds hung over us. "Claim those dreams and make them happen. You can do that in America."

When I started school and learned the Pledge of Allegiance, Papa had me teach my siblings how to face the flag at our doorway. I showed them how to place their right hands over their left breasts and recite the words: "I pledge allegiance to my Flag and to the Republic for which it stands; one nation indivisible, with liberty and justice for all." His baritone voice repeated each word with measured reflection, echoing down the street. Neighbors never complained about our nightly ritual. They, too, had emigrated to America and pledged their allegiance to a land of new beginnings.

Beyond the salute and lowering of the red, white, and blue each evening at dusk, he also made sure the Marzynskis celebrated American holidays with full gusto. A twenty-pound roasted turkey adorned the center of our table on Thanksgiving, complete with side dishes of stuffing, cranberries, and corn. We'd bow our heads and give thanks to the immigrants who had settled a new country, built upon the promise of religious freedom. On May thirtieth, Decoration Day, my mother would see us off to school with a reminder to offer a silent prayer when we walked past Mount Hope Cemetery and the graves of Union soldiers. We must remember those who had fought for the unity of our United States.

The grandest day of all—Fourth of July—rolled around with as much fanfare as a hora danced at Jewish weddings. Mother would dress David and Julian in short-sleeved sailor suits, inspecting every inch of the bright white cotton for telltale stains from a breakfast bowl of strawberries and blueberries. She'd smooth the navy-blue square, flap-style collars and adjust the black neckties into a loose knot. The white sailor's caps with navy trim didn't stay on their heads for long. David would wave his in the air. Julian, attempting to mimic his older brother, would inevitably drop his on the ground. Lillian and I wore matching white eyelet dresses with broad red sashes tied in perfect bows at our backs. Together, the Marzynskis would march the three blocks down Blue Hill Avenue from our home to the corner of Westview Street, where the annual parade ended and turned into Harambee Park.

How could I have known that 1912 would be the last Fourth we would spend with our father? I have committed to memory every precious moment of that day. Papa splurged on purchases from the street vendors. He kept six-year-old David occupied with a bag of popcorn. Lillian and I dug little wooden spoons into cups of flavored ice, mine lemon and Lillian's raspberry. An older Italian man with a pushcart had walked eight miles from the North End of Boston for the celebration and sure-fire sales of his icy treats. And for each of us, Papa presented an American flag, Old Glory stapled to a dowel. Our small fists curved around the wooden stick and waved it in smile-shaped arcs as the bands, veterans, and local politicians marched past the thunderous crowds. Mother tucked one flag onto the top of Julian's carriage. If we had streamers of red, white, and blue bunting for the carriage, we could have joined the parade, walking alongside the floats pushed and pulled by groups like the newly formed Boy Scouts.

On those days, my father's words, filled with instructions on how to live as a patriotic American, rang clear and true. But weeks after that glorious Fourth in 1912, a hidden malady seized him, sending him into the depths of dark madness. We'd find him sitting on the sofa, eyes wide and staring at nothing and everything. Often, his hands trembled, even at rest. Then he'd jerk with a twitch, which shuddered through his arm or neck. After the lowering of the flag, he'd mutter to himself, his words incoherent. Although once I swore I heard him say, "Stop following me. Find your own way home."

By the fall, after Papa's early morning departure for work, we'd often pass a store clerk on our way to school. I would pause long enough to hear him say to my mother, "He's not at the shop." We never knew where Papa went.

One day, Mother found him crumpled outside the house, weeping, with his jacket inside out. Untucked shirttails flapped behind him. She rushed to him, kneeled in the walkway, and stroked his damp forehead. "*Meine Sonne. Meine Liebling*," she whispered to the sun and moon of our family, her voice catching.

I stood frozen in the doorway, tears slipping down my cheeks as she purred the "Humming Chorus" from *Madama Butterfly*, her lullaby to call him back to her.

The doctor came. Then the men in white. They strapped Papa into a coat that crossed his arms over his chest and buckled tight behind his back. I stood by the flagpole and lowered our Stars and Stripes to half-mast. In my mind, I saw him pacing the padded rooms of the Boston State Hospital, raving nonsense in place of his proud speeches about liberty and freedom, fists flying instead of hands caressing maple bark, saluting the flag, or tousling our hair. We never saw him again.

A year later, Mother told us that his mind had gone still. After his burial in Temple Mishkan Tefila Memorial Park, I came home, loosened the halyard, and let his flag descend one final time. I buried my face in its folds, sobbing for Leopold Marzynski—the father we adored, the man who once stood so tall. Then I shook the flag out in the sharp wind, sending my tears to waft into droplets on the breeze upward to heaven.

Mother, numb with sorrow, never noticed the flag's disappearance. I took it, folded it into a neat rectangle, and tucked it into the bottom of my undergarments drawer, beside the smaller one we'd waved at the last Fourth of July parade with Papa.

From his desk in the corner of our living room, I stole a sheet of stationery from the *Marzynski Fine Furs* store. With Papa's fountain pen, and in my best cursive handwriting learned at school, I penned the words from *Genesis Rabbah 100:7* that felt like truth:

A society and a family are like a pile of stones.
If you remove one stone, the pile will collapse.

I folded the page and laid it on top of the flags in my drawer. Prayers and memories, I could hold them in my heart. The flags were tangible to hold in my hands.

SCENE IV

Grabbing a Dream

When the cornerstone of our family left us, I quenched my sorrows with song.

My love of music had started early. At night, Mother's lullabies soothed us to slumber. Her gentle arias wrapped around us like a warm shawl. Lillian, ever the dreamer, always requested "Un bel dì, vedremo" from *Madama Butterfly*. I think she fancied herself as the heroine, Cio-Cio San, awaiting Lieutenant Pinkerton. *Io con sicura fede l'aspetto.* (I with secure faith wait for him.) She clung to the dream that Papa would come back. I prayed her fate would not mirror that of Cio-Cio. Lillian deserved more. Full years, a loyal sister, and a love that stayed.

I preferred "O Patria mia" from *Aida*. If I had had prescient powers in my childish days, perhaps I would have understood why it resonated within my heart. Despite ending her training when she left Germany, my mother's lyric soprano perfected the tune. *O patria mia, mai più ti rivedrò!* (O fatherland, I shall never see you again!) How could I have known dedication to a fatherland would permeate my life someday?

As I grew older, listening to my mother's sweet voice stirred a passion for performance within me. By the time I was nine, I had begun elocution and acting lessons. I played in talent shows at Temple Adath Jeshurun in a variety of children's roles. Mimicry came naturally, for which I was grateful. After all, one could consider acting and diplomacy as close companions. These skills would serve me well in the years to come.

At age eleven, my mother urged me to take piano lessons. A proper young Jewish woman should be well-trained and eager to advance her education in all forms, including the arts. Yet I despised the endless hours of practice. I wanted to skip the basics and dive straight into playing. My teacher would not relent. Études after études until I thought I would scream. Whether I directed those screams at the keys or my teacher remains a secret I'll never tell.

Once I began my vocal training, it became the highlight of my week. I would race down Blue Hill Avenue to catch a streetcar to Miss Clyda Kendall's studio on Tremont Street in downtown Boston. Session after session, I and nine other girls practiced our scales, pushed our ranges and dug deep for the right balance of emotion for the magical scores. By April of each year, Miss Kendall selected three of us for the June recital. At the end of my first year, I performed in front of an audience of four hundred fifty in the magnificent Huntington Chambers Hall. I was eleven-and-a-half-years old. The thunderous applause of hundreds fell on my deaf ears. I knew I had a gift—one that deserved real training. My dream of a professional career in opera crept into the wings of that theater and the corners of my heart.

Five years later, the prestigious New England Conservatory of Music offered me a scholarship. But before I could grab that opportunity like the brass ring on a carousel, my world shattered. With the loss of Papa and his income, the economics of life shifted. At nearly seventeen-years-old and the oldest, my education would end. I would shelve my vocal training as a mezzo-soprano and tuck away my dreams. My family needed my help with a steady paycheck.

By September 1914, I found myself filing orders and invoices at a shoe factory in Chelsea. My once-bright hopes dimmed. For two years, I lamented my fate in a dusty, musty office. When I'd come home, downbeat and in a foul mood, my mother would remind me that my job was far easier than the factory work that thousands of other women throughout Massachusetts toiled at six days a week. I became thin and frail, barely weighing 115 pounds with my five-foot-six-inch frame. My skin paled. I felt hollow and disconnected from everything—my body, my surroundings, and life itself. Yet, a smoldering ember of ambition refused to die, even when everything else seemed to have lost its color.

At this point, you may think of the heroine as a Cinderella character, minus the evil stepmother and stepsisters. A young woman facing a life of drudgery. Suddenly, a puff of smoke covers the stage as a fairy godmother emerges to save the damsel from drowning in steel eyelets, tangles of shoelaces, cardboard boxes, and black smudges from an inkpad and rubber PAID stamp. The fairy in a blue chiffon gown waves a wand in a flourish, once, twice, three times, to re-ignite unrequited hopes and dreams. In my case, a fairy godfather, or rather, my cousin, Jack Meyers, in a dark gray business suit materialized on our doorstep. He carried no wand, but a plan and a promise from my mother's friends, the Müllers.

Twenty-three-year-old Cousin Jack worked for Riedel Pharmaceuticals, where my mother's childhood friend Klaus Müller held a senior position at their headquarters in Berlin. When rumbles of war spread across Germany in the summer of 1914, Klaus sent Jack to Amsterdam to open a branch office for Riedel to thwart any impending trade embargoes. As an unmarried man always ready for an adventure, Jack eagerly relocated to the Netherlands and traveled to America for sales meetings a few times each year.

By the time of Jack's visit, we had moved into a multi-family dwelling in the heart of Roxbury. Papa's death had forced Mother to sell our lovely home to raise funds to support her four growing children. I'll never forget the feeling when we walked out the front door for the last time. David ran to the maple tree to hug it goodbye. Lillian and I stood staring up into the reaches of its branches. Papa still lived there. Inside the house and outside in the yard. When we headed down the walkway toward the car that my mother had hired for us, I glanced back one more time. The house looked smaller. The maple tree seemed to sag and droop. I whispered to its leaves, on the cusp of turning to the vibrant oranges and reds of fall, "Leopold Marzynski, I pledge allegiance to your memory. I will never stop trying to grab my dreams and make them happen."

Our new home, a two-bedroom apartment in a noisy and crowded building, sat diagonally across from our temple. Mother had accepted a job as a linens laundress there, grateful for the extra dollars a week. I was thankful she didn't have far to walk. Julian was not yet in school, so she could leave him in the care of one of the elderly women in the apartment building. Whether Mother wrote in her letters to Jack and the Müllers of her employment, an unheard-of situation for a woman with her background and society standing, I don't know. Yet they must have drawn some conclusions about the change in our family's living conditions to prompt Jack's appearance on our doorstep that night in September 1916.

Jack sat at our dining table, his hands cradling the ceramic beer stein adorned with a folksy scene of a huntsman in a forest. My mother had kept our grandfather's stein, taking it from the china cabinet shelf only on special occasions. The colors of the carved figures caught the warm light from the chandelier. For a moment, Jack traced the raised patterns along its sides with his thumb, following the same tracks our grandfather's strong hands must have traveled. He lifted the stein and called out in the echoes of my grandfather Meyers. "*Prost!*"

After downing loud gulps of the frothy ale and over a plate of steaming potato knishes, Jack laid out Mr. Müller's proposal, outlined in a letter to my mother. *Send Josephine to us. With your musical genes and from the clippings of articles you've sent over* the years about her performances, she will have no difficulty in enrolling in the Konservatorium. *After training there, opera companies across Germany will vie to add her to their ensembles. We will cover the cost of her tuition and ticket. And since our Evelyn's wedding last year, her room has been empty. Josephine will find it comfortable. Once he concludes his business in Boston, Jack will see Josephine safely on to Berlin.*

I threw my hands in the air and hugged Jack so hard I think a rib creaked.

"*Mutter*," I said over my shoulder to where she sat in silence in her favorite Queen Anne chair, "you never let on about the Müller's cleverness and the depths of their generosity. This is a wonderful idea. We must reply right away so I can start with the January term."

Amid my surprise and delight, I hadn't thought to ask permission. Surely my mother could understand that the Müllers' plan would solve many of our problems. Wearied soft blue eyes scanned from me to Jack and back to me. Dry, chapped hands gripped the shepherd's-crook arms of the chair. "*Meine Liebling*, you are a young woman of nearly nineteen. I cannot forbid you to leave. Nor will I force you to go. Unlike my parents, I will step aside to let you make this decision on your own."

She pushed herself up from the chair, cleared Jack's empty plate, and bumped her hip against the swinging door from the living area into the kitchen. I tamped down her resignation and turned my attention to my fairy godfathers, the one standing next to me and the one sitting in a well-appointed parlor in Berlin with an open checkbook. In less than thirty seconds, I knew my decision.

"Tell me, Jack. What's next? Can we telegram the Müllers? I haven't much to pack, although I could use at least one or two new dresses if Mother will relinquish my next and final paycheck." I had to root myself to the floor as my legs longed to launch me into a jump of joy.

"Perhaps Lillian can take my job. I doubt they'll be sad to see me go. Further, she's much more compliant than I, and the tedium won't bore her into madness. In fact, it will be my pleasure to gather up an armful of those shoes and hurl them at their heads…"

"Settle down, Josephine," Jack said. "You'll have more pressing issues than a new frock to consider. And watch your language. You need to endear yourself to the State Department officers, not rile them with your sass. You do recall that Germany is at war with half of Europe? Rules for traveling abroad have tightened. Despite the neutrality, the Germans scrutinize every American who enters their country. Your passport application needs a more compelling reason than *to study music*. Your mother must still have the information for the attorney who handled Leopold's affairs. I can confer with him for guidance. We'll sort this out, hopefully before I sail on October sixth."

Within minutes, I had soared to the clouds, clutching rainbow-colored kite strings, imagining new possibilities. Jack's assertions cut those strings, crashing me back to a hard ground.

♪

The days until Jack's departure ticked by as quickly as my ten-year-old brother's hand snatching a cookie off the counter when Mother turned her back. True to Jack's assumption, the Department of State denied my first passport application when I filled in *to study music* under the *Object of Visit* space. On October second, Jack returned from another visit to the passport office, waving two documents in his hand. His dark wavy hair could not hide his merry gray eyes.

"Success," he called out, entering through our front door.

I jumped to grab the papers he flapped about in the air over my head. "How? What? Let me see. Let me see."

"I met with your father's attorney, Mr. Levy. His idea worked. He wrote a supporting affidavit that Mr. Müller and your mother agreed to the terms of their hosting you for the duration of your study in Germany."

Breathless, I placed my palms up, in front of him. As he laid the letter and folded card embossed with the United States Department of State on the front cover in my clutches, my heart skipped. In less than forty-eight hours, I would board a train to New York in time to catch the *Kristianiafjord,* bound for Bergen, Norway. For the first time in my almost nineteen years, I would leave my family, my city, my country. My dream of becoming an opera singer was within reach. My mother's dreams too. A means to heal our souls would pour forth in its purest form, the outpouring of every emotion through my singular voice.

I would leave and travel to Germany, while denying any thought of the impact of a war. Jack didn't seem concerned. Eighteen months had passed since President Wilson had called the sinking of the *Lusitania* an outrage but not a reason for war. Battles covered French land, not German. Why should I worry? Still, I knew the truth. Torpedoes hit passenger steamers and floating mines recognized neither friend nor foe. And Lillian. If I'd listened to her continual commentary that she expected never to see me alive again or to the fear whispering in the back of my mind, I might've torn up my travel papers and trudged back to the grind of the shoe factory.

I didn't.

I opened my dresser drawer, pushed aside my slips and stockings, and pulled out two flags. With a few quick snips of Lillian's embroidery scissors, I freed the smaller flag from its dowel. Folded tight, it slipped into the pleated pocket of my mother's valise. The larger flag, which had risen and fallen each day by my father's hand, I pulled close to my chest. I inhaled the memories before returning it to the drawer.

The red, white, and blue would travel with me, carrying the symbol of our people's courage and freedom to Germany.

SCENE V

Going Over

This story is not a travelogue. However, certain moments in my travels to Germany are relevant, especially as they portend the shadow of war. The rest I leave to your imagination. Most of us know tales of family members crossing on emigrant ships. Or have read recent newspaper accounts of German U-boat sightings in the Atlantic. Of course, I expect no one escaped the tragic news of the *Lusitania's* sinking.

I'll begin with our time in New York before Jack and I set sail on October sixth. There, I managed some last-minute shopping at the famed Macy's department store. After stowing our luggage at the dock terminal, Jack waited for me at a diner across the street. Wise decision on his part. I don't think he could have endured my oohs and ahhs while perusing rack after rack of stylish dresses, coats, and hats. Besides three simple shirtwaists, I selected a smart new suit of velveteen navy blue with a full skirt, deep pockets, a white satin collar, and a black silk tie. A wide-brimmed dark-blue felt hat with a slight curve downward at the edges and a cream-colored bow affixed to the front of the brim matched the suit. Its versatility in the neutral colors and refined style would allow me to match it to most any of my travel outfits. When the salesgirl said, "Miss, you won't find another shop that carries hats with such distinctive flair. And four ninety-six is a bargain. You should grab it before someone else does." I took her recommendation.

However, she may have laid her sales pitch on thicker than necessary. All it took was her placing the hat atop my head and turning me toward the mirror. I fancied myself the epitome of the fashionable young woman strolling down New York's sidewalks.

We made one more stop when Jack indulged me with a walk from Herald Square up Fifth Avenue.

"Josephine, there's another shop we should visit," he said. "If Bergdorf Goodman is good enough for the ladies of the Astor, Vanderbilt, and Rockefeller families, I'm sure Miss Marzynski can find a dress fitting for her upcoming performances in Berlin."

"Goodness, Jack! I don't have the means of those ladies. Look, there's a dress shop across the street. I bet it might have some fancier dresses at prices that won't wipe out the rest of my travel funds from Mother."

With a pat to his breast pocket, he said, "My treat."

Do you think an eighteen-year-old woman would refuse such a generous gift?

After our morning spent shopping, Jack planned our afternoon around my meeting with the German consulate. I wish he had inverted our schedule to have gotten through that ordeal first. My pleasant morning soured when I sat down in front of a gruff German.

"You, an American girl, want to go to Berlin? At this time?" His tone bordered on incredulity. He snatched my passport and affidavit from my hands. Narrowed, dark-hazel eyes studied me. Question after question, he tried to unravel the reasons behind such an unconventional decision. *Where were my parents from? Why I wanted to go. What were my intentions? Why now?* His skepticism grew as I unfolded the story of my journey from Miss Kendall's recitals to the offer of the Müllers in Berlin. My voice steadied. I sat assured of my answers. Seated next to me, Jack tapped my knee with his. He nodded that I should proceed with the lines we had rehearsed on our seven-hour train trip from Boston.

"Sir," I began. "My mother, Ricka Meyers, also attended the *Klindworth-Scharwenka Konservatorium*. At my bedside, she would sing to my sister and me. By the time I turned ten, I would join her for a shared favorite. Are you familiar with *Aida*, the opera about an Ethiopian princess?"

The Consul shook his head and said, "Fräulein, I have many appointments today. Enough of your nonsense about bedtime stories and African whores."

I opened my mouth, summoning courage from the deepest point of my diaphragm. *"O patria mia, mai più ti rivedrò!"*

My voice ascended, reaching for the heavens. I doubted this man knew the difference between a lyric and mezzo soprano. The words and meaning of the aria mattered more. I must convince this bull-headed man, irked by my presence, that I considered Germany my fatherland, the homeland of my mother, with its beauty and glory.

His eyes widened as the notes swirled through the air like fall leaves in the breeze.

"You hear it, don't you?" Jack said when I finished. "She has a gift, which she inherited from her German mother. She sings of the longing for her fatherland, afraid she may never see it again. We humbly ask that you allow Miss Marzynski to perfect this gift by training with the best in the world. In the land that birthed the genius of Bach and Beethoven. Brahms and Wagner. Strauss and Mendelssohn. In a country that sees a future built on the talents and sacrifices of the next generation. To permit a mother's dream to come true, knowing that her daughter will share her talent with other Germans. I promise you, the Empire will be proud to call Josephine Therese Marzynski one of its own."

My fingers tingled as I reached for Jack's hand, squeezing it tight with a thank you. The consul officer sighed and picked up a stamp. Etched into the rubber, I saw an eagle with its wings spread wide and a sharp angular beak opened, ready to attack its prey.

He tapped it on the ink pad and imprinted the ebony seal upon my passport.

♪

The *Kristianiafjord* weighed twelve thousand tons, a modest weight for a transoceanic liner. She sailed under two flags. The blue and white Nordic Cross of Norway heralded our approach, while the Stars and Stripes whipped in a frenzy at the stern. As we pulled away from the dock, again I asked Jack, "How can you be sure there's no ammunition on board? Are you sure we won't be attacked?"

"I can't say with one hundred percent certainty that Norway wouldn't strike up some type of deal on behalf of the allies, but after the *Lusitania*, every shipping company has issued assurances of their neutrality."

I wished he had said, "I'm one hundred percent certain."

After pulling away from the dock, I joined several other passengers who gathered at the ship's railings. As family and friends, who stood on the docks to see them off, faded into a jumble like discordant notes on a music sheet, we peered out over the waves. We plowed forward out of New York Harbor. Was that a piece of driftwood? A shark fin this close to shore? Or did a U-boat's periscope pop up, searching for the next target of its stealth torpedoes? A deadly explosive that could sink an ocean liner in eighteen minutes and drag over one thousand souls to watery graves. While none of us spoke, the quiet solidarity of shared uncertainty made it bearable. We might be strangers, but should the unthinkable happen, we had each other and our American-made fortitude.

A light breeze kissed my cheeks and tangled my hair. I swiped my tongue along the upper edge of my lip for a taste of the sea air. It reminded me of my father taking a crunchy bite of a dill pickle. He'd smack his lips and compliment my mother for following his

Polish family's recipe to a "t", using exact measurements of dill, garlic, coriander seeds, red pepper flakes, kosher salt, white vinegar, and water. Lillian and I helped by scrubbing the cucumbers until the dark green, waxy skins glistened. David would elbow his way in, too, saying his manly muscles were stronger to twist the Mason jar lids tight for the fermenting period. We'd laugh at his scrawny arms but let him have his moment of boyish bravado. A pang of missing my family had already entered my heart.

As the Statue of Liberty came into view, I tugged on Jack's sleeve and pointed toward her raised arm. The gold leaf covering the flames in her torch burned in the morning sun. I thought of the burning hopes that my parents and grandparents must have had when they first glimpsed the greeter to millions.

"Have you ever played tourist and gone up inside?" I asked Jack.

Jack's gaze followed mine up to the tip of the torch. "I did earlier this year. You can see for miles out to the Atlantic, to farmland in New Jersey and on Long Island, and across the island of Manhattan. From one angle, you can find the rectangle of Central Park. The greenery offsets the gray of the buildings."

"A glimpse of America in one viewing. When I come home, I'll tell Mother we should plan a trip for the boys."

"If tours still run by then. They closed off access to the torch in August. You didn't hear about the explosion?"

"What explosion?"

With a sweep of his arm, Jack turned me around to face the shore of New Jersey. "There, see that wide promontory area?"

I nodded, trying to piece together any sense of Jack's tour guide lecture.

"Black Tom Island. Its proximity to New York shipping lanes and the industrial land in New Jersey made it a prime location for armaments production destined for England and France. In July, an explosion on Black Tom sent shrapnel flying in all directions.

Several pieces hit Lady Liberty, including her right arm. The damage must have compromised the structural integrity."

"Have they determined a cause?"

"Lots of hypotheses. The press promotes the idea of a worker's carelessness. That's the theory the government wants you to believe. Any involvement of the Germans would demand a larger debate over whether the U.S. would consider a German-orchestrated explosion as an act of war."

It seemed to me the United States desperately wanted to maintain its neutrality.

♪

As the days passed, battles emerged of a personal kind. Although I had followed the advice given by a young woman who stood next to me as we departed New York harbor, seasickness wracked my body by the third day. Apparently, keeping my eyes glued to the Goddess of Liberty until she vanished from my sight did not ward off the evils of seasickness. Each time I heaved into the porcelain bowl in my cabin, I cursed the woman for her foolishness. I may have cursed the Goddess too.

Seasickness mingled with sleepless nights, my mind racing to and fro mimicking the waves lapping the ship. Under dark skies, could the crew watch for U-boats? My body would jerk up with a start as an image filled my head. Through murky seawater, passengers from the *Lusitania* with outstretched arms reached for me. They intended to pull me down to join them in their watery graves. I thrashed my legs into a tangle of the sheets as I kicked away from them, struggling to reach the surface, gasping for air.

On the sixth day, my nightmares turned real. That morning, I went on deck after another fitful night. The wind had calmed, yet a different disturbance consumed the air. I spotted Jack and a few other early risers pointing toward the horizon. The menacing gray shadow of a U-boat skimmed beneath the waves. The wreckage of a steamer lay low in the water. Like the giant squid of Jules Verne's *Twenty Thousand Leagues Under the Sea*, danger lurked. Evil kraken of the deep took many forms, each one with terrifying tentacles meant for destruction. Should a U-boat approach the *Kristianiafjord*, I hoped the crew had more than Captain Nemo's axes and harpoons at their disposal.

The night before our first stop at Kirkwall, Scotland, a fierce storm rolled in. The wind howled, and the sea pounded against the ship. A terrifying thought caught hold. If we struck one of the moored mines or met another hidden threat beneath the waves, we wouldn't stand a chance. The crew would find it impossible to launch lifeboats amid the chaos. Images of news photos from 1912 flashed through my memory. If the mighty *Titanic* sank from an encounter with an iceberg, how could the much smaller *Kristianiafjord* withstand these ferocious gales?

I retired to my cabin, undressed in silence and slipped into bed, bracing for what felt like a sealed fate. Fingers laced in prayer, I whispered, *In the name of Adonai, the God of Israel. Michael. Gabriel. Uriel. Raphael. Stand beside me. Divine Presence, please protect me.*

But sleep didn't come. I begged for protection, but hadn't I put myself on this ship, on this stormy sea? I hadn't hesitated when a dream had dangled itself in front of me. Why had I been so rash? Why hadn't I tempered my desire and waited out the war? Would I pay for the sin of pride by sinking with a ship and taking innocent souls with me? Somewhere between worry and weariness, I drifted off.

CRACK!

The sound tore through the cabin like a rifle shot. I scanned the dark, finding the porthole had burst open, the iron latch split clean through. Cold sea spray showered the cabin, soaking everything. Loose items scattered across the floor, crashing into each other with every violent heeling of the ship. I grabbed the coverlet, backed into the farthest corner from the open window, and curled in tight. The storm raged outside. Inside, it felt like my world spun in a tornado of turmoil.

The next thing I remembered, Jack's voice called from the other side of my door, "Josephine! We've reached land!"

I flung open my door and beckoned him in. He brushed past me to close the porthole, ignoring the damp nightgown clinging to my shivering body. The seas had calmed. In the distance, we could see golden light shedding a halo over a small shore village. Moors stretched beyond the cluster of buildings. On a rise, a majestic old Scottish castle stood surrounded by ancient stone walls.

As our ship drifted like a bobbing head at its mooring, I beheld a sweeping view of the entire harbor. At the entrance, a chain of mines seemed a warning and a promise. The bay bustled with movement, cradling ships of all kinds—neutral merchant vessels and countless other cargo ships. How many of these vessels, I wondered, would soon fall victim to Prussia's merciless submarines?

We reached Bergen, Norway, after a four-day delay near Scotland, where we disembarked from the *Kristianiafjord*. After ten days at sea, I thanked Jack for his decision that we would travel by train for the rest of our trip. We boarded a charming continental train. From the moment we set off, I felt like we rolled along tracks set in an enchanting fairy tale. We wound through gentle valleys, their beauty enhanced by sparkling silver lakes. As we climbed higher and higher, the landscape transformed. Snow-capped mountains rose to mighty heights. Peaks shimmered in the sunlight. When we reached Finse, Norway, over four thousand feet above sea level, Jack joked we might see polar bears. I smirked at his jest, happy for a touch of levity.

From there, the train began its descent, offering us breathtaking views along the stunning Norwegian fjords. At every turn, a new vista opened up. Rugged cliffs plunging into crystal-clear waters. Small villages nestled along the shoreline. And the boundless splendor of nature.

To my amazement, a long flatboat ferried the entire train across the Kattegat Strait to Denmark. Upon arriving in Copenhagen, the German Consul official waiting for us wasted no time in delving into every aspect of my life. Endless questions rattled my answers. Name my parents, grandparents, and even great-grandparents. After twenty minutes of tedium, he got to the point: "Why do you want to enter Germany?"

I explained my reasons.

"But why now? Why go to Berlin to study when the country is at war?" he pressed.

Again. How many more times must I repeat my desires to a man in a uniform who had most likely never attended an opera in his life? Who had never felt tears drip down his cheek as he witnessed the magnificence of art in any form?

I repeated my explanation. Still unsatisfied, he continued with, "How long do you plan to stay?"

This question seemed innocent, but Jack had warned me to give some thought to my answer. He had heard that even German citizens returning home for brief visits often found the word *DENIED* stamped on their passports. With the most far-away look I could muster, I replied, "I don't know. Perhaps forever."

How could I have uttered such lies? Looking back now, I realize that needing to say and do what must be said and done became a part of survival during wartime.

After some deliberation, he informed us that they would grant us permission to enter Germany within three days. Why the long wait? I wasn't sure. Maybe they wanted to cable America to double-check if I'd correctly provided my maternal grandfather's middle name.

When our probationary period in Copenhagen ended, we boarded the train for the last leg of our journey. My eyes focused forward.

This concludes my travelogue commentary. Let us return to the Müller home and the start of my time in Berlin, where I would commence a life under two flags.

SCENE VI

First Impressions

November 1916
Berlin, Germany

I blinked open my eyes. After a restless night, seeing the bedside clock pointing at nine-thirty didn't surprise me. Sun rays poured through a gap in the green velvet drapes at the large French window. Diamond patterns refracted the light into shapes on the floor. I climbed out of my warm, cocoon-like bed to peek through the beveled lead glass. Below, inlaid bricks wove concentric circles in a quiet courtyard. Neat privet hedges edged the yard, their small green leaves curled into tiny fists.

I turned back to survey the room. Exhausted as I was from travel, interrogations, and flea bites, I had barely glanced around before collapsing into bed. In one corner, a tufted lounge in burgundy satin beckoned a well-to-do lady for a luxurious nap. At that moment, I felt pangs of worry. Here I stood, surrounded by the trappings of an ornate and carefree life. Nearly four thousand miles away, I saw my mother. Late afternoon in Boston would find her trudging home after a day of wringing linens through hot, lye-filled water. One hand holding the lapels of her thin wool coat closed at her neck. The other, raw and red, clutching a drawstring bag half-filled with a lower-grade cut of brisket marbled with more fat than meat, pock-marked potatoes, skinny carrots, and yellow onions. If the Kosher grocer smiled at her with a wink, a pint of cream for her coffee would find its way into the canvas tote.

I brushed a tear from the side of my nose and headed toward the sleek washstand pushed up against the wall. Running water in the bedroom spoke of privilege as much as the brass faucets with porcelain white fixtures. For me. No elbowing my way into the wash closet, which my siblings and I suspected had been a broom closet before the Marzynski family of five moved in. With a splash of cool water against my face, I awoke with refreshed anticipation. Next to the washstand stood a massive mahogany wardrobe. Deep scrolls ran around the doors' perimeter. I tugged the glass knob and opened it. A set of curtains hung midway in its depth. Pushing aside the curtain revealed a second compartment. This one had its own mirrored door and shelves, like a grand bookcase, designated for hats and accessories. I imagined slipping inside and setting off on a grand adventure filled with fantasy and fancy.

I dressed in a collarless white blouse and pulled on my navy jumper with double-button detail and an asymmetrical crossover bodice. At the end of the hall, I entered an automatic elevator, which whooshed downward to the street level of the Müllers' home. I soon learned that this floor was called the parterre, an oddity, considering the Germans had banned most French terms from their language.

Frau Müller waited for me in the dining room. I noticed she hadn't touched a bite on her plate. I regretted I had risen so late, forgetting that Germans never began a meal until everyone had been served. Anna set down a fine bone china white plate with blue garlands swirling around its edges as I took a chair across from Frau Müller. Fresh, juicy blackberries, arcs of melon slices, a sunny-side up egg and a hard-crusted *Brötchen*. As I broke apart the roll, steam escaped.

"Wait," said Frau Müller. "Anna, fetch the butter."

"Butter, Frau Müller?" I asked. "I wouldn't think one would find even a pat here in Berlin."

"Oh, Klaus finds some...somehow. Last week, it cost him twenty marks for half a kilo." A grin spread across her face, smug and proud.

I tallied the calculations in my head. Twenty marks equaled five dollars! For half a kilo of butter. The last time I shopped for Mother in Boston, I had strict instructions to forgo the butter if it had crept to fifty cents a pound. Anna reappeared through the swinging door with precise creamy yellow squares arranged on a dainty dish. She seemed proud to serve in a household where butter and other delicacies graced the shelves of a well-stocked icebox and pantry. Her stocky build suggested she indulged in every meal that Greta, the cook, placed on the help's table.

Frau Müller sipped her coffee before launching into a one-way conversation. "Now, my dear, we'll want to keep you entertained, as I don't want you to be lonely. Most of the young men have enlisted. By their choice, or at the demands of the conscription laws. Our women's service activities keep the girls quite busy. And certainly, you won't want to spend your days doddering around this stuffy enclave alone with me. Klaus leaves quite early every morning, and my daughter Evelyn has young Rupert to attend to. She lost her *kindermädchen* a month ago to better pay at a factory. And Anna and Greta have their duties..."

I shifted in my chair. My back molars nibbled on the inside of my cheek. Didn't Frau Müller know about my plans? The one offered by her husband? Had a complication developed with my application to the *Konservatorium*? Why had I left my home and endured a voyage of seasickness, dangerous ocean swells, and fears of moored mines and U-boats if not to continue my musical study? My toe tapped in a molto allegro rhythm against the plush Persian rug under my feet.

"...although Greta, in her off-hours, could accompany you on a few outings. Did you know she's Polish, like your father?

Russian troops invaded her village shortly after the war began. Her father sent her to Berlin as a protective measure. She found employment with us two years ago."

Unable to quell my growing distress, I held up my hand. "Pardon me, Frau Müller, and excuse my confusion. Jack had informed me and my mother that Herr Müller would advocate for my enrollment at the *Konservatorium*, beginning with the January term. Has there been a change of plans?"

"Change? Oh, dear me, no. Herr Müller has made all the arrangements for you to start in January. I'm looking forward to hearing you sing. We could all use a spark of brightness these days."

With a sigh as loud as the tick of the banjo clock on the wall, I settled back into the chair. We lingered over coffee for another twenty minutes. "Now tell me, Josephine," said Frau Müller. "What are some of your favorite opera pieces? You'll want to prepare for your interview with answers that roll off your tongue. I think that will show your passion and commitment to training."

"Thank you for the suggestion. And I can tell you immediately that my two all-time favorites are 'Je suis heurese' from *Mignon* and 'Habanera' from *Carmen*. I've mastered both of them, as they're written for a mezzo soprano. Many in the opera world refer to 'Je suis heurese' as an ode to happiness, celebrating an innocent wonder. We all need some of those feelings, don't you think?"

"I do indeed. Especially during these times here in Germany."

From Frau Müller's remark, I realized that even in this well-appointed dining room with a bountiful breakfast spread, darkness could creep in. The impact of war lurked in every home. Finding beauty in the everyday may prove to be more difficult than I had considered.

As the clock chimed the half hour with a subtle ding, Frau Müller looked up. "I walk with Evelyn and Rupert at eleven. Go freshen up, grab your coat, and come with me. I think you and Evelyn will be fast friends."

By the time Anna cleared the table, I knew I had found my first steadfast German friend. The woman who had laughed, loved, and lived through childhood with my mother. How glorious are friendships that extend over generations?

♪

Eager to see my new world in daylight, I accompanied Frau Müller on the five-minute walk to her daughter Evelyn's home. On either side of the front door, decorative stone statues stood in recessed niches. A narrow stretch of grass, bordered by a spindly wrought-iron fence, separated the building from a broad street. Rows of balconied, stucco buildings lined the avenue. An expansive field with browned, trailing remnants of plant stalks filled the corner lot. I imagined summer days when the sun beat upon a patchwork of vibrant war gardens tended by neighborhood women. I could see them with their backs bent in curved C's. Heads kerchiefed with grayed linen scarves. Fingers scaly and red from digging in the earth and washing the crops' bounty. Eyes downcast, yet hopeful to find stems full of life, while black crepe draped doorways up and down the street.

Evelyn met us on the walkway in front of her two-story, wood-framed house. Rupert sat up in his pram. His chubby fingers grasped the edges while he rocked forward and back in a soothing sway. "Good morning, Mutter. I see you've brought your guest. I've heard all about you, Fräulein Marzynski!" she called, waving a pale-gray kid leather gloved hand as I approached.

"*Guten Morgen*," I said.

Evelyn swatted at the air between us. "Dearest Fräulein, your lovely voice needn't degrade itself with our harsh German vernacular. My father insisted I learn English from the time I was the same age as Rupert here. I beg you, a simple *good morning* is fine. And absolutely you must call me Evelyn." With a sweep around her, looking for whom, I don't know, she added, "As long as we don't see any officers. If they're within earshot, Ernst has advised us to avoid any English."

After tucking a blue knit blanket around Rupert's legs, Evelyn ceded the pram to her mother, seemingly thankful to let the grandmother take over. Like Frau Müller's eager conversations, Evelyn wasted no time in mentioning pleasantries about Jack, Rupert, and Ernst. "Father would have preferred that I marry Jack. But then he goes and sends him off to Amsterdam for the company. With Jack's constant travel, alas, out-of-sight and out-of-mind dimmed the candle of our attraction rather than flamed it. When I met Ernst in his Prussian army full dress uniform at a war bond fundraiser, I was a goner. Six months later, we married. Ten months after that, this little rascal arrived." She bent to tickle under Rupert's fleshy chin.

"A handsome little rascal," I said, peering at the cherub.

"He is, isn't he?" agreed Frau Müller, beaming down at her grandson's grinning face.

Evelyn said, "I love him to pieces. And it didn't hurt Ernst's standing in the army that we fulfilled our patriotic duty to the Kaiser so quickly. Ernst half-joked upon Rupert's arrival that I had satisfied my female version of military service."

I ran my eyes over Evelyn's trim body and firm, round breasts. I tried not to think of her as the German army did, a female Holstein to breed and bear offspring, keeping her in a pasture, ready for her husband's next visit home.

As we turned the corner to make our way back, I noticed a tall, slender girl walking toward us. She wore a Red Cross nurse's uniform. Beneath a crisp white cap, sorrowful dark brown eyes and heavy brown hair gave her the aura of a Madonna painted in grief. Raising her voice, Evelyn called, "Fräulein Duysen!" and motioned for her to join us. Gesturing toward me, she said in sharp German, "Fräulein Josephine Marzynski, please meet Fräulein Natalya Duysen."

Natalya shook my hand with an enthusiastic, firm grip. A slight smile attempted to battle a sadness that clung to her face.

"The opera student?" said Fräulein Duysen.

I nodded. "Yes, I hope so. It's an honor to be here in Berlin."

"I shall look forward to hearing you sing sometime. But now I'm late for my hospital shift." Her quiet grace and gentle nature seemed to conceal a heavy weight.

As she hurried away, Evelyn continued in English, "Her mother is Austrian and her father, Russian. I think she leans more toward her Russian heritage. How I envy those amazing, defined cheekbones."

"She's a beautiful woman," I said.

"A lovely, self-sacrificing soul. Besides the hospital, she works at the Settlement House, tending to German children whose fathers are away and the mothers employed in the factories and whatnot. Beyond those charges, the war weighs upon her as much as the next person, perhaps more so. She mentioned to me in strictest confidence that her father slipped away three months ago and made it across the border to join the Russian army. She's questioned by the police every week and worries they'll think she's a *spionen*."

"I've seen the signs everywhere. She may have a good reason to worry, yes? Perhaps her work is a cover?"

"Oh, Josephine, you don't know her. The way she cares for those children is genuine. She soothes their fears and works tirelessly to secure extra food for the breakfast and dinner they receive. One day when I helped in the kitchen, the cook added a rare luxury to the soup. Can you imagine simple grains of rice being called a luxury? Those poor children arrive at the schoolhouse each morning undernourished and with barely the energy to hold their schoolbooks."

I wondered if the pronounced sorrow Natalya bore stemmed from the children she cared for or the constant image of her father on the Eastern front? Or the incessant questioning by the police? How did she reconcile it? Did unsettled feelings hang over her every day? Would I someday walk in Natalya's brown, scuffed shoes, torn with combative sympathies?

SCENE VII

An Iron Shield is Raised

By mid-afternoon, we returned to the Müllers after a simple lunch and tea with Evelyn. Frau Müller, Anna said, napped at this hour, so I would need to amuse myself while she and Greta tended to dinner preparations. I asked if I could use the storeroom off the kitchen, two floors below Frau Müller's room. Anna nodded an assent. I took the stairs two at a time to my room. Habit and pleasure guided my hands to pull sheet music from its spot at the bottom of my suitcase. I rifled through the stack until I found Puccini's *Le Villi*. The story of Natalya and her conflicted allegiances to her Russian father and caring for Germans reminded me of the dark folk tale of tragic love and betrayal.

Closing my eyes, I recalled rehearsal times with Miss Kendall in Boston. I planted my feet in the center of the cool, dimly lit storeroom. With a deep inhale, I lifted every vertebra of my spine as if a string pulled taut from the top of my head to the ceiling. Exhaled out. Miss Kendall had instructed us to warm our voices first with breathy scales, using different vowels. I relaxed my tongue and jaw before allowing my body to melt into my shoes. The rich warmth of "Se come voi piccina" swirled within my diaphragm. With my hands clasped in front of my waist, I released the notes like tender, quiet rosebuds. Shifting into the next measure, my voice swelled as the rose petals opened at dawn. I summoned the longing and vulnerability Natalya must grapple with and channeled it into my practice. The music ebbed and flowed until I reached the full bloom of the piece, majestic and showy. My left arm lifted in a rhythm matching the notes.

Vibrations energized my body. A piece of me dissipated into the air as the final tones disappeared. Silence again filled the empty room. The plink of an imagined pianist faded. I clung to the musical moments as I opened my eyes. Overhead, I heard Anna tell Greta she would go wake Frau Müller. We expected guests for dinner.

♪

Jack, Evelyn, and I filled one side of the long dining table. Herr Müller at the head, Frau Müller at the foot. Across from us, two neighbors stared at me with thin-lipped suspicion.

"Herr Bachmann once ran a large export firm," Herr Müller said toward me as a means of introduction.

"But now I am honored to manage many parts of our commerce trade for the Kaiser," said the round, red-faced man seated across from me.

The air hung thick with the pungent scents of lentils and garlic. Smoky undertones of cardamom invited me to lower my spoon into the shallow bowl. The warm soup trickled down my throat as I detected an icy pride in his voice.

Bachmann leaned forward. "You are American, yes?" This man spoke English with assertive ease. So well, in fact, that I attributed it to a testament of German efficiency. Yet, before long, I wished he hadn't spoken at all.

I nodded.

"Then tell me, Fräulein," he said, his voice increasing an octave, as one might do when turning the page into a more dramatic operatic scene. "Why do you Americans pretend neutrality while you sell ammunition to Germany's enemies? But for your deception, we would have crushed France and England by now. The war would have ended months, years ago!"

The table stilled as the conversations faltered.

I stiffened. A flush rose in my cheeks as he continued in the same accusatory tone.

"Our son would be here at this table with us, instead of forging ahead across France. Think of the lives lost on both sides. I blame your country alone for this conflict's endless dragging on. Neutral? Bah! Your president has found a home in England's pocket—we know the truth!"

I sat here as a guest in a foreign country, uncertain in strange surroundings, and this man, this German, after mere minutes of pleasantries, jabbed at me. Like a bad habit, I felt Jack whack my knee under the table with his. He knew what my flushed cheeks could mean. *Say something, Jack,* I thought. Nothing. He picked up the napkin from his lap and dabbed at his lips. Business diplomacy seemed to rule his behavior. But I wasn't in business with Herr Bachmann.

"You cannot consider the sale of munitions to the Allies a breach of neutrality, Herr Bachmann," I managed. My voice trembled while a fierce desire to defend my homeland stirred within me. While not an expert in international law, I'd read enough in newspapers to recall arguments made on this very subject. I steadied my bristling. "As I understand it, Herr Bachmann, President Wilson never refused to sell to Germany. Rather, our ships can't reach you, for which you can thank the German navy and your insidious U-boats."

Herr Bachmann's lips curled into a sneer as he slapped his hand down on the table. The contents of his soup bowl splashed over the edges. The red-hued liquid fell like droplets of blood on the white linen. "Bah. You are both fools. Wilson tells lies. Supplying them and not us makes your neutrality a sham—a farce!"

His words sliced through the air with a finality that left me speechless. Logic, evidence. None of it mattered to him. He held his beliefs like an iron shield. Did I dare level an assault on his armor? The truth of eleven hundred bodies, including ninety-four children, at the bottom of the Celtic Sea—passengers and crew of the *Lusitania*—it didn't lie. I ignored the stare Jack leveled at me.

"Certainly, you can't call the *Lusitania's* sinking a sham. German torpedoes sank the ship and killed innocent people. It's common knowledge." A catch in my throat stopped me from going any further.

"An unfortunate situation. Yet, all could have been avoided if the crew hadn't loaded ammunition on board, bullets ready to take the lives of Germans."

At this point, I realized Herr Bachmann was impervious to anything I, or anyone else, might say. His certitude and perspective directed infallible beliefs. I had no desire to listen to one more utterance from the didactic Bachmann.

"Frau Müller, Herr Müller, please excuse me."

I didn't wait for acknowledgment of my request. Most likely, they thought my early exit far better than my arguing with their guest and neighbor, a man of obvious high standing in the community. As I rose from my chair, Herr Bachmann grabbed his wife's forearm. "Frau Bachmann. We will take our leave now too."

Eyes downcast, Frau Bachmann folded her napkin and placed it next to her soup dish. With a slight inclination of her head, she turned toward Frau Müller. "Our apologies. The time has escaped us. I've forgotten that my husband had mentioned a pile of papers awaiting his signature tonight. Thank you for the delicious soup."

With a precise turn on his heel, the German led his wife from the room. I headed toward the elevator, but paused when I heard Jack call to me.

"Wait, Josephine. We need to talk."

"I'm not feeling well, Jack. Can't you come by tomorrow?"

"No." He cupped my elbow and steered us into the pantry, closing the door as if to stifle me in the small room. I looked at him blankly. Now he had something to say?

"Cousin, I respect your American confidence in speaking your mind. But you need to realize you're not in Boston anymore, where freedom of speech is a right taught to you in school. Here in Berlin, people learn to guard their words. You've seen the placards posted on every street corner. You saw them when we entered Warnemünde. Germans assess every glance and exchange between two people. As an American, they'll whisper behind your back. They'll suspect your loyalties. Herr Bachmann could call the authorities tomorrow morning and put you on a watch list."

A warm flush returned to my cheeks.

I had read the newspaper every morning back in Boston before David took them out on his paper route. One article had disturbed me to the point where I could remember every detail right down to the name of a Belgian man who shared an unspeakable scene.

"I can't sympathize with the German army and all that it's done for the past two years. Doesn't the Amsterdam media report on the atrocities the Belgians have witnessed? Like Eduardt Ollivier, who watched German cavalry kill his wife? They then forced Eduardt and another man to dig Frau Ollivier's grave and two others. Smaller ones for children, whose noses and thumbs the soldiers burned with the ends of cigars before burying them alive."

Jack hung his head and lowered his voice even further.

"Yes, I'm aware of the brutality that ran through Belgium, and I grieve for those people. But I must think of you, whom my only aunt has asked me to take care of. I'm not asking you to sympathize with them, Jo. All I'm asking, telling you, is to mind your words. For your sake and the Müllers. Klaus' position at Riedel keeps him in good favor with the Reichstag. They need our products to supply the hospitals and to keep some lines of trade active for the German economy. He has learned what's necessary to stay in their favor. And my position there protects me from conscription. I'm of prime age for the Imperial Army to send me to the front. Would you like that? All it would take is for someone like Herr Bachmann to mention the Müllers are harboring a spy, and I'm related to you."

My heart beat faster when I envisioned my dear cousin dressed with a Pickelhaube atop his head. A spike sticking up like a mythical unicorn horn, its presence a harsh reality of battlefields.

"I'm not sure I can do this, Jack."

"Keep your opinions to yourself? It's not that hard, Jo. Just pinch yourself or something whenever you get the urge to blurt out commentary."

"I'm not sure I can stay here. Why didn't you tell me about the situation? Of the danger and suspicions? How difficult it may be for an American, neutrality or not?"

Jack let out a sigh. Shaking his head, he said, "You can stay here. You're stronger than you realize. Just keep your head down and focus on the reason you came. Your music, your dream. Ricka's dream. The Müllers brought you here expecting they could keep you safe. And they will. Hold up your end of this bargain by becoming the opera singer we all know you are meant to be."

He kissed my forehead and left me looking at jars of fruit preserves, tins of sauerkraut, and bags of potato flour. I tiptoed out of the pantry and up the stairs to my room. With my nightgown pulled down to my ankles and the ribbon at my throat in a loose knot, I slid my hand into the pillowcase and felt for my hidden flag. My fingers rubbed its silky cloth. I closed my eyes and murmured to the ceiling, *Lie us down, Adonai our God, in peace. Remove all adversaries from before us and from behind us, and shelter us in the shadow of Your wings. For You are our guarding and saving God.*

"Please, God, lay me down in this home in peace. Let me be thankful for the shelter under the Müllers' wings. Most of all, help me guard my tongue."

SCENE VIII

The City of Berlin

In the days before Jack's departure, he and Evelyn guided me on a whirlwind trip through Berlin. I needed immersive instruction to learn the local accents and to navigate the streets to and from the *Konservatorium*. During our outings, we glided through broad avenues in a taxi. That in itself was a minor act of rebellion, as the government had forbidden the use of taxis for pleasure rides. But, as Jack explained, Herr Müller's connections ran wide and deep, even to taxicab drivers.

For a full grasp of understanding my experiences, you must see through my eyes and walk in my shoes. I would like to share the initial truths as I understood them.

From an outsider's view, Berlin seeks to impress. Its ambition aspires to overshadow the glory of ancient Rome. For they have built a capital—a *Weltstadt,* a city craving status—where one can disappear into breathtaking and undeniable grandeur and ignore the larger travesties of the day. This magnificence makes the digression from noble ideals even more tragic.

As we headed toward the heart of Berlin, the city unfolded with a stateliness that amazed at every turn. Each new section presented a relentless parade of beauty and precision. My gasps of admiration began in earnest when we passed through the towering columns of the Brandenburger Tor. Evelyn launched into its one hundred-and-twenty-five-year history, explaining how the Roman styled triumphal arch, supported by twelve Doric columns, soared to a height of sixty-six feet. I craned my neck upward as we approached, trying to imagine eleven Jacks stacked one upon another.

"True Germans committed to the *Vaterland* will never tell you that Napoleon was the first to walk through the gate in victory," said Evelyn. "Instead, they'll regale you with Germany's defeat of France eight years later and the reinstallation of the copper statue, which Napoleon had taken for display at the Louvre as proof of his prior victory in 1806."

To our right, the imposing gray dome of the Reichstag rose as a stark reminder of authority and ambition. Every detail of the building that housed the German political machine fit into an exquisite whole. Jack pointed our attention through the taxi's front windshield. "Up ahead, do you see that glint of gold, Josephine?"

I narrowed my eyes to a squint toward the blur a mile and a half away. By the time my father passed, money had become too tight for frivolous expenses, like glasses for a girl with nearsightedness. As long as I could read sheet music on a stand or invoices on a shoe factory clerk's desk, my mother deemed my eyes functional. The bulk formed as we traveled an avenue bisecting Tiergarten Park. "Let's stop here and stretch our legs. You'll want to meet *Goldelse*." Jack tapped on the driver's shoulder and nodded toward the curb.

"Can't we pull up closer?" I asked. A fine, icy pelt had pinged against the windshield, and I preferred not to ruin my stylish new hat from Macy's.

"No," Jack said. "Too many police and I'm in no mood for an interrogation as to who we are and why we're using a taxi."

We climbed out and set off at a brisk pace for the two-block walk. At the monument's apex, a golden goddess of victory personified Prussia. An eagle helmet sat atop her head. In one hand, she held a laurel wreath, a field sign with the Iron Cross in the other. I wondered if an insatiable hunger to vanquish defined what it meant to be German?

The crowd around the plaza buzzed with energy. A group of Prussian officers standing nearby attracted my attention. Their close-fitting feldgrau uniforms gave them a sharp, almost theatrical air, as if they had stepped out of a military pageant. I elbowed Evelyn. "Look at that one with the monocle."

He looked like the funny character on packages for Planters Peanuts. Replace the gray felt cap on his head with a black top hat and swap out the silver sword dangling from his hip with a cane, and the costume would be complete.

Evelyn's eyes darted toward the officer. She placed her index finger over her lips. Too late. His gaze locked onto ours as he strode in our direction.

"Hauptmann von Lüben," Evelyn said in an even and composed tone. "May I present my friend, Fräulein Josephine Marzynski?"

The Hauptmann stood as rigid as a peanut shell. His polished boots clicked together with a sharp snap at his heels. He clapped his hands against his trousers before bowing low over my hand. Then, to my astonishment and mortification, he kissed it. The warmth on my face deepened. I stammered a greeting, "*Guten Nachmittag*, Herr Hauptmann."

"Gustav," he said, indicating he expected me to call him by his first name.

As Evelyn and Jack chatted with him, I stood to the side, struggling to find relevant remarks to add to their conversation. Instead, he turned to me.

"Let me show you our Iron Hindenburg, Fräulein," the Hauptmann said, taking my elbow in his hand and guiding me toward a colossal, yet awe-inspiring figure. As we neared the grotesque statue, he saluted with a quick jerk of his right hand over his brow. "Our idol. An iron man both in fact and in effigy.

Erected early in the war, it ignites patriotism to collect funds," he added with a sly smile.

I lifted my chin skyward to take in the totality of the imposing form. Countless small holes punctured its surface.

"Thirty-nine feet," said Jack, as my eyes strained to consider the height.

"Contributors buy a nail from that booth at the base and drive it into a hole. There's a man now, adding a gold nail. Naturally, the gold and silver ones come at a higher price than the steel."

The statue's stern, unyielding face loomed over the beautiful garden. To me, it embodied the relentless spirit of Prussian militarism—a harsh symbol of ruthlessness and hardened power. I imagined this Iron Man standing side by side with America's Mother of Exiles. She would lord over him in height and consequence. Her democratic ideals of freedom, opportunity, and enlightenment eclipsed his wartime call for rigidity, oppression, and sacrifice.

When I heard Jack mention we needed to head out, Hauptmann von Lüben reached for my hand again. He clasped it in his large mitts and said, "I hope our paths will cross again soon, Fräulein Marzynski."

I managed a slight nod as he turned on his heel and rejoined his group. The moment he departed, Evelyn leaned in. "He's quite rich and eligible, besides being an officer. And he's Frau Bachmann's nephew, so you're likely to see him often, Josephine," she said with a wink.

I scoffed, indignant. "Him? Really? He looks ridiculous wearing that monocle."

Evelyn raised an eyebrow. "He's a splendid Prussian officer," she said, her voice tinged with reproach. "And he's been wounded at the front, relegating him to office duties here in Berlin."

I blinked. It seemed impossible. His appearance so polished, so untouched by the brutality of war. Could he have committed some of the horrifying war atrocities from the early days of the war, that

I had read about? Like the story of the Belgian man forced to dig graves, other cartoon images from when the war started in July 1914 also remained embedded in my mind. German soldiers stabbing Belgian men, women and children with bayonets. *Burning them, burying them alive.* Innocents baptized in a bloodbath on their neutral soil. Had this von Lüben held one of those pointed takers of life? Driven by bloodlust and the madness of war? I'm not sure I wanted to find out.

We continued along the Unter den Linden, an enchanting boulevard. The city unfurled treasures in a deliberate display. We crossed an ornamental bridge that looked like a gateway to a foreign world. A cluster of imperial buildings surrounded the Kaiser's palace. A fortress of stone, it personified the spirit of a warlord who sought to dominate the world.

As we rode back to the Müllers, I confronted an unsettling truth: I had to recalibrate my perception of the world. So different from Americans in their drives, Germans' habits and thoughts existed on a different plane. This profound divergence had kept Americans from understanding them. We had been blind, not only to their intentions but also to the gulf that separated us. A gap loomed larger and more insurmountable than I had ever imagined.

I went straight to my room when we returned. My heavy heart ached with a stabbing pain I couldn't ignore. As I recalled my thoughts of Lady Liberty next to the Iron Man, a wave of nostalgia for home gripped me. Its hold so strong, I thought I might crumble under its weight. Then, a painful realization struck me: I had no photographs of my parents, nor my sister, nor my little brothers. We had never kept family pictures, and now that absence felt unbearable. Only those who have found themselves alone in a foreign land could understand the depth of my sorrow that night.

Something deep within me stirred every time I saw the United States flag. Whether hanging in the home of an American acquaintance or fluttering in front of the American Embassy, the sight left me with the overwhelming pull of a homeland I couldn't reach but carried in my heart. Yet, as Jack had instructed, I needed to look forward to the challenge of my schooling, not backward to the safety of home.

SCENE IX

The People of Berlin

More important than buildings, statues and parks were the people. Let me take a few more moments to share my first impressions of Berliners. Like any major city, wartime or not, crowds of women and men teemed through the streets. Seeing men in the mix surprised me, as Jack mentioned the army had conscripted from age seventeen to sixty. Yet, I found them everywhere, carrying on their business with restless fervor. Many of them, like Herr Müller and Herr Bachmann, had received exemptions from service to keep the German economy humming. How many worked for the armaments industry under the control of the Prussian War Ministry as compared to civilian industries? I assumed the percentages tilted toward the war effort.

These businessmen strode down avenues with an air of detached confidence and import. Splotches of their glaring blue neckties, bright yellow waistcoats, and bottle-green suits, with spats, disgusted me. Herr Müller's conservative gray suits made him stand out like a simple pigeon among a flock of strutting peacocks. I much preferred the steady rhythmic coos and loyal ways of a pigeon who always found his way home.

Military boots scraped the cobblestones with hesitancy in their steps. I wondered if the soldiers shuffled because of injuries or as a defiant statement against years of heel clicking and precision, instep marching. As time passed, I understood statements of defiance could never be the reason.

Fresh recruits marched by them in an eerie inversion of circumstances and posture. Straight backs passed slumped shoulders. Stiff legs kicked out in precision while others dragged along on legs of jelly. Pale, gaunt faces looked as if a razor blade had yet to scrape the peach fuzz on cheeks and chins.

One afternoon, as I stood waiting for a column to pass, an elderly man beside me bowed his head. He spoke to the sidewalk under our feet. "More signed death warrants. Turn around, *meine jungs*. Run back to your *mutters*. Find your *geschwister* for games. Run back to life."

I glanced sideways, heart thudding, checking if anyone else had heard the old man's treacherous words.

As the formation continued its way down the street, the sounds of their singing chilled me. Their lips formed the memorized lines. But I saw no pleasure in their expressions, the way my heart filled and spilled across my face when a melody consumed me.

"*In der Heimat, in der Heimat, es gibt ein Wiedersehen.*" (In the homeland, in the homeland, we shall see each other again.)

Would they? Or had death warrants already been signed for each of them?

♪

Among the businessmen and soldiers, and despite the government's attempts to hide them away, vagabonds lurked in the streets' shadows. Now and then, a wandering minstrel sat with them. Their mournful tunes mingled with yells from the market. Voiceless by choice, as if their words held no meaning, the beggars shrank into the hard stone of the buildings. I considered whether they drew comfort from the solid permanence of the granite, when their days of troubles offered little in the way of security. Through sunken eyes, they held out cups or caps for *pfennigs*. Children huddled next to some of them. Small hands outstretched. Their eyes round and knowing. Dickensian scenes played out in German alleys and tenements where families dwelled in squalor.

On the morning before my interview at the *Konservatorium*, Natalya invited me to join her Red Cross rounds. On the outside, the apartments looked neat and presentable. The interior told a different story. Because of severe shortages of skilled workers and high maintenance bills, critical repairs went undone. Broken windows and leaking roofs marred the lives of those who called these hovels home.

In one cramped room we visited, six people lived together, including three young children. Walls stained from years of soot and dampness revealed patches of bare plaster beneath peeling wallpaper. A single grimy window provided little sunlight. If you reached out the window, you'd touch the building next door. The few breaths of air the window brought in mingled with scents of a week's build-up of sweat from multiple bodies in the small space, rancid food, and a musty odor. Two of the adults, the grandparents, slept on a sagging bed in one corner. Moth-eaten blankets strewn on the floor created a sleeping space for the children and their mother. I imagined how she must pull the wraps close over the children's shoulders. After tucking in the children, she would tug a bulky sweater, thinned by holes at the elbows, over her own misshapen torso and bent shoulders. Ragged clothing hung on a thin line stretched across the room. A few pots and pans sat on a shelf alongside mismatched dishes.

The children, two boys and a girl, stood in front of Natalya for inspection. I feared a gust of wind could topple their skeleton-like bodies onto the hard wooden floor. Chapped toes with long, unclipped nails poked through the boots of two of them. Dirt smudges hid sallow complexions. Yet they smiled when Natalya spoke to them in tender tones. At her request, they rolled up the sleeves of thread-bare coats and thrust their pale matchstick arms forward for Natalya to check for open sores from flea bites. I drew my gloved hand to my chest and turned away for a moment, remembering the itch from flea bites my first night.

The girl teased her braids apart for Natalya to run a comb through, hunting for the invisible invaders who preferred a child's scalp. Satisfied that this week's visit yielded no lice infestation, worsening of conditions, nor any additional concerns from the mother, Natalya hunted in her satchel and sent them off to play with a carton of pick-up sticks.

As we made our way down the stairwell, I said, "What a tragedy. I don't know how they survive living like that. Are you worried?"

"Fräulein Josephine, I am not. It's clear to me that the mother stays vigilant in supervising them and does her best to keep them clean, warm and fed what she can manage. It's when a mother loses that instinct, when she succumbs to a sense of hopelessness and helplessness, that's when I worry."

With a murmur under my breath, I sent the little ones a quiet line sung by the Sandman, from the *Hänsel and Gretel* opera, which I knew so well. My voice lifted and traveled up the stairs. "*Damit ihr schlaft in sanfter Ruh.*" I hoped they would find sleep in gentle peace. Their mother too.

♫

Unlike the insides of the tenements, the streets of Berlin appeared as sterile as our Boston apartment after one of my mother's frenzied cleaning sessions. The next day, after my morning walk with Evelyn, I remarked to Frau Müller, "How do the streets stay so clean?"

"Of course they're clean," she said. "The city employs women to keep our streets tidy and spotless."

"Yes, they seem quite industrious. Today, I saw a woman wielding a pickaxe while another stood next to her with a massive steel shovel. They looked as strong and brawny as an American lumberjack."

A tittering tee-hee emitted from Frau Müller as she considered the comparison I drew.

"We're fortunate that these women take on the jobs. They collect garbage, work in stores, operate elevators, and serve as conductors and subway guards. They understand women can do the job of almost any man."

"From what I've seen, I dare say they do a better job!"

Frau Müller nodded. "Indeed!"

You might expect to find confidence among those who held steady jobs in the metal and electrical industries. Women who ran equipment and kept the ever-turning cogs of the German war machine well-oiled and humming. Instead, everywhere you looked, faces seemed etched with suspicion or despair. How different these crowds were from those at home in America! I took for granted the cheery smiles and lighthearted chatter found up and down Boston's streets. Here, every street became a stage as the people of Berlin played their part in a city under constant surveillance. Civilian workers. Students. Beggars. Soldiers. Foreigners. A heavy weight of fear or puffed-up pride directed their movements. They hit their mark for each scene and moved on to the next. Which one wore the mask and costume of a *spionen*?

One evening at a bustling café, I witnessed an incident that laid bare the chilling efficiency of the surveillance system. A woman seated at the table next to us began speaking in English. Her words carried over the low hum of conversation, drawing *tsks* and glances. I caught snippets of her sharp remarks.

"...arrogance, nothing more, nothing less. Thinking they could sustain fronts in the East and the West..."

Within moments, a police officer appeared as if summoned by the collective discontent of the room. Without a word, he placed a firm hand on her shoulder and escorted her out. Where she went was anyone's guess. The swift removal of the woman left an indelible mark on me. I took heed of Jack's admonishments to tread carefully and to hasten my lessons of the local dialect.

During my first weeks in Berlin, others disappeared too. Regulars whom I would see walking to the corner store vanished without another mention of their names. People whispered, but never too loudly. Each disappearance served as a stark reminder that no one was above suspicion. Fear bred silence, and silence bred more fear. Footsteps and voices filled the streets of Berlin to create a cacophony of noise, but beneath it all lay a suffocating, watchful stillness.

SCENE X

Klindworth-Scharwenka Konservatorium der Musik

Fog pressed thick against the window. Vague shapes hinted at the outline of a tree branch. An otherworld had settled, hushed by a dense, swirling mist as if Berlin held its breath. Inside my bedroom, my chest tightened too. Jack would leave this morning. His meetings with Herr Müller had finished. The last thread tying me to my family would unravel and spin away like a spool rolling across a dressmaker's floor.

Evelyn, sensing the weight of Jack's departure, offered to accompany us to the Charlottenburg Bahnhof, the station from which Jack would leave for Amsterdam. Afterward, she'd take me to the *Klindworth-Scharwenka Konservatorium der Musik*.

For three weeks I had waited. Now I would step into the place that had pulled me across an ocean. Back in Boston, my family waited for news. My hopes and dreams had become theirs. My mother had staked as much on this as I had. A failure to realize my goal of becoming a professional opera singer would shatter both of us.

That morning, I slipped into the dress Jack had bought me at Bergdorf's. Blue topaz charmeuse, Brussels netting at the bodice, hints of gold at the sleeves and a cluster of rosebuds at the waist that I couldn't stop touching. It made me feel like a princess. I'd twirled in it back in New York to model for Jack, lifting the skirt in soft waves. He had grinned. "Dress to impress, Jo. You must wear it to your interview at the *Konservatorium*. It makes you look like an opera star. Ready for the stage to awe your audiences."

I held that thought now. Not for Jack. Not even for me. For the ones waiting back home, who believed I already was a star.

When I met Evelyn in the Müllers' foyer wearing the dress, she placed her hand over her heart. "Stunning! Oh, I'm jealous. We haven't seen new styles for years. How I wish I could visit America, if only to shop!"

"Thank you, Evelyn. Jack bought it for me. I daresay it was more than I could have afforded," I said.

"Not as much as it would be here. Jersey and cotton are in short supply. The more luxurious fabrics are available, but only at the right price. That dress would go for four times what you must have paid in New York."

♪

Jack waited for us at the station. Steam hissed from beneath the iron wheels on the tracks. Soldiers swarmed nearby. Coming home or going. To where? Eastern front? Western front? Life? Or Death? The whistle blew with a long, sharp, blast. We heard the conductor cry out, *Alle an Bord.*

Tears welled in the corners of my eyes as I flung my arms around Jack's neck. He pried them loose from my tight clasp. "Josephine, I can't miss this train," he said. "My papers note today's date for departure. Dry those tears and buck up. You have the Müllers and Evelyn."

Jack, always with the right words at the right moment. I did not need to play the distraught damsel. For three weeks, Frau Müller and Evelyn had shown me nothing but friendship and kindness. Herr Müller had assumed a father's role without hesitation. I drew back from Jack's embrace and swiped a coat sleeve to sop up my tears.

"Yes, of course. And I am so grateful for their hospitality," I said.

"Good. And please, Jo, remember what I told you." He bent his head and whispered in my ear. "*Spinonen gefahr*. Eyes and ears are everywhere."

In a louder and cheerier voice, he continued, "The next time I see you, I expect you'll have a slew of girlfriends asking about the good-looking gentleman who calls on you. Pick one out for me, eh?"

"Ha, I don't think so. I'll just tell them, 'Ladies, he's just my cousin. Don't get all agog over Jack Meyers. He's nothing special.'"

A laugh and a tip of his hat sent him swinging up onto the train. I glimpsed his brown fedora, making his way through the train car. His destination in the Netherlands, a neutral state, allowed him to escape. The land where I stood, with its war widows and orphans, incessant marches down city streets, and enough suspicious characters to fill a *polizist's* notebook in an afternoon, had ensnared me, for better or for worse.

Several streetcars passed Evelyn and me without stopping as the queue of passengers grew from a couple to a mob. Loud grumbles of frustration invaded the heavy air around us. Evelyn shifted from one foot to another, the delay beginning to wear on her. "With the shortage of drivers and coal, our transportation system isn't what it used to be. When you start classes, you'll need to arrive at the station early enough to make sure you get there on time."

When one screeched to a stop, the crowd scrambled to board. Evelyn and I stepped up, elbowing our way past three other women. At the driver's wheel sat a woman dressed in awkward, knee-length bloomers paired with thick stockings, a regulation jacket, and a dark gray cap with her identification number. A most unflattering uniform.

One woman we had elbowed past climbed aboard. "*Besetzt,*" barked the conductor, signaling the car was full. The pushy passenger planted her legs in place, their thickness resembling two sturdy oak tree trunks. The conductor's voice rose another octave as she repeated, "*Besetzt.*"

"I've waited two hours. I'm not getting off," said the woman. She crossed her arms over her chest and looked up and over the conductor's head toward the expanse of tracks lying ahead of us. A standoff set in. Woman to woman, as if they vied for the attention of a dashing young soldier instead of a spot on an overcrowded streetcar.

"We won't move an inch unless you get off," said the conductor.

"*Nein,*" said her opposer. "Who do you think you are? A piece of nothing! The lowest cur slinking through an alley. As filthy as the *dreck* it leaves at the curb."

Her fury crackled in the air like a live wire. The noise swelled from a volley of impatience and anger between the conductor and passenger. I waited, thinking if a resolution didn't present itself soon, a duel would unfold, not unlike the one that closes Act I in *Il Trovatore*. The conductor already wore a uniform like Ferrando, Captain of the Guard.

Still, the woman claimed the spot. A red flush seethed across her cheeks. The rest of the passengers sighed with collective annoyance until I heard one call out, "Enough. She's not moving. Just go." Others joined in. "She's already on and there's room. Go!"

GO! I screamed in my head. I couldn't arrive late for my appointment at the *Konservatorium* in a city that craved and celebrated precision.

The car jolted forward. A battle lost between Germans.

Once the streetcar jerked ahead, I noticed many eyes staring at my feet. What did they find so interesting? Then it dawned on me. My sleek, pointed American boots stood out against the clunky, square-toed footwear the others wore. The contrast was unmistakable. In Berlin, I soon learned, one's shoes could identify a status quicker than presenting identification papers. With a hint of playful defiance, I stretched one toe out for a display of my Americanism. Until I saw a poster plastered over the side of a window. Bold text directed people to save soap and oil with suggestions on how to do so. I pulled my toe back.

♪

The exterior of the five-story *Konservatorium* left me underwhelmed. On either side of it, buildings crammed the space of Genthiner Strasse, a nondescript city block. Its conformity and blandness seemed designed for utility rather than an inspiration for artists. My world had narrowed to this spot of sidewalk in front of pale gray bricks. Evelyn started toward the door. My mouth went dry as I gasped for air. A lump rose in my throat like bubbles from a drowning person as the water pulled from below. In the window's reflection, I adjusted my hat, pulling the brim down a tick into a jauntier angle. I squared my shoulders and reminded myself that my muses came from libretto and musical notes, not from a box of granite squares.

A young woman close to my age sat behind a desk inside the entrance door. She checked my name against a ledger listing and gestured for me to follow her, leaving Evelyn on a bench next to her desk. We passed through an empty hall lined with practice spaces. At the door with the nameplate of Herr Direktor Robitschek, she knocked.

"*Betreten,*" boomed a voice from the other side of the door. She pushed the door open and left me to enter. My nerves swirled in an eddy. Since arriving in Berlin, I had found limited time for solo rehearsal sessions in the storeroom off the kitchen. The harsh late fall climate had also taken its toll; a persistent cough had plagued me for the past week, leaving my throat raw and irritated.

The Herr Direktor greeted me with an unhurried cadence. He exuded the air of a polished and self-assured man. His graying hair neatly combed. An upturned mustache of his hair's former dark-brown color adding to his dignified appearance.

We conversed for a few minutes about my background and former training with Miss Kendall. When I asked if he had heard of the Boston Symphony, he scoffed. And to my surprise, he said in English, "Of course I have Fräulein, since it has the best leader in the world. A German."

"And on behalf of the city of Boston and all music aficionados, I say thank you to Kaiser Wilheim for releasing Herr Muck from his position at the Royal Opera House. Berlin's loss is Boston's marvelous gain," I said, thinking it best to show an appreciation of all things German. I hoped I would also remind him how music could bridge divides, even in turbulent times.

"I'm not sure I should say you're welcome," he winked, which helped to ease my distress one notch down the anxiety pole.

"Now, you will please sing, Fräulein Marzynski. You have brought your sheet music?" he asked, nodding to the young woman who had met us at the entry and who had slipped in without my notice to take a seat at the baby grand piano in the room's corner.

I had rehearsed Pamina's aria from *Die Zauberflöte* for the past two weeks after deciding I wanted a short piece for my audition. The composition would showcase my abilities with breath control, purity of tone, and an emotional connection to the music, the words, and an audience. The slow tempo would reflect my longing. I handed the sheets for "Ach, ich fühl's" to the pianist.

Would my lips find the same magic possessed by the flute? I swayed to the delicate entrance of the orchestration before lifting my eyes to an empty spot on the blank wall over Herr Direktor's left shoulder. My lips parted, and I allowed my tongue to relax. "*Ach, ich fühl's.*" I stretched the phrase, letting the notes linger like a sigh. *Ahhhh*. Pamina's lost love, her happiness, took control of my own longings. As I finished placing my hand on my heart, I felt optimistic that Herr Direktor would think my performance satisfactory. I studied his face as he tapped two fingers against his chin.

"You have a pleasant voice, Fräulein, but you sing too *American*. We must correct that distraction."

My optimism sank to the point of my Boston-made boots. Although hearing that Herr Direktor described his daughter as *too American* would have delighted my dear father, I realized my classical training might require many lessons of the mundane. I would need to soften my flat vowel sounds, transform an uneven delivery into a smoother legato, and enhance my emotional nuances and fluidity.

Herr Robitschek placed his hands together, flat palm to flat palm, and jabbed them toward me in a forward thrust. "However, if you work hard—and I believe you will—I am confident you can succeed."

A renewed glow of confidence spilled from my upturned lips. "Thank you, Herr Direktor. I am not afraid of hard work. With training from the *Konservatorium's* esteemed instructors, I will make you proud to call Josephine Therese Marzynski, a student of *Klindworth-Scharwenka*."

An eagerness gripped my heart.

"Herr Müller contracted for the first year's tuition on my behalf. I know that starts in January. But if there is any way I could come back tomorrow to begin, I'm ready."

Over the course of our brief meeting, Herr Robitschek set in motion the arrangements. My rigorous schedule would include lessons in the theory of harmony, the history of music, and Italian. Even Germany couldn't deny that Italian reigned as the language of all music. The academic classes demanded hours of daily study, supplemented by vocal instruction four times a week. Though the journey ahead seemed daunting, I felt a flicker of hope. Challenging? Yes. But the rewards? Oh, so immense. And they awaited me in the sparse, cold rooms of *the Klindworth-Scharwenka Konservatorium der Musik*.

SCENE XI

Ready for New Beginnings

Miss Kendall's voice echoed in my mind as I set out early the next morning for the *Konservatorium*. "One more time. Less air. Push it. Punch it. Again." She had been critical, yet constructive, and never demeaning. Decisive yet creative in her approach to teaching. Boston felt a lifetime away. How would I fare here in Berlin? Would the instructors, like Herr Direktor Robitschek, also find my voice *too American*? What if they deemed my person too American, an enemy-in-waiting? Unworthy of their time or attention? Would they suspect my intent, commanding every move I made? Every word I spoke?

Three streetcars rattled past without stopping. I kept walking. What about the other students? Would they accept me as a kindred soul dedicated to a passion for beauty found in musical notes? Or would they deem me an unnecessary competitor, to be hushed and ignored, or even berated and labeled? Herr Bachmann's words rang cold and sharp: "You are a fool, a liar. Like all Americans."

Lost in a sea of self-doubt, I whipped my head around when a wool-gloved finger tapped my shoulder. "Natalya! My goodness, you gave me a fright."

With one swift, light glance, like a flickering candle flame, the Red Cross nurse's eyes swept the surrounding street. "Forgive me," she said, voice low. "I didn't mean to scare you. You looked as if you were somewhere else..."

"I start at the *Konservatorium* today. Guess I'm more nervous than I thought."

She nodded, her eyes downcast. "Change is scary—not knowing what's ahead. Feeling powerless, I understand."

For a moment, I considered what Natalya and other Berliners had seen and experienced in the past two years. They had no way of knowing when the war would end. Who would be the victor? Regardless of who won, more changes to uproot lives would follow.

"Where is your *vetter*? Herr Meyers? You would want family with you on your first day, yes? I've met him before, with Evelyn. He seems the type to lend moral support."

I watched as her mind seemed to drift away. Did she harbor an interest in my cousin? According to Jack, many women did.

"Jack left yesterday morning for Amsterdam. I hope he'll return for another visit soon. His work with Herr Müller seems to call him back for frequent business meetings."

A clang of the streetcar interrupted us. Only ten or twelve people stood on the platform queue. "I must run. This one has room. I can't be late for my first class! Perhaps I'll see you another day after my classes? May I join you on a few more of your home visits?"

"I'd like that, but yes, hurry. I'll stop by the Müllers at the end of this week. Good luck!"

I high-stepped down the block to the waiting streetcar, clutching my bag filled with sheet music close to my chest. Taking my spot in the queue, I watched Natalya linger in the spot where we spoke. A gust of wind blew across my face. I reached up to clamp my hat down and re-pinned it. A late November day had arrived with a frosty nip in the air. Imminent changes in the weather and the world around me awaited.

♪

The same student and pianist from my interview directed me to a cold, unwelcoming room. A baby grand piano, bench, and four chairs crammed into the small space. My new teacher, Frau Julie Trebicz, introduced herself. I had heard about her illustrious past. Miss Kendall often spoke of the grand dames of opera, including Frau Trebicz of the Austrian Grand Opera. A celebrated singer in her prime, her voice, though softened by time, still retained a remarkable richness for a woman of fifty.

She was a short, solid woman with dark brunette hair streaked with gray. Her face, expressive and alive with motion, bore countless fine lines that spoke of years of passion and performance. Over the next weeks of study with her, I would learn she had the "artistic temperament" in every sense. She would jump up with "Bravas" as quickly as she would clap her hands together and demand, "Again."

Three girls seated in the chairs fixed curious gazes upon me. Frau Trebicz explained that she gathered pupils together to observe each other's lessons, a method she believed fostered learning through shared mistakes and group critique. I doubted her theory. Instead, I considered it a tactic, showing us the abilities of our competition.

She nodded to the girl on the far left of the row of chairs. A tall young woman whom I pegged as several years older than me rose. "*Guten Morgen*, my name is Zara Shenski. Second year. Contralto. From Minsk, Russia." She brushed back a flop of dusky hair, which had fallen over her large, dark eyes. With a tight tug, she pulled the flowing fabric of a navy-blue woolen skirt into a side clutch and resettled into her chair.

Ah, another foreigner, a German enemy, no less. The tight knots in my stomach eased and calmed into a lighter flutter.

The next two girls stood, matched to each other, with blonde braids coiled atop their heads and pallid complexions, pocked with the remnants of teenage acne. I wondered if they might be sisters. Both had heavier builds than the svelte, well-proportioned Zara. One stood a tad more rigid. She introduced herself first with the same stark details.

"My name is Paulina Hermann. Second year. Soprano. Berlin is my home and my heart." Her chest expanded, and her chin lifted. Her icy blue eyes surveyed me from the plum velvet hat on my head to the pointy toe of my well-polished boot.

The third girl began her introduction. "My name is Hannah von Strauss. I am first year. Soprano." I caught a slight eye twitch as she tilted her head toward Paulina. Did a lively tête-à-tête echo in the halls between the first-and-second-year sopranos? A wave of confidence washed over me. I was content to remain in my position as a mezzo-soprano.

"From Frankfurt by way of time in Paris." Her face colored at the mention of Paris. She must have recalled a pleasanter time there with its rainbows of flowers, artist easels on corners and bridges. The latest fashions adorning cosmopolitan women, strolling arm in arm with each other or draped across the dark suit sleeve of a mustachioed gentleman who would murmur French endearments in her ear.

Frau Trebicz reached for my hand in a customary German handshake. Her touch calmed the quiver in my fingers. "Thank you, Fräuleins. Please meet our newest student, Josephine Therese Marzynski, from Boston in the United States."

A sharp gasp from Paulina. A quiet exhalation from Zara. Hannah, sitting between the two, remained composed and neutral without a reaction.

"You are a mezzo-soprano, Fräulein?" asked my new instructor.

"Yes. I spent five years at the best school in Boston before friends of my mother arranged for me to come here. I'm excited to join you all."

Paulina's clasped hands in her lap turned white. "How did you dare come to Berlin?" she said. "Are you able to sing every piece in German or Italian? Frau Trebicz, I will not tolerate listening to an exalted German opera tainted by traitorous English or French."

The loosened knots in my stomach re-tied into themselves. "I can sing in German, Paulina," I replied in my perfected German. "And Italian, English, and French. In fact, I have plans to master Wagner's *Die Meistersinger Von Nürnberg*."

Lying to a German at a first meeting. Maybe not my wisest move. Every opera student knew that tackling Wagner with an inexperienced voice could ruin one's vocal cords. There was no turning back once I started down this path of deceit.

"I most often trained for the role of Magdalena, the mezzo-soprano. But before I ended my studies, my Boston teacher suggested I might aspire to the soprano role of Eva." Gauntlet thrown down. If Paulina felt threatened, so be it.

The day marked the start of a strange, challenging, yet enriching chapter, filled with personalities as vivid and complex as the music we meant to conquer.

♪

For the first class, I sat and listened to the three other women. I refrained from adding a critique, fearful of how they might respond and unsure of voicing my opinions. The next day, Frau Trebicz asked me to sing. I requested time for my routine warm-ups. With her assent, I faced the wall, searching for a private corner to transport myself back to Boston and my training with Miss Kendall. She believed a singer should consider her larynx like a muscle. As such, all muscles should stretch and loosen before activity. I reached my arms overhead to send my fingers wiggling toward the ceiling. My shoulders rose as I inhaled through my nose. I fell forward at my waist like a rag doll. With my fingertips brushing the wooden floor, I swirled them in a semicircle at my feet. Then, up, up, up. Stretching again, I lifted my head.

"The *turnhalle* is a street over. She should go there for her gypsy acrobatics."

I ignored Paulina's behind-her-hand comment.

As I lowered my chin, I began my series of chromatic hums and lip trills. *Hmm, hmm, hmm. Hm, hm, hm. Brr, brr, brr, brr.* I always thought of bumblebees flitting between snowflakes during this exercise. I massaged my neck, pressing my vocal cords up and awake. Lips firm and tongue neutral and relaxed, I reminded myself. *Hmm, hmm, hmm. Hm, hm, hm. Brr, brr, brr, brr.*

With a quick step backward, I pivoted forward to face Frau Trebicz and the students. I pressed my shoulders down and moved on to a foundational exercise of rote transitions between vocal registers. Punch out the *aah, aah, aah.* Ascend with *ah, ooo, ah.* Brighten each vowel. Project a series of *a, e, i, o, u.* Now, wobble along a sliding scale. Release locked knees. Open chest. Hit that high C. Control it. Slow it down. *Oooo, eeee.* Ground my feet into the floor. *Aaa, aah, aaa, aah.* There. A controlled balance, which I had worked years to own.

I dug deep for the memory of a special performance in Boston when I sang "Habanera" from *Carmen*. Paulina could fume all she wanted over my choice of a French aria. I agreed with Georges Bizet's idea of describing love as a rebellious bird that no one can tame. Loving with wild abandon. That libretto deserved the smooth, flowing melody of the French language with its soft consonants, rather than the guttural harshness of German. *L'amour est un oiseau rebelle, Que nul ne peut apprivoiser.* My carriage lifted to hold, hold, hold, the *garde* before descending to the *à toi* of the final line, "*Si je t'aime, prends garde à toi!*" I resumed a statue-like pose, waiting for the praise I felt forthcoming.

Frau Trebicz stood, a copy of the sheet music in her hand, now riddled with marks she had made as I sang. "Thank you, Fräulein. Your voice is pleasant, but you're too prone to *portamento*. We'll work on more distinct separations in your slides and discipline in your pitch control. And next time, in German or Italian. If Herr Direktor hears a French rendition seeping over the transom, he won't think twice to oust both of us on our ear. You may sit down."

She filled her first commentary with rules, rules, rules. For the rest of the day, she worked us through exercises which demanded strength and fullness in our voices, while insisting on flawless *pianissimo*. She also emphasized the need for balance between technique, expression, and temperament.

After Paulina's last exercise of the day, Frau threw up her hands. "Ach, you are hopeless! The tonal range has improved. You covered both the octaves from F_4 to F_6, but the stage presence? Below average. Your expression? Bah. You look like a Norse wooden idol. Shall I call you Odin?"

I quenched the snicker at the back of my throat. Although I had to agree. Paulina had chosen the "Mild und leise wie er lächelt" aria from *Tristan und Isolde*. I couldn't fathom how she managed to take a piece meant to show a moment where love conquers death and turned it into a funeral dirge. As if the German government had added emotion to its long list of all things *verboten*, Paulina, the ever-sacrificing German, obeyed. How could she have stood there lifeless and solemn while Isolde stood over the dying Tristan? Themes of intimacy and tenderness during radiant climaxes demanded an all-consuming vitality. Paulina's performance lacked all of those emotions.

Over the first few weeks, I sometimes grew impatient with the endless technical drills. But I found genuine joy when Frau Trebicz gave me songs to work on—simple yet beautiful compositions by Franz and Mendelssohn, followed by pieces by German greats, especially from von Weber's *Der Freischütz* and Mozart's *Le nozze di Figaro*. Every day, despite increasing challenges awaiting outside the walls of the *Konservatorium*, I clung to the joy of singing, finding solace and purpose in each new piece. Music remained my refuge and my voice. My guide for the days and weeks to come.

SCENE XII

Two Friends, One Foe.

December 1916
Berlin, Germany

As the weeks went by, Zara and Hannah drew me into a circle of companionship and compassion. Their kindness filled the corner of my heart that ached for my mother and sister. After morning classes, we settled with our lunch sacks in the break room, where they would bombard me with questions about America. Since we lived in Berlin during a war, food delicacies often became the topic of conversation.

"I wish you could both taste my mother's veal schnitzel," I said one afternoon as I pulled a slice of dark bread with a spread of blackberry jam from my lunch sack. The day before and the day before that, I had pulled out the same.

Zara leaned back in a hard wooden chair. The smell of stale, burned chicory coffee hung in the air. "Mmmm, I haven't had veal in ages. Go on, torture me a bit and describe it."

"She makes the most perfect silky, creamy mushroom sauce, which spills over the top of the breaded veal and pools across the plate." I could almost feel the tickles of the tender meat and the soft mushroom chunks between my teeth, the savory warmth melting across my tongue.

Hannah moaned. "What about dessert? Does she make *Pflaumenkuchen*? Or do plums not grow in America?"

"Oh, we have plums, and peaches, and pears. Citrus grows in the southern states. Oranges, limes, and lemons. But my father's favorite was apple pie. Mother makes it every weekend in the fall for us."

"Like an apple strudel?" asked Zara.

"Better. Mother tossed the apple chunks with sugar and cinnamon…"

"Sugar!" both women exclaimed, like a duet singing of tasty treats.

"Yes," I continued. "A squeeze of lemon juice and then poured into the pie shell with a latticed dough covering. Steam would curl up from the soft filling when she'd pull it from the oven."

"I could climb right inside that pie and lick the tin plate clean." Zara closed her eyes. I wished to join her at the spot she must have gone to: a land of apple smiles, flaky crusts, lemon zest, and cinnamon sticks. A spot in a Boston apartment

More often, however, our conversations turned to the realm of young women, regardless of where they lived: fashion and men.

Hannah, with her experience of living in Paris, would launch into a discussion about my clothes. "Josephine, your suit is divine. Is the semi-fitted coat with the flare below the waist a new trend? And the fabric! I may have to sit next to you every time you wear that velvet on Monday's Theory class just to slide my fingers across your skirt. That kitten-ear softness could calm anyone's nerves before we're called upon to answer questions about musical modes."

To Hannah's delight, I would commiserate with her about Theory class. Who could remember, or care, what was the starting scale for a Dorian mode? It was all Greek to me. I wanted to sing, not read about mechanics. To her fashion question, I'd reply with a demure smile that the suit also came in deep wine, black, or green. She'd sigh as I imagined a green velvet covering her shoulders, her blonde hair loose and flowing over it like sunbeams hitting a meadow.

Zara held a fascination for American men. She amazed me every day with inquiries about the mythical creatures she thought lived in the great United States. I don't know how her silly notions washed ashore from the Baltic Sea and wafted inland to Minsk. Nevertheless, I found them amusing.

"It must be wonderful to live in a country where men place women on thrones and worship them," she said one afternoon, her eyes affixed upon a faraway fairy-tale image. I enjoyed playing along with her, not having the heart to shatter her romantic musings.

"Chivalry lives in the States. Why, a woman cannot walk down a city street without a gentleman offering his arm or laying his coat down to cross over a puddle."

Hannah tossed her blonde braids like a filly shaking her mane after a prance around a paddock. "Well, my Friedrich has never been to America, but I can assure you, he's just as chivalrous. He always makes sure he's on the outer edge of the sidewalk when we walk. Always stops for a quick pleasantry with anyone we know, even the old, miserable crone who lives across the street from me. That is when he's in Berlin..."

She trailed off with a sigh. Hannah's beloved, Friedrich Vogel, served in the Prussian army. Hannah would often comment on the number of days since his last leave, not knowing when she'd see him again.

"Do you have a beau in Boston?" Zara asked, careful to pull Hannah from her despair over Friedrich's absence. "Someone who lays down his coat and makes sure you're on the inside of the sidewalk? Ready to whisk you away to a life of music, leisure, and lapdogs?"

I dropped my gaze to my lap. *Josef Bonime.* He barely knew who I was. The moment I saw his elegant, long fingers dance across piano keys at Jordan Hall as an accompanist for the famed violinists, Mischa Elman and Eugene Ysaye, I had tucked his name away in the recesses of my mind. His passion for music spilled over the keys, stroking and commanding them into a splendid opus. One day, somehow, I would meet him again, even if I had to travel to New York and hunt him down. To look into his dark eyes. To intertwine my hands in his gifted ones. Imagine his full, soft lips upon mine.

I had never mentioned Josef to anyone, not even my sister. My new friendship with Zara, however, warranted sharing secrets. "I can't say he's my beau, but there is a pianist. I met him once backstage at a Boston music hall. He was exiting after a magnificent rendition of Schubert's Sonatina in D Major."

"Pianists are a dreamy sort," said Zara, her fingers wiggling in the air over the lunch table as her body swayed to a silent concerto.

"You could say that," I agreed, recalling the way Josef poured his soul into those keys with warmth and grace. "This one, though, was not your typical egotistical musician. You could tell he respected his position in accompanying the violinists. His notes sang out in a refined balance, rather than any attempt at a virtuosic dominance."

With every crescendo, I dreamed I soared alongside him with an intimacy meant for me alone. At each transition, a tenderness enveloped me like a cashmere shawl pulled tight over my shoulders. That night in Boston, Josef's lively steps offstage steered him smack into me. I watched his full lips lift and part. "My pardon, Miss." His voice, a breathy undertone of apology. Those three words I've kept in my heart.

Zara tugged on my sleeve. "Josephine. Josephine. Where are you? What else can you tell me about this pianist?" She winked as a slow smirk spread across her face and added, "Perhaps he has a friend for me?"

I shook myself, returning my senses to Berlin. "Come to think of it, when I asked about him around the music hall the next day, I learned he had immigrated from Vilna."

Zara's eyes widened with the possibility that my pianist from Russia could have a friend for her, a fellow Russian to boot. She extended her hand to me with her right pinkie poised like a single quotation mark and the other fingers curled into her palm.

"Let's agree right now. When we finish our studies here, I will go with you to America. You will find this pianist, and he will introduce me to one of his friends. We'll have a double wedding to two handsome, musical paragons who'll buy us homes next door to each other where our children will play together as you and I lounge in chaises and sip glasses of claret after an afternoon at the theater. How does that sound?"

"Like a dream," I said with a forced smile, for my friend's sake.

With all my heart, I wished Zara's play scene might happen someday. But the incessant ringing in my ears of German troops marching through the streets of Berlin, singing their proclamation of devotion to the Fatherland, *Lieb Vaterland magst ruhig sein,* would keep dreams suspended like the fluffy clouds that filled the pages of fairy tale picture books.

Whereas a growing friendship developed between me, Zara, and Hannah, Paulina maintained an aloofness of the staunch, self-assured Prussian type. Her assertion of the superiority of *Deutschland über alles* became excessive in my opinion. Each morning, she regaled us with tales of working with the *Nationaler Frauendienst* the prior afternoon and evening.

The German women's service moved like a machine, as well-oiled as troops on the battlefields. Both toiled in the name of the Empire. Paulina flitted from soup kettles, ladling thin broths to hollow-eyed children, to visiting hospital wards where rows of still bodies lay. Painted tin covered gaping holes where helmets had left jaws and noses exposed. I wondered if the tin masks Paulina described came from the same factory that made tin bowls. It seemed to me that the factories molded the before and after effects of war.

The morning Paulina declared a new mission upended all three of us. As Zara, Hannah, and I drew our sheet music out from our leather satchels and arranged them into neat piles on the music stands, Paulina launched into her newest desire to support a frenetic sense of patriotism.

"Singing opera and dedicating my gift to entertain the masses during these bleak days is well and good. But sometimes I wonder if I shouldn't be doing more to contribute. As a young woman, a desirable one with comely features..."

Beauty was in the beholder's eye, I thought. Hannah was the comeliest one in our group.

"...with broad hips and a healthy heart, I might extend my hand to a soldier at the *krankenhaus*. When I sit next to him, many times a tent in his sheet forms below his waist. His face is terribly disfigured, but other parts of his body appear to be working just fine. I would marry him in a simple ceremony and fulfill the call to address our falling birthrate."

Hannah's hand flew up to cover her mouth, dropping her music to the floor. Zara's face turned as red as the borscht the Russians loved to make for dinner. Me? I let loose a full-throated laugh of hilarity.

"Thank you, Paulina. Most days, your stories bore me to death. However, this *well-endowed* one," I chuckled at my wit, "makes me think you should pursue that idea. Tell us if your assumptions about what's hidden under his sheet are correct."

This time, all four of us broke loose, laughing until tears ran down our cheeks. A moment of levity shone around us. For a fleeting minute, a reminder of humanity amidst the chaos soothed our frayed nerves.

SCENE XIII

Rations

January 1917
Berlin, Germany

"Who's had carrots this week? Weren't they delicious?" Evelyn asked.

The group of neighborhood women gathered at the Müller's parlor, sewing baby clothes for the *Nationaler Frauendienst*, dropped their needles mid-stitch. Heads swiveled like a line of tops. Left turn, right turn. Each one faced Evelyn with mouths agape. As Evelyn chuckled, the others joined in with tee-hees and groans.

Frau Bachmann clapped her hands together, straight palm to straight palm. In a prayer-like motion, she bent her head and said, "*Mein Gott*. I swear an orange tint has crept into my granddaughter's cheeks. I fear as she toddles down the street, neighbors will think her one of those dreaded Celtic pumpkin-heads."

Our strained laughter petered out. We had all eaten carrots at least three times that week and most likely twice a day. The truth stung from a place born of shared suffering. In those long winter months of early 1917, gnawing pangs of hunger, the weight of grief and suspicion, and shades of despair laid claim to Berlin. A city far from rural farms, its people did not gaze upon laden dishes of plenty on their tables; they endured with barren plates of want.

By nature, Germans enjoy simple and robust diets, accustomed to four or five hearty meals a day. Over two years of war, however, abundant varieties and quantities dwindled into scarcity and monotony. Food became an obsession. Even for me, spared much of the suffering as a member of the more affluent Müller household, bitter memories linger. Although I hesitate to dredge them up, I'll share a few vivid details about the plight of rationing. Like an open sore that never heals, its presence festered inside every home.

♪

Meal-planning started on Saturdays. While we kept to our Jewish faith as close as possible during those trying times, we didn't consider collecting our ration cards from the *Brotkommission* office as violating the Sabbath. Further, with all Berliners under the same directives, we expected even the local rabbi or his wife "carried" home their ration cards.

Those precious cards determined our entitled food allotments based upon precise household records. Officials documented the age and needs of those living under the Müller's roof and every other dwelling up and down Berlin streets. Careful calculations transformed cards into lifelines, as vital to one's existence as a pardon to a prisoner on death row. Each household received two types of rectangular pasteboard cards. The first one, divided into equal squares, denoted a specific number of grams for staples like bread, meat, and potatoes. The scarcer, colored slips afforded us "specials."

Each Monday market visit greeted us with an even measure of ambiguity. The omnipresent carrots and parsnips may have spilled over the tops of wooden-slatted barrels. Or their scarcity would cause women to fight for the last one at the bottom of a basket.

Even staple foods ran out, rendering our cards useless. Worse, counterfeit cards flooded the market. Grocers grew suspicious, inspecting every card like a police forensics report.

When the morning paper announced that holders of pink card No. 40 could purchase enough oatmeal to fill five breakfast bowls, we hurried to the grocer for an early spot in line. Hesitation meant loss. Forget cravings for beans, rice, or barley. There was none to be had. Butter, though available, sat on a large platter awaiting cuts into greasy, foul-smelling lumps that were more unidentified filler ingredients than from fresh dairy sources.

We accepted the half-kilo of hamburger steak the butcher offered on one miserable Monday in January. Using breadcrumbs, we'd stretch it to make one meal. Then we moved on to the grocery to ask about potatoes.

"Four kilos," the grocer said. He slapped our ration card onto the counter. That he wielded power over us based on potato sacks sickened me.

Anna took the card back, stuffing it deep into her reticule. "Yes. We understand. Thank you."

He didn't answer, just passed the sack over the counter and waved at Anna to step aside for the next customer. A woman in a worn blue coat sidled up. She passed him her own card. I watched her flick her wrist and slide a small envelope into his hand. He turned to scoop more potatoes into a sack. It strained the seams of the burlap as he hefted it onto the counter.

I tugged on Anna's coat sleeve, pulling her closer for a quiet remark. "I noticed that woman's card. Allotments for five people as well. That's not four kilos." I nodded at the bulging sack.

Anna didn't meet my eye. With a slight shake of her head, she whispered back. "Of course it's not."

Bribery reigned. We all knew it. I set aside my angst over potatoes when we heard another clerk call out, "Eggs today. One per person." A rare triumph.

Outside the baker's shop, we stepped into a long line without complaint. We had resigned ourselves to patience. Our bread ration card allowed one hundred grams per person for our household of five. A small, dark, coarse loaf must last an entire week. Greta exchanged our card for the heavy loaf, handed over the marks, and clutched it with bittersweet relief. Next to us, a woman requested flour instead of the loaf. She cajoled her daughter. "Never mind the loaf. Our card states *Ausland* flour; the Scandinavian wheat is superior. We'll just need to sift it a few extra times to remove the worms."

As we boarded the tram to go home, others stared at us. Wide and vacant eyes glared at our baskets. Compared to the empty ones next to the feet connected to empty eyes, you would have thought Moses had blessed us like the Israelites with a bountiful harvest. The ones with the empty baskets also received the issued ration cards, but one must also possess the mighty mark. Carrying food felt like a badge of honor, a sign of survival and wealth. Fewer and fewer full baskets sat on the tram's floor each week.

Evelyn also relied on Greta to secure Rupert's quarter of a liter of milk ration. The rest of us went without. When Herr Müller learned of the skimping on his grandson's milk, Greta received instructions to find a new milk girl. His request: one amenable to sneaking in larger portions. After two weeks, Greta announced, "She says she can't spare any milk this morning unless new stockings find their way into her pail."

The next day, Herr Müller slipped out on a solo trek to a destination he would not reveal. Yet we knew where his mission would take him. The ancient law of self-preservation reared its ugly head. If anyone could secure more for himself and his family by whatever means available, he acted. While sought after by the police and a hungry populace alike, illicit speakeasies thrived. As long as well-filled purses and pockets strolled through those underground channels, farmers and dealers took their chances of incurring heavy punishments. An illegal back-alley transaction exchanged a pair of stockings for an extra serving of diluted and grayish milk to feed a baby.

♪

On Friday nights, my longings for home peaked. The rituals and food of Shabbos dinners had always brought me comfort, both before and after my father died. I'll never forget the year Papa suggested Lillian and I join our mother in lighting the candles. "You are responsible young ladies now. Repeat after your mother and pay attention." *Blessed are You, Lord our God, King of the universe, who has sanctified us with His commandments, and commanded us to kindle the light of the holy Shabbos.* At the Müllers, Evelyn would join me and Frau Müller, taking care not to waste a single match. Everything was in short supply.

As the candles burned low and Frau Müller fretted over the ability to replace them, we would stare at the meager portions on our plates. We rarely found bread at the bakery. We made do with coarse black bread. Every Friday, I noticed Herr Müller's deft touch of dipping our bread pieces in the salt bowl for the scarcest amount to provide a hint of flavor and make the salt last for as long as possible. Most weeks, Greta pulled together a potato or carrot kugel. The lack of sugar and eggs set her off, muttering all day as she tried to create something out of nothing, or at least with less than what she needed.

At home, I thought of my family, gathering around the table, saying prayers, and digging into one of my mother's many chicken recipes. Honey roasted with dried fruit. One-pan, *herbes de Provence* style. Orange glazed. Seasoned with fennel, coriander and lemon. My tongue would glide over my lips, thinking of the spicy aromas wafting from that Boston kitchen. Waiting for the tangy and sweet fruit. The tart, earthy, and nutty undertones of spices.

Coffee, bread, milk, eggs. The daily supplies I took for granted in America became precious commodities. I should have rejoiced on the market days when we placed those items in our baskets. Despite our more fortunate situation compared to many others, by late January I developed bouts of dizziness. My fingers and toes went numb when I walked to the *Konservatorium,* forgoing the streetcar to save on the allowance Herr Müller gave me every week. A shortness of breath developed with that mild exertion. To maintain my breath control during Tuesday and Thursday performance lessons, on those days, I splurged for a streetcar ride. When Frau Müller found me on a couch after a walk home, quivering and kneading my stockinged feet, she sent for a doctor who diagnosed I suffered from anemia. Although I saw the distress on her face, we both knew a remedy wouldn't be forthcoming while rationing remained in place.

I punished myself further when I daydreamed about the fried doughnuts my mother made. Golden edges crisp and perfect. Centers doughy and sweet. Swallowed in two bites, the taste tantalizing as sugar crystals swished over my tongue. Nothing seemed capable of satisfying my craving for something fried.

My inane longing spilled into a letter to Cousin Jack in Amsterdam. Ten days later, a package arrived. A newspaper, rolled into a tight coil and enclosed in an ordinary wrapper, that he had left open at both ends. Hidden within those curled pages, tucked between sheets of waxed paper, I found a thin slice of fat matching the size and shape of the newspaper itself. If the postman suspected the precious parcel held anything beyond a newspaper, I presume the inspectors would have confiscated it. Or a sly postman's family would have enjoyed a meal of fried delicacies, even if they were carrots.

SCENE XIV

Other Necessities Dwindle

Food is but one of life's necessities. When I think back to the winter of 1917, I shiver, recalling how fuel and clothing joined the parade of hardships. Everyone suffered. Even in the Müller's comfortable home, the cold seeped in and settled into our bones like a hawk's talons, unwilling to let go of its prey. We took to wearing our cloaks indoors and nestled under extra blankets at night.

Despite the biting January weather, I would often join Natalya on the ten-block walk to the hospital. While my nursing skills were limited to wiping a fevered brow or spooning warm broth to cracked lips, I think I helped. One morning, when we heard that eggs scrambled with water were available, I had one soldier say to me, "Please, can you scrape my eggs into my handkerchief? I'd rather give it to my wife when she comes by this afternoon. I don't think my kids have had eggs in weeks." Sacrifice came in all forms. From losing a leg to giving up a plate of eggs.

As Natalya and I set off another morning, we stopped to watch three city officials enter the Bachmanns' home. "What do you think that's about?" she asked.

I shrugged, curious too since Herr Bachmann exuded the confidence of a compliant German, eager to support the war cause at every turn. The answer came when the men stepped out through the front door, each bent under the weight of coal sacks slung across their backs. Fine black dust trailed them like smoke from a dying fire.

"Aha, Frau Bachmann's bragging caught up with her," I said. "I heard her boast about their stockpiled coal at one of Frau Müller's sewing circles. Someone must have reported they were over the mandated allotment."

Natalya caught my sleeve. Her grip was hard, her eyes harder. Her mouth twisted, and for a moment her gaze drifted past me to somewhere far colder than Berlin. "Well, good." She spat, the sound sharp in the frozen air. "Let their grand parlor feel as cold as the ice-covered trenches on the Eastern front."

I hesitated. "You should tell the social office. Who knows what those men may do with it. Probably take it home for themselves, along with their paycheck. I'm sure many of your families need it more than the Bachmanns or those men."

Natalya's eyes returned to the retreating coal men. A slow smile tugged at the corner of her lips. "Oh, I'll make sure the right people know," she murmured.

The wind caught her scarf as she turned away, and I couldn't shake the feeling she wasn't talking only about coal.

♪

Electrical use, too, had to adhere to strict directives. One time, unbeknownst to Herr Müller, we exceeded our level. Upon receiving a sharp written warning that if it happened again, we would have even less the next month, Frau Müller rose from the table and dimmed every burner and bulb. The ghostly glow over the vast rooms felt as heavy as the winter itself. When Anna complained her eyes strained to clean and dust to expected standards, Frau Müller told her, "You'll have to make do, or we face a total cutoff. Although if that happens, I guess it won't matter. No one will notice the dirt on the floor or the dust in the corners." I wondered if Anna held secret hopes for a total cutoff.

For me, I cared little about darkened rooms; far worse conditions affected my daily routine. Early on, we received orders to use hot water only between noon on Fridays and midnight on Sundays. The Saturday night bath appeared not just as a cliché but as a grim reality. As the days grew colder, soaking in a tub of warm water became as rare as sprinkles of ice shards on a summer's day.

Soap also vanished from the market along with fats. Laundry became a constant scrubbing battle with scant scraps of soap and cold water. Ironing, an indulgence that required coal, was out of the question. Most households adapted by forgoing tablecloths, using paper napkins, and embracing the simplicity of unpressed clothes. On the streets, it became common to pass by both men and women dressed in rough-dried and crumpled shirts or shirtwaists. To Germans who craved precision and order in every aspect of life, this new normal must have irked them to no end.

I understood the enforced shortages of food and fuel. Those fed and propelled the army forward. But the constant inspections of our wardrobes exceeded my comprehension. We had to prove beyond any doubt the need for a new dress, suit, boots, or even underwear and handkerchiefs before we received the ration cards.

While we scrimped and scavenged, rationing rules exempted luxuries such as hats, furs, and jewelry, since most citizens lacked the means to purchase those luxuries. The wealthy, however, indulged with abandon. One afternoon, Frau Bachmann swept into the Müllers, draped in an extravagant broadtail Persian lamb coat.

"Why," said Frau Müller, "you already have that stunning sealskin coat. Why would you need another?"

Frau Bachmann replied, "Oh, it's fine for everyday. But I couldn't resist. It was a steal at only thirteen thousand marks."

I thought of the countless poor souls freezing in rags. Powerful stirrings of socialist sentiment rose in me as Frau Bachmann took another spin around the living room to flare the folds of the ridiculous coat.

Beyond clothing, metals, string, and cork also disappeared into the war effort. The simple pleasure of reading drifted like smoke wisps up a chimney as magazines and newspapers deteriorated, printed on flimsy paper with foul-smelling ink. Churches and synagogues stripped their bronze for bullets. Gold and silver coins all but vanished, replaced by a fragile paper currency and five-*pfennig* aluminum coins.

In late January, I walked into the kitchen, hopeful for an extra slice of bread after my classes. I no longer packed a lunch pail to tide me over until dinner. Even if I had to spread the bread with a greasy dollop of the vile lump the grocer called butter, I would relish an afternoon snack. To my amazement, instead of finding bread or butter, I watched a battle unfold in the Müllers' kitchen. Greta held one side of the looped handle of a large copper pot in her meaty, chafed hands. Across from her, a gloved hand gripped the other side of the handle. I followed the hand into the sleeve of a worn, gray topcoat and up to the dour face of a city official.

"You will not have it," said Greta. She tugged her side of the handle closer to her bosom as if she clutched a dear child to her heart.

"Fräulein. I've placed the two marks on the table. You have no authority here. I have collected from all your neighbors. They understand the need to surrender all but two pans per household. Let it go."

With a gentle stroke of her fingertip around the pot's rim, Greta released the handle.

♪

Leading up to the war and throughout the first years, Germany had flaunted a sense of superiority as the center of learning, culture, and intellect. By 1917, the grand facade cracked. The realities of life struck hard and sharp. Many nights, I burrowed beneath the layers of blankets and coverlets and asked myself the repetitive question: *Why?* Why did I stay? Even cold Boston winters, with snowdrifts that towered over my head outside, still offered a well-lit, warm living room inside. A hearty dinner would beckon the Marzynski family to gather at the dining table and rejoice in the retelling of each one's day at work and school. Light laughter would rise, mingling with the scents of a meal cooked with love.

The music sheets, tied up with baker's string and tucked into my satchel, answered my question. Each week, I pushed myself through the academics and the training. Words of praise and corrections from Frau Trebicz lifted and empowered. I had come to Berlin to train as an opera singer. The day I heard Frau Trebicz clap and call out "Brava!" as I struck a coveted high note, my decision to come, and to stay, fell into place like a curtain dropping at the end of a triumphant aria.

I don't recount these details of rationing and self-doubt to evoke pity or sympathy for myself. Rather, I share them as an example of Germany playing with fire. Its flames of greed, mistrust, and misunderstanding rose to the heavens. Like children, they needed to learn the lesson of what happens when you play with fire. Its people were being scorched. No cooling balms would soothe their raw, burned flesh until one heard the call for retreat, surrender, and peace.

SCENE XV

A Question, An Answer.

I hope you will stay with me for a few more descriptions of life in Berlin in 1917. For my story would be incomplete without a picture of the people's glorification of the military and titled classes.

Soon after my arrival, I realized that war fever consumed Germany. The people obsessed over rank and formality. At the top of the ruling class, people held the Kaiser and his entourage in esteemed honor, almost god-like. Their devotion seemed blind to the flaws behind that authority. I also discovered a fervent obsession with uniforms. Even a single insignia on a chest or upper arm commanded respect and admiration. They also revered titles with an unhealthy fixation. A title attached to a name ruled with as much power as the Kaiser himself. Those without lived at a subpar level of disdain and disregard.

After class one afternoon, I waited for the streetcar outside the *Konservatorium*. An older woman stood in front of me, her maroon wool coat pulled tight across her ample bosom. Her ramrod-straight posture kept her as immobile as a statue in Tiergarten Park. A subtle curl of her lips and a lift of her chin suggested her disgust at having to stand in a line with plebeians and students like me. Striding across the platform, Paulina marched to a spot in line behind me. I watched with half amusement, half annoyance, when I saw Paulina bow her head in reverence toward the woman.

"*Guten Tag,* Frau Hauptmann Lange," Paulina said.

The woman's eyes shifted for one quick glance at Paulina before she turned her back away from us.

I leaned in to whisper, "I've not heard of any women in the army, let alone of a rank of captain."

"Don't be ridiculous, Josephine. Of course she's not in the army, but she is the wife of a captain. They live down the block from my family. She would take great offense if you called her simply Frau Lange." The spectacle of arrogance and ignorance from both Frau Lange and Paulina left me disgusted.

Behind Frau Lange—I refuse to refer to her as Frau Hauptmann Lange—a small boy, no older than eight or nine, wore a complete uniform. From the *Stahlhelm* on his head to a feldgrau tunic covering his torso to the black leather riding boots which rose to his mid-calf. As the streetcar emptied, another boy with a similar outfit approached us. The two lads eyed each other before, in unison, they exchanged formal salutes with the precision of seasoned officers. The sight of these children, steeped in the rigidity of rank and uniform, reflected a society that worshipped authority even in its youngest members. These boys would learn by the time they entered the military academy or university that picking up a dueling sword to defend one's honor would mark the measure of his worth. Those who failed to meet this standard faced immediate ostracism.

Beneath the surface of this childish pantomime, a sinister undercurrent simmered. Militarism thrived, woven into the nation's fabric and ingrained through generations. The mindset cultivated and shaped identities and values from birth.

♪

I escaped from the suffocating military uniforms, children in costumes, and faux Hauptmanns when I attended my classes and met up with Natalya. As I waited to cross the street on a mild Tuesday in late January, I saw her standing on the curb. Her Red Cross uniform—white apron and gray-blue skirt—flapped at her ankles under her unbuttoned, army-issued wool coat. A splotch of dried blood spotted the hem of her apron. Its maroon blot resembled a smashed red poppy. I thought of the poem "In Flanders Fields," which had appeared in *Collier's* in early 1916. Written by a Canadian doctor after witnessing the aftermath of hellish battles in Ypres, Belgium, his lines juxtaposed blooming red poppies with dirt rows of white crosses. Natalya moved like the poppies, alive among the dead. Those in the hospital beds, dead in their bodies. And those in the tenements, dead in their souls.

I caught up with her as yet another military parade in tight formation stepped off at the end of the street. Boots struck the pavement in rhythm. Rifles gleamed. Medals attached to the chests of the feldgrau uniforms shimmered in the weak sun. A small group gathered, cheering as they passed.

One infantryman turned his head toward us. Our eyes met for a fleeting second. He looked barely seventeen. "It must end," Natalya said. To me? Or to the young boy?

"You're not alone, Natalya. I sense more and more people feel the same but are too scared to say it out loud." I lowered my voice. "The casualty lists. Rations. The uncertainty. They bear down, bore in, and are slowly killing us all."

With a quick scan of the area, she pulled me into an alley. A scrawny rat surrendered its hiding spot to us. She stepped back from me for a head-to-toe evaluation. "Josephine, you look dreadful."

I didn't consider her remark unkind. She spoke the truth. My face had paled to an ashy white, like the crusty snow pile at our feet. "The anemia is worse."

"I thought Herr Müller had gotten iron pills for you?"

"He did. Enough for a couple of weeks. But when the supply officer at Riedel questioned him the next time, he told them the pills were for me. They denied his request saying all supplies must go to the army."

She picked up my hand and gazed into my eyes, deep and questioning. "Josephine, why are you still here? Living in these conditions? It's madness."

My trembling and icy hand in hers felt the warmth of her concern.

"I can't leave the *Konservatorium*. There's too much at stake. The Müllers have paid for the year. And my mother…"

"If your mother knew the full extent of the situation here, of your condition, I'm sure she'd want you to come home."

Would she? My grandfather had forced my mother to sail away from her dreams. No one forced me to stay in Germany. Nor did they call me home. In Mother's most recent letter, she had asked for as many details as I could fit on a page about my classes, which pieces I was studying, and how I was getting along with my new German friends. I leaned back against the brick wall, steadying myself against a wave of dizziness.

"My mother never got the chance to feed her dreams. She neither forbade nor pressed me to come. But I know. She believed I shouldn't fritter away this chance. I need to stay for her, and for me."

A silence hung heavy between us, broken only by the scuttle of the rat poking through discarded newspapers. Natalya pulled me closer, her breath warm against my ear. "You're braver than I give you credit for," she murmured.

She paused. As if she had taken a top rail off a split-rail fence and laid it on the ground, she said, "I wonder if you might help me."

Whispered words of a mighty request slipped from my friend's lips. In a city filled with mistrust and deceit, Natalya Duysen, an Austrian-Russian, working for the German Red Cross, asked for my help. I, Josephine Therese Marzynski, an American Jew, studying opera at Germany's finest music school, said "Yes."

SCENE XVI

Pomp and Propaganda

I had mentioned my first encounter with Hauptmann von Lüben at Tiergarten Park. In the months following, he called on me several times at the Müllers. Despite Frau Bachmann's accolades about her nephew's eligibility as an officer attached to Headquarters in Berlin, I found him pompous and blinded by devotion to the Kaiser.

One afternoon, Frau Bachmann invited me to her home for a chaperoned visit. As she greeted me at the door, she leaned in closer, taking my coat. "You're looking lovely today, Josephine. The plum suit magnificently sets off your hair. I'm glad you chose it. Gustav will find you even lovelier than he already does."

Under my breath, an inaudible groan escaped. The Planters Peanuts man arrived as we took our seats in the parlor. As he had the first time we met, he snapped to attention. His heels clicked together, hands at his sides, before he lifted my hand and kissed it. I summoned the control and presence of mind I used before taking the stage for a performance. I needed my acting skills; otherwise, I might burst out with laughter loud enough to rattle the Bavarian crystal glassware in Frau Bachmann's corner curio.

During his theatrical display, I studied him beyond the exaggerated formal gestures. He was tall and slender with a well-built figure, broad-chested, thick neck and arms defined beneath his uniform. A predatory boldness, however, hovered below his smooth-shaven, narrow face. An aquiline nose and thin lips hinted at a perpetual sneer when he surveyed his surroundings.

Once he removed his hat, his blond hair, styled into a frozen pompadour, made his narrow face look even longer. When he had kissed my hand, I noticed well-manicured nails. The ridiculous monocle perched over one eye. A silver bracelet gleamed on his wrist. These foppish features and accessories contrasted with his martial bearing. He was a contradiction: a man who seemed equal parts predator and dandy, strength and affectation.

Whether it was his uniform or his nature, my dislike for him sharpened when I thought of the letter Anna had received that morning from her brother at the front. She'd let it fall to the floor before fleeing the dining room in tears. I'd picked it up, meaning to save it for her. I hadn't meant to read it, but no shield would mask the black ink and the heavy hand that penned the words. The few lines I saw spoke of anxious fear, nibbling at frayed nerves.

...the earth quakes from the incessant shells that rain down, day and night, with no place to escape in these godforsaken trenches. Some days, I'd like to pick up my shovel and dig deeper into the depths of the dirt. Let my body lie straight, my back pressing against the slick mud until it swallows me. My last view that of a blue sky. A calmness until it's punctured by the scream of incoming shells and streams of burst gunpowder. Then, the Stabsoffizierre raise their arms and call out to muster our rifles. When there's a break in the shelling, we advance toward the next line of barbed wire. On the hunt, for what? I've lost track, but shoulder my rifle I must. With my gas mask swinging from my belt, I heave myself up out of the trench and reach behind to pull another man up to face his fate. Life or death within the next hour. Which of us will close the eyes of the other?

"You look chilled to the bone, Fräulein Josephine. May I pour you a mug of Glühwein?" said Hauptmann von Lüben.

His offer broke me from thinking about the letter. I could use a mug of Frau Bachmann's famous winter drink. Just like she did with their coal, I suspected she'd stockpiled the wine and brandy. The spiced blend of spirits, cinnamon, and cloves might warm me, but it wouldn't thaw the icy images from Anna's brother's trenches.

We settled on the couch with Frau Bachmann launching into a discussion of von Lüben's return from Frankfurt. "Now, *Tante*," he said, "you know I cannot reveal the purpose of my travels. Suffice to say, we had successful meetings, and you can rest easy that all signs point to more German victories in the coming months."

The confidence of the Germans' right and might. Why did I expect anything different? I sipped from my mug, allowing the tingle of the spices to awaken my senses, while the alcohol dulled my reaction to the Hauptmann's declarations of assumed victories. Encircling the warm mug and with my eyes lowered, I remembered Jack's instructions. "Do not prod a raging bull." While von Lüben's demeanor remained calm through his conversation with Frau Bachmann, I sensed a rage ready to roil with the slightest provocation.

"I'd love to visit Frankfurt, see more of Germany," I said, not looking up from the mug cradled in my hands. "It's so much closer to France. Would it be safe to travel there? I mean, for me, as a tourist?"

The Hauptmann raised an eyebrow as he studied me. Did he trust my innocent interest in tourism?

"To see where Goethe lived and wrote would be amazing. Or the Römer. A building in use for over six hundred years? Remarkable. The oldest buildings in America, in Plymouth close to Boston, where the first settlers arrived, are barely three hundred years old."

"The Römer buildings have stood for hundreds of years. They'll stand for hundreds more. Better that you wait until the war is over before any sightseeing trip." Although he answered in a smooth tone, I also heard a steel edge beneath it.

All unclear details about the happenings in Frankfurt, but I hoped they might help Natalya. If the Germans sent a significant number of troops there, it might mean a build-up of a new offensive, crossing through Luxembourg for a different route toward Paris, further south than the Somme.

Von Lüben's gaze lingered on me a moment longer. But I had seen the faint twitch in his jaw. A flicker of discomfort behind a mask of composure. My interest in Frankfurt had struck something. I smiled and leaned back, content to let the conversation drift back to learning whether he could help his aunt secure an extra bag of coal.

After we washed the crumbs of decadent butter spritz cookies down with the last drop of Glühwein, Hauptmann von Lüben asked for permission to escort me home. Forgetting Jack's advice and driven by an irresistible impulse, I told him, "No, thank you, unless you would please remove that ridiculous bracelet from your wrist and silly monocle from your eye."

To my surprise, he laughed with a snort, but complied without hesitation. As we walked together, he showered me with deferential bows whenever we passed another officer on the sidewalk. With each one more exaggerated than the last, he seemed to emphasize his silent gallantry. It felt less like an honor and more like a performance. I prayed a curtain would fall right on top of his blond pompadour head.

For the two-block walk back to the Müllers, I allowed myself to disappear into a different scene. Accompanied by a different man. *I wonder what Josef Bonime is doing tonight? A real performance somewhere? New York, Boston, Chicago. Or practicing, as he must, for hours on end. Perfecting his talent. His fingers alighting on the keys. Coaxing the notes.* I put my fingers to my cheek, imagining him, a Russian who fled the pogroms. An

American who lived as I do, driven by passion. His fingers stroking my cheek with the same gentle, yet commanding touch.

Could I dare hope that wherever he was, whatever he was doing, he also wondered if a woman waited out there for him? Someone brave and feisty, as Natalya and Jack described me. A woman with a pleasant voice, willing to work hard to perfect her gift, as Herr Direktor Robitschek had said. A woman who embraced the American ideals of democracy and happiness.

♪

My afternoon spent with Hauptmann von Lüben heightened my awareness of other instances of the Germans' blind beliefs fed by ubiquitous examples of blatant propaganda. The same party line always crossed his lips. "The Fatherland must fight for its very survival."

This attitude lived large among the people, regardless of class or position. After reading another German newspaper article espousing the wrongs of their enemies, I couldn't contain myself. I poked the hornet's nest, otherwise known as Paulina Hermann. I intended to ferret out a more meaningful understanding of the German brainwashing machine.

"Please, Paulina, if you will, explain why Germany invaded Belgium, a neutral country, minding its own business, eating waffles and chocolates," I asked one January day between classes.

Without hesitation, as if the words had formed on her tongue from rote repetition, she replied, "France was mobilizing. They were preparing to attack us. The most direct route to Paris meant a march through Belgium. We offered them a generous guarantee of safety and indemnity, but they refused. That was their foolishness."

I have no doubt Paulina's father presented this rationale over their dinner table while, steps away, her brother suited up in his feldgrau, ready to join the ranks of the righteous. Rare is the day a girl defies her father's proclamations.

As for the alleged atrocities committed against the Belgian people? On more than one occasion, the affected Hauptmann von Lüben pitched his rehearsed lines to me when he noticed my lingering skepticism. "Lies, Fräulein, foul lies. Belgian women poisoned wells. Young boys fired at our troops from the houses. We needed to end such actions with an iron hand. Executing the offenders taught them a lesson."

I attempted another topic. He couldn't prove this one was imaginary. "What about liquid fire and poisonous gas? Germany has not denied its use of them."

"Yes, they are horrible," he said. "But war is war. And if the most ingenious side should profit by its ingenuity, it must. Yet, we did not use it in Belgium. We waited until forced to as a last resort at the Marne. The week's battle had gone on too long."

Justification to the point of absurdity. I couldn't listen to any more of his morbid drivel.

That was the spirit of the people among whom I lived, whose lives became entwined with mine. You may agree with them that war is war. But I hope I have helped you grasp how an autocracy and its self-deluded citizens can believe, think, and act as they do. War is destruction, grinding a society beneath its iron tread until nothing is left but bloodied dirt.

SCENE XVII

Rumors, Rumblings, and Reality

January 1917
Berlin, Germany

Homesickness for family, friends, and America festered like a rash. While I delighted in my voice training, the kindness of the Müllers, and my friendship with Hannah, Zara, and Natalya, my heart ached for news from Boston. Yet, the sporadic letters from home that reached me in those months focused on superficial matters.

Did I read the line correctly that Mother said my brother David had begun preparing for his bar mitzvah? That little cherub, or Beelzebub depending on the day or hour of his whims, was growing up without me. And Julian. Probably running Mother ragged with his seven-year-old energy and inquiries. And what of Lillian? Forced to leave school to work so I could come to Berlin. She wrote fleeting sentences. I imagined Mother standing over her shoulder, commanding her to write in the name of being a dutiful sister. I didn't care that walking the boys to school made her late for work and she received harsh reprimands from her supervisor. Did she have a beau? Did she resent me? Would she forgive me for leaving? How did Mother manage? Did she have enough funds to set aside for David's bar mitzvah celebration? My worries deepened with every day that passed without news.

On the rare occasions I received a Boston newspaper, which my mother had sent, I devoured every word. Even the advertisements entertained me. Trimmed hats marked down to ninety-five cents at the Magrane Houston store. *Little Women* ran with matinees on Tuesday, Wednesday, and Saturday at the Castle Square Theater. I wondered if Lillian had found the fifteen cents for a ticket to go with her girlfriends. I would have loved to have sat in the seat next to her, watching our favorite book come alive on stage.

War news in the Boston papers came in scraps. A German censor's shears had sliced out entire columns, making neat holes on every page. Harmless information remained: reports on thick ice harvested from Massachusetts ponds or the culinary thrill of five new ways to serve canned salmon.

Here in Berlin, my extended family faced changes too. Frau Müller fretted more when Evelyn's cheeks paled as she began surrendering her own ration cards to keep Rupert fed. Anna still had no word from her brother since the letter I'd picked off the dining-room floor weeks ago. Greta clattered about the kitchen, making do with two battered pots. Herr Müller's rare appearances with black-market parcels under his arm felt as unlikely as spotting a palm tree in Tiergarten's winter frost.

I saw less and less of Natalya. She'd rush by me, her cheeks flushed from the cold, eyes sharper than usual. She didn't invite me to join her rounds nor did she say where she'd been. More than once, before anyone else noticed, I'd seen her fold a piece of paper and pocket it.

One evening in late January, Herr Müller came home with exciting news. No, he had not secured a dozen eggs for us. He had received an invitation to a state banquet at the Hotel Adlon, where Berlin's business leaders would welcome back Ambassador Gerard from America. I forced a smile as he shared the news, but envy hummed beneath it. I longed to be surrounded by the American faces and voices that would also attend.

When the day of the banquet arrived, my longings escalated like the rising steam from a teakettle's spout, and I feared I'd bubble over with emotions. With a swipe at the tears forming in the corner of my eyes, I straightened Herr Müller's bow tie and tugged on the ends to pull it taut. With a quick flick of my fingers, I brushed the flecks of dandruff from his shoulders. I repositioned and smoothed the wrinkled handkerchief in his top pocket and extracted a promise that he recount every moment of the night to me upon his return.

As midnight approached, the front door opened. I stirred from my spot by the fireplace, where I had waited alone. Throwing off the matted quilt I had burrowed into, I greeted him in the entry.

"Tell me all," I said, breathless and eager.

Herr Müller shrugged out of his topcoat and handed it to me. "My dear Josephine. I wish they had allowed you to accompany me. You would have been a star. In fact, they should have had you sing. An American woman studying in Berlin would have reinforced their statements about our amicable relations. Hold on while I rustle through the liquor cabinet. I think I hid a bottle of *Asbach Uralt* from the prying and disapproving eyes of Frau Müller. Then I'll tell you all about the banquet."

I winked at him for his suggested after-dinner digestif. The smooth notes of vanilla and chocolate mixed with almonds made the German brandy a favorite among the sophisticated set. We settled onto the divan where Herr Müller regaled me with every detail of the magnificent scene. His descriptions of opulent decorations, glowing lights, joyful music and elegant speeches whisked me away to that state room.

He concluded, exhausted but still beaming, "Ambassador Gerard said relations between the two countries have never been more cordial than they are now! Oh, and they took a flash-light picture standing beneath the interwoven German and American flags hanging on the wall. I stood almost directly next to the Ambassador."

That night, with my flag still tucked into the pillowcase, I closed my eyes, content and secure that all was well between the countries. My happiness grew when I saw the next morning's papers had run a full-length article detailing the banquet—complete with the photograph, printed large for all to see.

♪

As January advanced, classes passed with preparation for a grand staging of *Mignon,* showcasing Frau Trebicz's past and present pupils. My humble role in the first row of the chorus did not diminish my excitement, even if we had to sing in German rather than Ambroise Thomas' original French. The exquisite lead aria brought beauty to life. Resplendent rose bushes, full golden oranges, birds flitting in soft breezes against a cerulean sky. *Das ist da bei dir, würde ich schweifen.* ('Tis there with thee, I would wander.) At the end of each practice session, I found myself transfixed in my spot on the stage. I'd stare out at the empty seats of the theater. How I wished I could wander off to that place where nature reigned and mankind's evils evaporated into the air. Alive in the moment without a care in the world.

On the night of the performance, I stood shoulder to shoulder with seasoned artists from the opera houses of Berlin, Frankfurt, Essen, Hamburg, and Breslau. Musical talent connected us. Despite the very different lands we called home. As the chorus reached its crescendo, my thoughts floated to my home. To the places I remembered well, with those I loved. Our comfortable home at the Blue Hill Avenue address in Roxbury. America, with its spacious skies, fruited plain, alabaster cities, and purple mountain majesties. *'Tis there I would wander. 'Tis there I would wonder.*

I recognized his silhouette against the theater's granite wall. The tall, proud, unyielding posture of Hauptmann von Lüben. His voice when he spoke held an almost careful softness.

"Fräulein Marzynski, I believe this is yours? You may want it as a keepsake."

In his gloved hand, he held out a folded program from the night's concert. I hadn't realized I'd dropped it on my way out.

"Thank you, Hauptmann von Lüben. I didn't know you were in attendance."

"My tante mentioned it. I wanted to see the American on stage among the Germans." His eyes lingered on the program.

"I saw you in the chorus." He tilted his head, considering the right words. "You stood out. Not that you are an American but by the way you carried the music's emotion into every gesture, every turn of your head. It's clear how deeply the music moves you."

We stood inches apart. I studied his gloved fingers, the precise line of his jaw. Something unspoken trembled between us.

"That's kind of you to say. Thank you."

"Will you be performing again soon?" he asked.

"I hope so. The *Konservatorium* may schedule one more concert before the summer break."

He gave a slight bow, his voice dropping low. "I hope it does."

And then he was gone. My breath caught, as if the air itself had left with him.

♪

The cordial détente Herr Müller reported from the Ambassador's banquet vanished as quickly as early season snowflakes melt on a pavement warmed by an afternoon sun. On February 1, 1917, I joined the Müllers for breakfast. Delighted to discover a bowl of oatmeal and a dollop of brown sugar on top waiting for me, I pounced on my spoon and began shoveling the creamy heaven past my lips. Not until I scraped the bowl for the last sticky remnant did I notice a somber pall hanging in the room.

Herr Müller shook his head with a pained expression. As he folded a copy of the *Berliner Tageblatt* and placed it on the table, bold headlines leaped out at me. Admiral von Tirpitz had announced an unrestricted submarine campaign.

"This is bad," he murmured, almost to himself.

"What does it mean, dear?" Frau Müller asked the question on the tip of my tongue. German *Unterseeboote,* U-boats, had ceased maneuvers nine months ago. After the Germans torpedoed the *Sussex*, a French passenger steamer crossing the English Channel in March 1916, the United States had requested Germany send out adequate warnings to ensure the safety of passengers and crew on non-military ships.

"Wilson warned Germany that America won't tolerate these types of campaigns. The banquet was a sham. Trouble is brewing."

The sweetness of the brown sugar treat soured into a dark lead ball. The Germans had transformed themselves once again. Their callousness had risen like an insidious phoenix, resembling the eagle of the German Empire. Black and menacing, with its sharp red beak, curled tongue, and dagger claws. Its wings spread and feathers flapped to rule over all beneath its flight path. As I set out for class, I walked down streets electric with celebration. Black, red, and white flags fluttered at every corner. Swarms of smiling faces surrounded me. Strangers exchanged the news with eager excitement.

At the *Konservatorium*, Paulina greeted me with wide eyes and uncontainable joy. "Isn't it wonderful?" she exclaimed.

"Wonderful?" I asked, shaking my head. Had Frau Trebicz announced the selections for our next concert? Had she cast Paulina as Mimi, the coveted role of all opera singers in *La Bohème*? We didn't expect that announcement for at least another month.

"Don't you read the papers? Has Herr Müller slipped so that he cannot afford the *Berliner* every day?"

"We receive the papers, Paulina. I saw the disturbing report that the Germans have reneged on their *Sussex* pledge by reactivating an unrestricted submarine campaign. It's a serious misstep."

"Misstep? Hardly. It's a step in the right direction. The end is near. The government promises that the war will be over by April. Our greatest weapon will not fail!"

"By killing hundreds, thousands, of innocents on passenger ships?" My voice rose an octave, spurred by the vehemence in her words.

"Possibly, yes. More likely, we'll starve England into submission." She spat the word like a curse. "Just as she's tried to starve us for three years. No neutral ships, and that means American ships, will dare to deliver supplies through seas overrun with *Unterseeboote*. The pasty patsies of England will fall to their knees. The Allies will follow, crumbling like a house of cards."

Paulina's unwavering confidence spoke on behalf of a delusional nation. They believed that the flash of bared teeth, swarming toward innocents like steel sharks, would send the world cowering in fear. I refused to accept a misguided belief. Would America stop sending ships? The thought never crossed my mind. Until now.

♪

"Americans don't want war. The Peace God knows it. After all, wasn't that how he won re-election? By promising neutrality? Of course, he did," said Herr Bachmann.

The Müllers entertained frequently and expected me to join the evening discussions. As I sat still in the living room, I seethed with rage listening to Herr Bachmann espouse his opinion of American cowardice. I summoned the breathing exercises I used to calm myself before singing. The idea of Wilson as a "Peace God" had become a running joke in Berlin. Before Frau Müller could stop me, I stomped up to my room. I took my flag from its hiding spot. The time had arrived to reveal its power. The silky fabric slid through my fingers as I spread it across my chest. Holding it flat, I re-entered the living room.

"Herr Bachmann, you had best pray that President Wilson doesn't change his tune." I traced my index finger over the horizontal stripes. "America speaks through these stars and stripes. Red is our strength. White, our pure belief in American democratic ideals."

My palm spread across the top left corner. "We are united in thought across our forty-eight states. The white stars sit upon a field of blue. Vigilance and justice thread us together. We will not abandon our battered friends in the face of evil."

Turning on my heel, I left. My American right to speak freely regardless of what line I lived behind was as much a part of me as my desire for librettos with words that moved a soul.

That night, I took four straight pins from my sewing kit and tacked Old Glory to the wall over my bed. I would no longer bury a love for my country inside a lace-trimmed pillowcase.

♪

Two days later, my world collapsed.

February 3, 1917 --- America Severs Diplomatic Relations. Ambassador Gerard Demands His Passports from German Officials as U.S. Secretary of State Robert Lansing Orders Count Johann von Bernstorff to Leave Washington Immediately.

The newspaper headline collided with a whirlwind of fear and confusion in my mind.

My knees buckled. Frau Müller grabbed me by the waist and eased me into the dining chair. A chill seeped through me, as icy as the sleet that had fallen over the city.

I eked out a question, my lips trembling, my throat scratchy. "If Ambassador Gerard leaves, what about the rest of the Americans here? What about me?"

"Poor dear," said Frau Miller, her voice laced with sympathy.

More questions swam as the image of "Little Britain" surfaced in my thoughts. Would Germany round up American citizens the way they had the British ones when war broke out in 1914? Would they send me and others to an internment camp? Converted sheds and stables at the Ruhleben racetrack on Berlin's outskirts had housed 5,000 British civilians for two and a half years.

"The camp..."

Herr Müller patted my arm. "No, Josephine. The Brits are formal enemies of the state. It won't come to that. You are a young woman with valid documents proving your enrollment at the *Konservatorium*. You should be fine."

Should, he said.

I couldn't eat, despite the gnawing inside me. I slipped away to my room, seeking solitude. Standing before my beloved Stars and Stripes, a fleeting scrap of doubt crept in. Should I take it down? No. Now, more than ever, I would let my colors fly. Its power would watch over me. Remembering a reading from my father's funeral, I repeated it aloud for no one to hear but myself.

I am the One who will sustain you. I have made you and I will carry you; I will sustain you and I will rescue you. - Isaiah 46:4

SCENE XVIII

Closing the Door

February 1917
Berlin, Germany

After my initial shock at the severing of diplomatic relations, I embraced a new resolve. I had come to Berlin to study opera. Onkel Klaus and Tante Helga, as I now called them at their insistence, had paid my tuition for the year. As I had promised Herr Direktor, I worked hard every class. Frau Trebicz noted fewer American tones in my singing as I focused on the mechanics of each piece in German. A mere coincidence? Or a fated skill developed at the right moment?

The morning after the news, I chose a German-made dress that Evelyn had left in the closet. Four years out of date, the narrow, blue skirt with a matching long, thin wool overcoat would help me blend in on the streetcar. The extra length would also cover most of my American boots.

Downstairs, I heard Tante Helga greeting one of their neighbors. Mr. John Weil had arrived in Berlin in 1906 as a representative of an American mercantile firm. Over time, he had established a self-sustaining German branch. His father joined his business, bringing his mother over to Berlin to settle into German life. As a result, the Weils became well-connected in the local community. Relief at hearing his voice eased my nerves. I hurried down the stairs, eager to learn if he had any information regarding Americans in Berlin.

"Good morning, Miss Marzynski. I'd be happy to accompany you to the *Konservatorium* on my way to work today," he said with a slight nod.

In agreement, Tante Helga added, "The extra precaution is a wise idea. But I suggest neither of you speak English on your way."

In silence, we walked to the streetcar station. As we boarded, I couldn't shake the unsettling feeling that every passenger gazed at me, heavy with suspicion and reproach. I crossed my legs at the ankles and scrunched my feet under the seat and out of view.

To my dismay, Mr. Weil seemed to forget or ignore Tante Helga's suggestion. He prattled on in English about an upcoming pianoforte recital of some acquaintance or another. I added no comments, nor did I answer the questions he asked about my interest in attending with him. He continued until a stern-faced passenger leaned over and whispered, "You fool, this is no day to speak English."

Around us, I heard the humming of other passengers' remarks.

"A devil in angel's clothes."

"Wilson has played a dirty trick."

"*Ach*, I expected nothing else. Didn't I say that Ambassador Gerard must be a spy?"

More than once, my burning ears caught remarks to the effect of, "Oh, if Wilson visited the Reichstag, he wouldn't make it the two blocks from Friedrichstrasse to Potsdamer Platz."

What did they expect would happen to him? I shuddered to imagine Germans grabbing my president's trademark pince-nez glasses and stomping them to smithereens beneath Marschstiefel jackboots. German women waving loaves of bread in his face, only to snatch them away with a scream. *Now, you'll see. No bread for the fat Americans.* A ringlet of German children, holding hands, dancing around Wilson in the center of their circle, chanting, *Lügner, Lügner.* (Liar, Liar.)

The taut strings in my neck pulled tighter as I entered my first class of the day. Zara and Hannah dashed to my side. Each picked up one of my hands as they soothed me with endearments of, "We're so happy you came," and, "You mustn't worry. You'll continue your studies as planned," and "We're here."

The patriotic Paulina, however, stared me down with a piercing glare. From the corner of her mouth, she hissed. Her words slimy like a snake slithering across a garden path. "Yes, don't worry, Fräulein Marzynski. You have nothing to fear. Even if you declare war on Germany—which my father thinks unlikely—there would be no proper battle. How could there be? An army of a hundred thousand American men against our millions? Our well-trained and formidable soldiers, the finest the world has ever seen. The very idea is laughable."

I stepped out of Zara and Hannah's embraces. "Paulina, please do not assume our army would be any less well-trained, strong, and committed to an objective than your German one. We are not at war. We should hope it won't come to that. I think it's best we keep our thoughts to ourselves and focus on next month's performance. Don't you?"

Frau Trebicz had not yet announced roles for *Hänsel und Gretel*. But in my mind, I selected the perfect cast. Sweet, angelic Hannah as the Dew Fairy. Zara, the broom maker's sturdy wife. Of course, I would be Gretel, savoring the moment when, with one little shove, wham! I'd close the oven door on Paulina the Witch.

Schwaps! Geht die Tür—klaps! Nun ist die! (Whoosh! Goes the door—slap! Now the witch is dead.) If only we could vanquish the fear and distress of war with one gentle push.

♫

As the weeks unfolded, my resolve faltered. Walking home from our Monday market outing, Anna and I neared the central train station. A somber crowd mingled at its entrance. A procession of automobiles and taxis lined the curb. I watched as more than one hundred men, women, and children emerged from the vehicles. The American ambassador's entourage of family, consuls, and clerks. Hushed goodbyes in Spanish, Dutch and Greek from colleagues of other foreign embassies filtered through the air. A mass exodus of Americans was underway.

Leaving me behind.

As they vanished into the station, my heart tucked itself into one of the valises. I told Anna to go on ahead of me, wishing for time alone. I wandered down one street then another. A debate echoed through my head.

Should I drop my market basket and run? Grab hold of the cool steel pole by the doorway and swing myself up and into a train car? Not only for my security and sanity, but what about my mother? Had her worries escalated since the threatening news? I did not know. Correspondence had dwindled as tensions intensified. I believed she still wrote, but I had no faith the Germans processed her letters. I tossed every night since the severing of relations, thinking of her, lying awake, paralyzed in fear. In the morning, did she send David racing to the newsstand while dreading headlines about another U-boat sinking?

As Natalya had asked, why was I here? Worry over my mother's situation gave way to a slow build of anger. Mother hadn't said ten words about my plans. She must have realized the risks. Didn't she care about my safety? Did she think more about my chance to live out her dreams? I realized then the difficult position I had placed her in. Choose what was best for me or what was best for her? Mother's silent sacrifice burrowed deep like a mole, blinded by impossible choices as they stabbed, stabbed, stabbed in the dark for the right decision.

I faced the same dilemma now in the streets of Berlin. Should I leave or should I stay? As my thoughts clashed against one another, I stopped and looked up at the hulking, three-story

Blücher Palace, which had housed the American Embassy offices. Flags from Spain, Greece, and the Netherlands flapped on poles outside the main entrance. One pole stood alone in stark nudity. Stripped of its purpose of flying the flag that had greeted me on my walks. Its whispers of strength packed away in a crate. On its way home.

SCENE XIX

Stand By Me

March 1917
Berlin, Germany

While I lived beneath a veil of uncertainty, a sliver of happiness bloomed as springtime lifted her head from the weary winter. My German friend, Hannah, announced she had said yes to a proposal from her longtime sweetheart. A new future awaited her at the end of the aisle, filled with love, commitment, and hope. Her intended would be home on leave long enough for a ceremony and two days together afterward. Then, he would return to the Western front and she back to her study at the *Konservatorium*. Her courage and confidence in her decision amazed me. I wondered how long it might take for her to exchange a white wedding dress for a widow's black veil.

I cast aside my personal reservations when Hannah asked for Zara and my help. Zara volunteered her costume-designing skills to refashion Frau von Strauss's outdated wedding dress for her daughter. I took charge of assembling a decent bridal trousseau under the pall of clothes rationing.

We set out for the *Kaufhaus des Westens*, where we found a pair of low-quality cotton stockings, priced at only five marks. Woolen ones commanded thirty, if one could find them. Wool had joined the scarcity list, and the once-common practice of knitting socks for soldiers vanished for lack of yarn. A wedding night for any bride also demanded a new chemise. We hunted and hunted until we found a delicate, simple, fine cotton one with lace trimmings. It was worth every one of Hannah's ninety marks to welcome her husband into their marriage bed.

Holding up the chemise in front of her bulky dirndl, I teased, mimicking a man's lustful voice, "Hannah sweetheart, you look ravishing. Come to me." I slipped her fingers into the lacy straps, stepped back, and held out my hand.

As if performing on stage as Susana in *The Marriage of Figaro*, she pursed her lips and winked at me, "At last comes the moment, When, without reserve, I can rejoice in my lover's arms." She wrapped her arms around herself in a tight hug worthy of her fiancé's embrace.

For the ceremony, I loaned Hannah my boots with a strong request that she return them after her two-night honeymoon. A gesture of friendship only went so far. I had no desire to clomp to and from school in a pair of clunky, chunky German shoes. After three years of outfitting German soldiers with boots to withstand the terrors of trenches, the quality of leather had deteriorated. Shoemakers resorted to fabricating wooden sandals with leather straps. Among young women, wearing that hideous footwear and forgoing stockings became another statement of patriotic sacrifice.

On a Thursday afternoon, Tante Helga and I gathered at the Berliner Dom Lutheran church. I had never set foot inside any church, let alone one of such prominence in the German *kultur*. The cathedral's dark stone rose above the gray streets in defiant majesty. Tante Helga flanked me as we entered the cathedral. I prayed I wouldn't burst into flames, not as an American in a city wary of my political allegiance, but as a Jew. Hannah's friendship with me, however, outweighed the Torah's teachings. Inside, the air smelled of wax and old incense. Murals of angels, saints, and golden-framed apostles watched from heavenly perches. I felt like an intruder in a painting and hoped those Christian idols wouldn't point me out to the other guests.

When the officiant started the service, he spoke in tongues. Not of my God. And yet, a familiarity seeped into the space between the pews and the altar. Hannah von Strauss and Friedrich Vogel uttered their vows of love, honor, and endurance. To remain true to their union while the world urged defeat and retreat. Those words transcended any religion.

Throughout the brief ceremony, I wanted to yell "Mazel tov" to my friend, waiting for Friedrich to stomp on a glass, lying on the floor under a cloth. I didn't get the chance. No such ritual existed in a Lutheran ceremony. Instead, I reached for her hand as she passed by, exiting the magnificent church. I squeezed her fingers tight, a slim band of gold rubbing against my palm. "You look radiant, Frau Vogel. Mazel tov!"

I stood watching two people now joined as one. Would my boots that Hannah wore today ever walk me down an aisle to take the hand of a betrothed? Perhaps, some day. But to whom? And would Hannah witness my wedding? *If I married a German, of course she'd be there*, I thought. At that image, I shuddered. A German man standing next to me under a chuppah, his hairy hand placing a glass on the floor, and smashing it to smithereens beneath the heel of his polished jackboot.

As Hannah hailed from a prominent Berlin family, seeing Hauptmann von Lüben escort his aunt Frau Bachmann to the wedding didn't surprise me. On the sidewalk outside the cathedral, we waved our best wishes to Herr and Frau Vogel. The Hauptmann paused next to us.

"Fräulein Marzynski, I understand the reception is for immediate family only. Would you care to join me in toasting the Vogels at the Zur Letzten Instanz?" he asked.

Tante Helga nodded at the invitation. "Herr Hauptmann, my daughter's husband is also on leave, and I promised I would watch my grandson to give them some time alone. I cannot chaperone Josephine today."

A perfect excuse. I was in no mood for an evening with the Hauptmann as I eyed his polished jackboots.

"Frau Müller, I understand, but please know, I have the utmost respect for Fräulein Marzynski. Our Kaiser commands me to represent his army as a gentleman. We will have dinner, and I will see her home before eight o'clock. Nothing more."

I stepped closer to Tante Helga. "Wouldn't you like help with Rupert? He's becoming quite the handful these days," I said, hoping she would sense my disinterest in the dinner invitation.

"Oh no, I love watching him. Go along. You deserve a night out. I think we can trust Hauptmann von Lüben." I detested the wink she gave him. With no other excuse on the tip of my tongue, I placed my hand on his proffered arm. At least I might glean some information from him to pass along to Natalya.

Inside the café, warmth rose from coal stoves and porcelain cups of bitter coffee. I had never developed a taste for liver. But I didn't say "no thank you" to the plate of *Ganseleber* that the server set down between us. The gray block of paté with thin slices of dark rye bread beckoned with promises of the protein I had missed from too many meals. *Thank you, Mother Goose, for your sacrifice*, I thought.

"That was a beautiful ceremony, don't you think, Gustav? Hannah beamed through every minute."

"Indeed, it was. Herr Feldwebel Vogel has demonstrated his commitment to our cause. I'm glad we could reward him with a leave to come home."

"And Hannah too. She will give up her husband for the cause within two days. I hope Friedrich stays safe for both of their sakes."

"That's an impossible hope during war, Josephine."

His eyes turned downward as his ever-squared shoulders drooped a noticeable inch. A dent in his armor appeared for the first time since I had met Hauptmann von Lüben. I leaned upon the table, the rough cotton napkin under my elbows and my chin on my fists. With a slight bend forward, I asked, "Can you tell me, Gustav? Anything about your time at the front?"

I gazed over at him, noticing his jaw clenched and the muscles in his neck drawn taut like the strings of a cello. He looked at me with the light from the overhead oil lamp casting a shadow across his brow, deepening lines carved there by time and command. A faint breath escaped his lips.

"If you insist. My last battle tour ended with the second campaign in Aisne last May. After two weeks of daily skirmishes, the *Franzosen* released poison gas. I hadn't changed the filter on my *lederschutzmaske* in over a week. The gas odor leaked into my nostrils. A sergeant with a gaping hole in his stomach lay in the trench next to me. I took the man's mask."

"Oh, how could you?" I gasped.

"But why not?" he replied, his voice calm, as if explaining simple logic. "The man would die if not within minutes, then within the hour with no medical aid nearby. Why should we lose two German lives?"

The cold practicality of his words sent a shiver through me. Could I be friends with a man with such callous disregard for life? Or must I consider his situation and wonder, would I have done the same?

"In the end, it didn't matter whether I wore his mask or my faulty one. A shell exploded before I slipped it on. The force tore it from my hands. I breathed in so much gas, dirt, and small pieces of shrapnel that it should have killed me."

"But it didn't." Did I dare to admit? I was glad Gustav had survived the sufferings of a mud-filled trench.

"The gas inflamed and weakened my lungs to the point where the doctors deemed me unfit for combat. Now I'm bound to an office chair for the rest of my service. Hearing every day of our men's sacrifices. And yes, wondering about the safety of each one of them."

He paused. A twitch at the corner of his mouth belied the regrets in his eyes. He looked older, not in years, but in weight. The sharp edge in his spine, the perpetual discipline in his bearing, gave way to something fragile. More human. A man emerged whence a soldier had stood.

Hauptmann von Lüben hoped for things he had told me were impossible to hope for during war. I would not ask him anymore. In fact, I didn't think I could probe him for any information to share with Natalya. Gustav trusted me to tell his story. I wouldn't betray that trust.

SCENE XX

A Proclamation: War

April 1917
Berlin, Germany

I strolled down streets lined with blooming cherry trees as I headed home from classes the first week of April. Fragrant vanilla scents and soft pink petals wafted on a warm spring breeze. On the fringe of the city, I imagined fox kits emerging from dens and frolicking through beds of pine needles. In the parks, yellow finches flitted to and fro, interrupting their trills to drop an insect into tiny open beaks in twig-woven nests.

The beauty of nature dissolved as harsh man-made realities seized the land on the sixth of April, 1917. At five o'clock on that Friday afternoon, a military band lined up in front of the equestrian monument of Frederick the Great in the middle of the Unter den Linden. In the spot on that famous boulevard where I had admired the majesty of German history in my first weeks in Berlin, drummers began a 3-6 beat roll of their sticks against the toms. An Oberst, with two brass pips on his braided shoulder boards, stood on a raised platform, as straight and rigid as the Iron Man. This colonel—by now I knew the distinctions of rank insignia—boomed to the gathered crowds. "By all highest order: A State of War against the United States of America is proclaimed in Berlin, the Province of Brandenburg, and throughout our great Kaiser Wilheim's mighty German Empire."

My satchel slipped from my shoulder and hit the pavement with a dull thud, sheet music spilling out at my feet. I pressed my hand hard against my chest, as though I could steady the pounding inside. The sharp, finality of the words rang in my ears. My fears materialized with one long sentence. The Imperial German Government had declared my country, my people, as its latest adversary. I buried my face in my open palms and wept.

♪

Over the next two weeks, the Müllers attempted days to retain the fragile illusion of normalcy. Friday nights meant Shabbos dinner with Evelyn, followed by bedtime stories with Rupert. After a meager meal of ground chicken and a hearty reading of another tale of the mischievous imps, *Max und Moritz,* Evelyn and I stepped into the black April night toward her house. The air bit at our cheeks. We quickened our pace until I left them at her doorstep, eager to nestle deep under down-filled quilts waiting for me at home.

More ice-cold fear, however, met me upon my return to the Müllers. Anna stepped forward, her eyes wide and forehead creased as deep as the fissures in a sidewalk crack. She thrust a paper into my hands. "Oh, Fräulein Josephine," she burst out, "a policeman came looking for you. He left this."

I unfolded the document, its official seal at the top mocking me. Tante Helga peered over my shoulder and read the words I could not utter aloud. "You are commanded to report at your local police station at eight o'clock in the morning, Saturday, April 21. Bring your passport with you."

My hands shook. Seeing the words printed in crisp black ink with my name at the top of the page made the floor buckle beneath me. Tante Helga rested her hand on my shoulder. I swallowed, but my mouth went dry. My eyes darted back to the paper. No explanation. No choice. A command. The embossed eagle's wings spread over everything it sought to control. Including me.

My quilts would not protect me from the cold that night. Nor would the Stars and Stripes hanging above my head. Dreams blurred in scenarios from hope to despair. One moment, I stood at the railing of a great ship, pointed toward a fiery red setting sun, its fading rays glinting off the pale green robes of Lady Liberty. The next moment, I clutched the black bars of a horse stable like where British men had been held now for two and a half years. I'd kick at brown wooden slats, screaming white-hot demands for my release from an internment.

That Saturday morning, Anna offered to accompany me to the *Prasidium* police headquarters. I accepted the moral support and presence of a German girl at my side. We sat close together on a waiting bench in a small, gloomy basement room. Five overbearing officers stood along the wall, keeping watch over us and three other aliens. A door opened every twenty-minutes to admit one of us to learn our fate. After a silent hour of unease and dread, I heard my name. "Fräulein Marzynski." Too late to ponder whether I should have taken my mother's maiden name of Meyers for my passport seven months ago. I relinquished the summons paper to the gnarled hand of an older gentleman seated behind a scratched desk.

"Ha! Another damned Yankee! Well, give me your passport."

He eyed the Seal of the United States with a sneer. "What are you doing here in Berlin?"

I pointed to the line on my passport, Nature of Business: Music student.

"I'm studying music, sir."

"Oh? Every American woman who comes here claims to be a music student, and every man says he's a dentist." A sense of skepticism laced his statement.

His tone burned. I swallowed the sharp words rising in my throat. Jack's warning from months ago echoed in my mind: wiser to stay silent and safe than to land yourself in a Prussian prison.

"Sit," he said. I obeyed like a dog.

"Why come here during wartime?"

I answered patiently, although I knew he didn't care. Then the real interrogation began. He wanted to know about my parents—where had they emigrated from? What did they do in America? I recited the familiar details with expanded notes about my mother's family and my father's mother, who was also German although she had moved to Poland. I explained my father's untimely death and my mother's work.

"What of siblings?"

I tried to focus on his questions, this man with my fate in his hands, but I couldn't. The rote answers lulled me into a sense of limbo. I glanced toward the door, waiting for an open escape route. I pressed my sweaty palms onto my thighs. Harder and harder, I pressed, feeling the tension rise through my arms to my shoulders. The tight coil ready to snap.

"Fräulien, siblings. Where are they?"

"A sister, Lillian, and two younger brothers, David and Julian. They live with my mother."

He raised his head from his note-taking. "So, two brothers."

I nodded.

"Ages?"

"Julian is eight. David is twelve."

"Not old enough to fight us, then?"

"No, not yet…" The words slipped out before I could stop them.

His eyes darkened. He leaned over the desk, jabbing a manicured finger in my face.

"Well, listen to me, Fräulein." He drew the title out into two syllables that sounded like the longest semibreve rest I'd ever heard, more than the four beats of a whole note.

"If we haven't won this war five years from now," he continued, "your brother David will probably fly over Berlin, dropping bombs from airplanes. And I hope the first one lands right on you!"

The air in my lungs stalled. Is this how Gustav had felt with the useless gas mask dangling from his hand? My body wavered in the chair. I gripped the armrests to steady my sway. Before I could respond, not that I had any rebuttal to his caustic remark, he moved on to his next question.

"Where is your residence?"

"The Müllers, at Niederlagstraße 15. They are dear family friends of my German-born mother and offered lodgings to me during my study at the *Klindworth-Scharwenka Konservatorium der Musik*."

His head snapped up. "Herr Klaus Müller?"

A flicker of recognition, perhaps even respect, crossed his face. At that moment, I understood how important the right connections could be to save me. I exhaled with a cautious sigh.

Moments later, I watched him add his signature, *V. Boehn*, to the bottom of the page with a flourish. He handed me a printed two-page document marked with fresh notes. "Here," he said. "These conditions will allow you to remain with the Müllers. For now."

The words struck me as something between a residency permit and a set of rules—permission to remain in Berlin and a stark warning of how fragile that permission was.

Ausweis (Identification Papers)
For the American citizen, *Josephine Therese Marzynski*.
Born: *30-12-1897*
Current Residence: *Niederlagstraße 15, Berlin*
All persons over fifteen years of age, male or female, who are citizens of an enemy country MUST:

1. Always carry this pass.
2. Report to this police station ~~twice daily~~. *(hand marked once daily)*
3. Remain indoors between ~~8 P.M. and 7 A.M.~~ *(hand marked 10 P.M. and 6 A.M.)*
4. Not leave this district of Berlin *without permission* from the Supreme Police Court.
5. Any violation of these rules will be punished by the Supreme Kommandant under the regulations of January 21, 1916.

Signed,
The Chief of Police of Berlin
V. Boehn, Cavalry General

"Thank you, Herr Polizeichef Boehn. I appreciate the consideration and accommodation. The early morning and the late time in the evening allow me to attend my classes and performances."

"Just understand, Fräulein, that you are in our power. Be careful what you say, or..."

He waved us away and called for the next alien. I doubted that man had the same high-level connections to afford him the luxuries given to me.

In between classes the following day, I shared my news with Zara and Hannah. Zara, from Minsk, lived with her Russian grandfather on the outskirts of Berlin. She agreed that the extended hours boded well for me. At the end of last year, the police in her neighborhood released her from daily check-ins, but not her grandfather.

"Despite living in this country for twenty years, my grandfather has had to report *every single day* since August 1914. Sometimes he comes home frightened and quiet. If he so much as shifts his weight in line waiting for his appointment, they bellow at him, 'Stand still, you!' And he's an old man. A weak old man. And our neighbor, an Italian, drags his entire family, even the youngest children, to mandatory twice a day appointments."

Hannah squeezed my hand as I tensed at Zara's account. "Don't let her scare you. Herr Müller commands great clout here in the city. You'll be safe."

I blinked back a tear and turned to the sheet music on the stands in front of us. Frau Trebicz had cast me as the Sandman, not Gretel, for our next performance. During practice and at home each night, I lifted my voice to the heavens to call upon the angels to bring me sweet dreams. *Und bringen holde träume*. I hoped they'd find me behind my curtain of anguish.

INTERMISSION

January 1918
Boston, Massachusetts

A waiter in a black suit appeared at our table. "Have you decided?" asked Mr. Robinson.

I propped my elbows on the white tablecloth, scanning the vast menu. The choices filled the oversized sheet, edge to edge, top to bottom. Cotuit oysters, thirty cents. Twelve different soup selections. Fish and seafood. Oatmeal muffins for a dime. Luncheon entrées, salads, vegetables, potatoes, spaghetti three ways: Italienne, Milanese, au gratin. I wanted a bite from every column and row.

My eyes drifted to the desserts. Boston cream pie. Éclairs. Peach melba. Ice cream, sorbets, sliced fresh pineapple. Bananas! Camembert. Coffee with cream, orange pekoe tea. A bottle of pasteurized milk for ten cents. A month ago, my choices fit on half an index card, rations deciding for me. Now, the choices were mine to command.

Careful to avoid dishes swimming in cream or melted butter—I didn't want to lose those delicacies to a stomach which would reject them after a year of bland, small servings of the most basic staples—I pointed to the breaded veal cutlet accompanied by a side of spaghetti Italienne. As my mother had taught me, never choose the most expensive item on a menu; it's poor form. At sixty cents for the plate, the combination should fill me without overextending the generosity offered by my lunch companion, even if he had mentioned Page Publishing would pick up the bill. "Can you also bring a dish of dill pickles? Are they made with kosher salt?"

The waiter confirmed they were, took Mr. Robinson's order of the lamb chops with mint sauce, whipped potatoes, and a cup of coffee, and headed to the kitchen. We would resume our talks, this the sixth day of our meetings, as I unfolded my story to an eager listener.

My ghostwriter pulled a fresh pad of paper from his briefcase. "Yesterday we left off with the declaration of war, and you received the directive to check in at the police station. You had thought when diplomatic relations were severed, you should leave. But you stayed. Now, it was war against America. Didn't you think then you should leave?"

"My first reaction bordered on hysteria. I calmed myself after Onkel Klaus reiterated I should continue with my routine and my studies. He had become like a father to me. I trusted his every word. He gave me no reason to doubt his decisions."

"So, you went on with your classes without interruption."

"Correct. Life continued. The war marched on."

I picked up the menu, waving it at the waiter as he had forgotten to take it with our order. At the top of the page, above the restaurant's logo of two large entwined "C's" for Copley Café, a statement reminded me the war continues now, in January 1918.

BUY WAR SAVINGS STAMPS—FOR SALE HERE.

Here, at a gentlemen's dining club, one couldn't escape the omnipresence of the war effort now that the United States was fully engaged. But the food. Oh my, did I relish my return to the land of plenty. May I never see a ration card ever again.

ACT II

SCENE I

Friends and Enemies

May 1917
Berlin, Germany

Shadows of unease shifted just beyond my sight. To be treated no differently than a common criminal ate my soul. Like acid trickling down my throat, scraping and damaging my precious vocal cords. I longed to resist the law's grip on me. But Jack and Onkel Klaus' warnings echoed in my mind.

Throughout the spring of 1917, I reported daily, as instructed, to the police station. I mustered every ounce of willpower to answer the same questions day after day, despite attempts to catch me with an inconsistency. *Where did I live? How long did my term at the* Konservatorium *last?* On an afternoon in early May, another blow fell. The mail arrived with a stark, official envelope addressed to me. My hands trembled as I opened and read the clear, inescapable message. The *Kommandantur* (headquarters) had summoned me to appear no later than noon the next day.

Evelyn accompanied me to the massive stone building, holding my hand and talking of the spring blooms and chatter that Monday's market might have mutton available. I appreciated her efforts, but no bouquets of flowers or hanks of fatty, salted meat could quell my nerves. At the entrance, I pulled the new summons from my reticule for inspection. The soldier handed me a numbered card, forty-five, and gestured toward a small room off the main corridor. Above the door, a sign read AMERICANS.

"Wait until we call your number," he instructed.

As we walked down the hallway, I glimpsed other rooms marked with the names of other nationalities. In these makeshift holding pens, the enemies of Germany sat trapped in agonizing limbo. Inside the room, a family huddled on a bench next to me. The father, a tall man with a handlebar mustache, dressed in a dark suit, stood hovering over his little family. The mother held an infant in her lap. When the baby mewled like a hungry kitten, the mother hushed her and swayed her body to a silent lullaby. Two older boys both wore suit jackets and knickers with knee-high socks and polished boots. One would poke the other the same way my brothers would annoy each other for amusement until the father flicked his middle finger against the back of each one's ear.

When the attendant called "Twenty-eight," the family rose and disappeared through a different side door. A strange fascination took hold. As if I had stepped into a surreal tale from *The Arabian Nights,* I wondered. What lay beyond that door—fate or fatality? Retention or release?

Three endless hours crawled by. The tick of the wall clock pinged like the hammering of a nail into a coffin. Turning to Evelyn, my voice taut with exhaustion and dread, I said, "I can't. I'm going in next, whether or not they call my number."

I burst through the doorway where I had watched countless others enter. None of them remained in the room on the other side of the door. A single officer sat at a lone desk. His heft spilled over the edges of the chair. Blond hair lay in combed waves across his head. A stiff mustache in the same yellow tones looked like a gold bar cemented above his thin lips.

Laying the summons and my identification papers before him, I said, "I'm here as requested." He scanned each one, then opened a thick black ledger. Row after row contained names and dates.

English, French, Italian, German, Greek, Polish, Irish, Danish, Slavic surnames. All of them American or Americanized.

The stubby finger paused on the ledger sheet at the letter M.

Evelyn entered the room and stood by my side. I nodded a thank you for her reassuring presence.

"Yes. Yes. But who are you?" he asked. He turned his sharp eyes to Evelyn.

"Pardon me. I am Frau Hauptmann Schmidt. My father is Herr Kommerzienrat Müller, and my husband was recently appointed..."

"I recall, to a Stabsoffiziere," he interrupted. Ernst's elevated rank worked like magic. In an instant, the stern demeanor melted. The inspector sprang to his feet, bowed deeply, and, in a voice now thick with charm, exchanged exaggerated pleasantries with Evelyn before escorting us into another small room. Here, another official wasted no time. "Passport," he demanded.

I handed it over, heart pounding as my empty stomach groaned.

"Fräulein, this passport has expired," he said, his voice wasting no words.

"Expired?" I repeated. My mind raced. How did I miss the three-month validity date? How did the countless other inspectors since April miss it?

"*Ja, ja*, it is worthless," he continued. "I could have you interned."

My dread, no longer a mere wave, strengthened into a tsunami, ready to consume me. Evelyn encircled my waist and flicked a gaze toward the first inspector.

"Ahem," he interrupted. "May I introduce you to Fräulein Marzynski's close acquaintance, Frau Hauptmann Schmidt?"

He gave another slight bow.

The second official completed his inspection. "Under the circumstances, I will overlook the expiration. But you must renew it immediately."

"Yes, of course. I'll go this afternoon," I assured him, already edging toward the door.

♪

Every morning before heading to class, I pored over the *Berliner Tageblatt*, and every evening, the *Vossische Zeitung*, desperate for any shred of news about what was happening across the Atlantic. But why did I bother? Line after line of blatant misinformation filled the newsprint. Frustrated, I would crumple the deceitful pages and hurl them to the floor. Under my breath, out of earshot of my gracious and proper hostess, I cursed.

By mid-May came reports of an American draft. The German papers refused to call it "Selective Service" which Onkel Klaus explained would call upon young men to fill the ranks of American troops. Instead, the Germans sneered at it as "Conscription." One morning, as we sat at breakfast, Frau Bachmann breezed in under the pretense of wanting to borrow Anna for the afternoon. Her maid had fallen ill. Despite Tante Helga's quick agreement to help a neighbor, Frau Bachmann turned to me and said, "I thought you called America a *free* country. What do you think now? Your government has resorted to conscription. I guess it proves what Herr Kommerzienrat Bachmann has always said—your people will fight only when they're forced to."

Later that week, she arrived again with another smug comment. "I suppose you've read in the *Tageblatt* that your compatriots have seized all our magnificent ships from American docks? Even the magnificent *Vaterland*. That ship cost us sixteen million marks!"

This time, I would not remain silent. I met her eye-to-eye. "I think the United States did what Germany would have done."

"But what good are those ships to you?" she snapped, her tone an octave lower than before. "I understand our sailors disabled every single one before the Americans seized them."

I tamped down my mix of rage and unease. This woman didn't warrant my fury. Anything I said would fall on her closed ears and mind. I knew then that the people of Germany would not voluntarily abandon beliefs. While misguided, those beliefs ran through their veins, rooted in generations of tradition, shaped by education, and reinforced by relentless propaganda. How would they ever come to see, as I did, that they worshiped false idols, as deceptive and hollow as Baal?

Again and again, the papers mocked America's slow enlistment and downplayed the first Liberty Loan's success, calling it a scheme by Wilson and his wealthy allies to drag a reluctant nation into war. I knew in my heart that America would fight like the devil to free her allies from the Prussian grip. What I craved was the truth. An American paper in my hands. Better yet, I longed to see the familiar slant of my mother's handwriting on a thin sheet, folded in thirds, stamped *Boston, Massachusetts.*

Every night, I thanked Elohim in my prayers that David and Julian were not of age. For I knew my brothers, in honor of my patriotic father, would join the Selective Service as its first enrollees. This war must end. It couldn't continue for another five years. The words of the officer during my first police station visit could not become a reality. I cringed to think of David flying over Berlin, dropping bombs on the city where I lived, trapped behind bars of my own doing. A target for my brother to destroy.

♪

My gloom descended like a moonless night when one afternoon Hauptmann von Lüben called on me to accompany him to the theater. The mere thought exhausted me. A relentless heat, reported as the worst Berlin had seen in seventy years, had sapped me of any energy. Sensing my reluctance, instead we visited in the Müller's living room. I tried to keep our conversation lighthearted, sharing news of my next concert and the hope of landing the role of Elsa in *Lohengrin*. The demands of the role exceeded my range and ability, but I needed a dream to latch onto during those trying days.

Gustav let out a low whistle as he lounged in the chair opposite me. "Whee-hee, fair maiden, Josephine. You needn't dream. It is I here, your knight in shining armor, ready to ease your fear, defend your name. If I recall the final scene, the knight asks Elsa to marry him in exchange for the pledge of his loyalty."

To keep him amused, I teased, "Such the dramatic. Perhaps you should be on a stage instead of behind an army desk. However, your voice would never reach the tenor needed to play Lohengrin to my Elsa."

"Nor do I have the patience to train the way you do, Josephine. I am constantly in awe of your dedication to your studies. What's your favorite aria from the opera?" he said.

"That's easy—'Elsa's Dreams.' It reminds me of the Swan Boats in a lagoon we have in a Boston public park. Do you recall the scene when Lohengrin arrives at Elsa's side, drawn up a river by a swan pulling a boat?"

I slipped back into the memory of Boston. Our beautiful Public Garden, lined with majestic elms, maples, and oaks blazed fires of red and gold in the fall. In spring, flower petals burst open in every ribbon of color along walkways. Hot summer days when my brothers, sister, and I would race over a bridge, through the gates, and across Tremont Street on our way to Brigham's ice cream shop. A scoop of chocolate nestled in a chilled pedestal dish awaited my poised spoon to dig in.

"Swan-pulled boats. You'd best hope the American army won't try to use that mode of transportation for its soldiers. They'll be doomed for sure."

"Gustav, don't be ridiculous. The swans are made of wood to look like swans."

My casual tone encouraged a wink from him. "I'm glad we're becoming friends, Josephine. We won't be enemies much longer."

"Why not?" I asked, wary of his confidence.

"You read the papers," he said, spreading his arms wide, palms up, as if he held a precious present out for me. "Russia is on the verge of making peace. Once we pull our troops from the eastern front and send them west, we will wrap this up in no time."

"You forget America," I interrupted.

He threw back his head and laughed—a grating sound that set my teeth on edge. "Oh, no, I don't. It will be years before those troops have any real impact."

I held his gaze, my frustration boiling over. "Gustav, I know my country, and we wouldn't have entered this war without cause. If you think we'll quit before finishing the job, then you don't know us at all."

With a toss of my chestnut locks, I rose from the sofa. As any great diva would do for her exit scene, I nodded a curt good night, brushed past him without a glance, and left the room with my head held high.

SCENE II

Fourth of July with the Red, White, and Black

July 1917
Berlin, Germany

Across the ocean, in my beloved homeland, I could almost see my brothers waving their hand-held Stars and Stripes as marching bands tooted, blared, and drummed. Taste the tang of blueberry pie washed down with tart, freshly squeezed lemonade from a sweat-covered glass. Ice cubes clinking against the sides with every gulp. An electric fervor in the air as bodies pressed together along the parade route in unity and anticipation. July Fourth, 1917. Americans, being Americans, on American soil, celebrating the birth of our independence. Here in Berlin, I lived under a webbed snare, waiting for a spider to descend on a filament of silk and devour me whole.

Onkel Klaus set aside the morning *Tageblatt* as he sipped on a bitter cup of chicory. Super-charged, caffeine-laced coffee had become a distant memory. With a sigh as long as the column of names of war dead in today's edition of the paper, he said, "July Fourth. Your parade will include new soldiers this year. The wild enthusiasm surrounding them will be magnificent."

Across from him at the dining table, Tante Helga's voice quivered. "Do you think they'll reach the Western front? Everyone, well, Frau Bachmann, says the U-boats will sink every transport before they hit French shores."

I had also heard Frau Bachmann's ill-guided observations: "Then again, perhaps we shouldn't waste our U-boats' time on your troopships with such small numbers of men. Even if a thousand Americans should reach the front, so be it. We'll show them what an actual war is. One skirmish and they'll be writing home in a panic, begging their government to pull them out and warning others not to come."

There was no arguing with such warped, blind, twisted reasoning. Logic is powerless against a mind determined to ignore it. Yet the dreadful image Frau Bachmann painted of eager young soldiers, half-covered in seaweed and sea froth before they placed a boot on foreign shores, chilled me. I saw their faces: boys from my school, men who raised their voices at Temple Adath Jeshurun, pleading with heaven in song and prayer.

What of Josef Bonime, the pianist I'd met backstage for mere moments? Would he chance his gifted fingers to the grip of a rifle, a bayonet aimed at a Boche soldier? What if that soldier was a German Jew with the same musical talent? Would they recognize a kinship between them? Would they lay down their arms and turn away? Or would they lie mangled in the mud of France, their music lost forever?

Those types of thoughts followed me when I set out for my daily duty. I—a so-called free American on the day of our Independence—would report to a Prussian police station like a criminal on parole. Germany's red, white, and black banners dripped from building eaves, each one a taunt. The officer glanced at my papers before stamping them hard and tossing them back.

The date, *4 Juli 1917,* would burn into my memory, seared like a brand to remind me of my time as an enemy of the state.

I tucked the papers into my reticule and trudged home to the sanctuary of the Müllers.

♪

School was out, and empty hours passed with no distraction from the weight of my isolation. When the telephone rang, I lunged for it. Mrs. Weil's warm voice invited me to spend the evening with her; John and her husband were away, and she didn't want to be alone on the American holiday. Today, my thoughts refused to bend into German. We spoke in English—until a sharp voice cut through the line.

"Kein Englisch!"

A click. I set the receiver down, pulse racing. Rather than give them the satisfaction they had severed my connection to a friend, I put on a brave smile and set off for Mrs. Weil's home. Inside, she had drawn the drapes lest any prying eyes see an American flag hanging from the bookcase in the middle of her living room. We poured wine, clinked glasses, and toasted our forty-eight states and everything they stood for.

"I remember when Arizona and New Mexico became states five years ago. That year, my father rushed out as soon as the new flag with the forty-eight stars came in stock. He handed over his seventy-three cents at the dry goods store with only a minor grumble at the cost. Plenty of men at the store pointed out that in Alburquerque, subscribers to the local newspaper received a free one," I reminisced, regaling Mrs. Weil with stories of past July Fourths.

"When Papa came home, he snapped it onto the ropes of our flagpole and hoisted it up. For dinner that night, he sent my sister and me off to the store in search of traditional foods from the southwestern states. Our kosher grocer laughed, claiming he didn't stock chili peppers."

Mrs. Weil chuckled with me. The hard lines of worry around the corners of her eyes had softened. "I wonder if we'll add any other states?" she asked.

"I don't know. Although I have to admit, geography was not my favorite subject. I couldn't name any other territories, even if you paid me with a new pair of stockings."

For hours, two solitary women in the heart of Germany tried to lift each other's spirits with stories of home and the loved ones we longed for. But the more we spoke, the deeper our homesickness grew. At least, I knew mine did. Even the rare indulgence of a box of chocolates from a hidden stash of candy boxes did little to console us.

"John has a true American sweet tooth," Mrs. Weil admitted, half-laughing, half-apologetic. "When they started cutting back on sweets, he stocked up before the famine hit."

She lifted the lid from a half-pound Cadbury's Milk Tray. Neat rows of chocolates nestled in ribbed paper cups. For half an hour we studied their shapes, guessing at the fillings without taking a bite. At last, I chose one. "Hurrah!" My tongue met smooth milk chocolate, then strawberry cream over vanilla. I'd found the coveted Strawberry Temptation.

The evening stretched on, our conversation tumbling forward until I glanced at the clock. "Goodness, it's almost midnight! I should have left hours ago!"

Mrs. Weil said, "You can't walk home now, unescorted. It would be best if you spent the night."

"It's only a few short blocks. I'll be careful and quick. The police have more to worry about at this hour than a single woman hurrying home."

"Let me call Helga, so she knows when to expect you."

I agreed and stepped out alone into the quiet, darkened streets. I wore a thin white flannel dress, which made me look tall and slender, like a lighthouse. Although I wasn't afraid, I realized how easily I could be seen, even in the dense darkness that cloaked Berlin's streets at night.

While scanning the shadows for a policeman, I quickened my pace. At each corner, I slowed. Would a policeman protect me from the lawlessness that lurked along the streets at this time of night? Or turn me in for breaking curfew by over two hours? At the end of the block, I spied the Müllers' stately home. Almost there.

After a lovely day with Mrs. Weil, I slipped into a blissful calm. The peace of the day embraced me as I thought of the aria "Deh, Vieni, Non Tardar" from *The Marriage of Figaro*. Composed for a soprano, the words held comfort.

Come, do not delay, oh bliss,
Come where love calls thee to joy,
While night's torch does not shine in the sky,
While the air is still dark and the world quiet.

Lost in the libretto, I didn't see two powerful arms, which shot out from behind me. They wrapped around my neck like a snake, sinewy and slick with sweat from the sultry summer night. A thick tongue slurred the German equivalent of *"Hello, girlie."*

Terror locked my throat. My mind flashed with nightmarish visions. I twisted hard, trying to break free, but his ironclad grip held me like a vise. He pulled me tight against his chest. I felt the round knobs of the steel buttons running up his torso. His fingers loosened just a fraction, enough time for me to drive my elbow into his ribs. I wrenched free. He snarled and lunged at me again.

Out of the corner of my eye, I saw him. A hulking figure clad in a soldier's uniform. I bolted, galloping like a wild mustang across the Great Plains of America. My hair loose and flowing behind me. I bucked and lurched forward. My pulse roared in my ears. Then, out of the blackness, a different sound of footsteps pounded behind me. Another figure materialized, sending my stomach plummeting to the ground. I pulled myself up short. As I looked up, my terror eased. I had never been so relieved to see a police officer. I stumbled, righted myself, and gasped out my story.

"Did you see him? Aren't you going after him? He attacked me!" Shaking, I stammered the words out.

And the police officer? He laughed.

HOW DARE HE! He couldn't have known I was an American girl out past curfew. With my simple white dress and chestnut hair, I could have been any German girl. My fury surged hot and fast, drowning out my fear. When he spoke, his tone shifted to something gruff and suspicious.

"Fräulein, why are you out at this hour?"

"Returning home from an evening with my friend's mother. She was especially melancholy tonight. I wanted to take her mind off her son's absence with a game of Klabberjass. I let her win every round."

Let him think John Weil was a soldier, not an American businessman. Let him think I was a kind German girl thinking of the well-being of an older woman, alone in her grief for her son at the front. But in my panic, I slipped. My foreign accent betrayed me.

His eyes narrowed into a squint. "American? Where do you live?"

"With Herr Kommerzienrat Müller." I pointed to the house.

"Go. Don't let me find you out past eight o'clock again. You'll lose more than a round of Klabberjass if I do."

I nodded my acknowledgment and hurried up the street without looking back.

Tante Helga opened the door for me. With anxious waiting etched into her face, she peered over my shoulder.

"Did I hear you talking to someone?"

The moment I stepped inside, the dam broke. I collapsed at her motherly knees, sobbing out the whole terrifying ordeal, my nerves unraveling like a ball of yarn rolling across the floor.

"Please, I want to go home," I said. After eight months in Berlin and three as an enemy of the state, my entire being teetered and my nerve waned. I longed for the grace of God to send me home. Like a snuffer placed over a candle flame, the Germans, with their relentless inquisitions and suspicions of me, had extinguished my passions. My desires disappeared like wisps of smoke from a blackened wick. Swirling up and away as translucent tendrils, taking my dreams of becoming a professional opera singer into an air of nothingness.

And that…that was my Fourth of July in 1917.

SCENE III

Travel within Borders

July 1917
Berlin, Germany

I resolved to leave Germany as soon as possible. By this point, Onkel Klaus agreed and offered to purchase my ticket. I learned, however, that securing a ticket involved much more than sliding a few thousand marks across a counter.

Two days after my breakdown on the Fourth, he came home with the news I dreaded. "Absolutely impossible, my dear Josephine," he said, shaking his head. "Ships have been sold out for weeks. Even those with means have booked themselves into half of the steerage accommodations. I've added your application to the waiting list. But we won't know when a spot will become available."

His words sank like a stone in my chest. Rather than packing my valises and saying heartfelt goodbyes, instead I would endure summer in Berlin. I loathed the idea as much as the prospect of the July sun beating down on us. Zara had taken a factory job when news hit that Russia had redoubled its efforts to oust the Kaiser. "I need to show my allegiance to the German war effort. Further, I can't chance the Germans deciding my grandfather and I are spies, or worse, assassins. As if an old man and young woman, weak from food rationing, could take on a well-fed German soldier or police officer with a firearm at his side."

Evelyn had left with her husband's parents for a summer visit to Salzbrunn Springs. On a chance meeting with Natalya, I learned she had stopped her visits to the tenement families. When questioned, she replied, "The hospital ward overflows with delirious soldiers." My fears for her safety escalated when she added in a lower voice, "Many times they confide more than they should to a quiet, dutiful Red Cross nurse."

The week following the Fourth, Tante Helga asked me to join her on a hunt for summer clothes for Rupert. After two weeks in the country with fresh air and access to garden harvests, dairy cows, and fewer ration restrictions, Tante expected he would have outgrown all his clothes. As I laced up my boots, she looked down at my declaration of American fashion.

"I think, Josephine, you should shop for some shoes too. Pack your boots away until your trip home."

Recalling the glares I had received on the streetcars for months now, I nodded. Although the thought of the chunky wooden boxes the Germans called shoes made me shudder. One more reason I couldn't wait to get home.

We cobbled together extra ration cards and set out for *Kaufhaus des Westens*. Once inside the store, I nearly tripped into the arms of Hannah. The moment she saw me, her face lit up. "Oh, Josephine," she exclaimed, "Mother and I are about to leave for Bad Elster, a renowned health resort, on our annual six weeks summer outing. It's a stunning place in the mountains near the Austrian border."

She gazed upon my sallow complexion and heavy-lidded eyes, encircled like a raccoon's mask. "I think it's exactly what you need. Would you like to join us?"

Before I asked Tante Helga her thoughts, she interjected, "Hannah, you're an angel. That's a magnificent idea and a magnanimous offer. The mineral waters and baths would work wonders for Josephine's anemia. Of course, we'll need to ask Herr Müller for his opinion. If Josephine's application for passage moves ahead, can she get back in time?"

While I appreciated her optimism, I don't think Onkel Klaus had told his wife the waiting lists covered several pages before the name *Josephine Therese Marzynski* appeared. A smile lifted my lips for the first time since my afternoon with Mrs. Weil. "I'll take that risk. I have little hope that an opening will arise within the next six weeks."

We talked of plans as excitement bloomed within me. By the time I returned home, I sensed a skip in my step. Only one maddening obstacle arose. I needed a set of documents that would allow travel within Germany.

At the *Kommandantur*, the official who daily stamped my documents instructed me to submit a formal written petition requesting permission to leave Berlin with details of where I planned to go, who would accompany me, who I would stay with, and for how long.

Bureaucracy sought to entangle me with countless questions and unsatisfactory answers. But I was determined. I could almost feel the soft mountain air in Bad Elster kissing my cheek. I'd hunt down the largest pair of scissors from Greta's sewing box and slice through every piece of red tape until they fell on the floor in a heap.

German decisions moved with astonishing speed when urgency demanded it. In my case, however, it required endless, painstaking deliberation. Days crawled by. Hannah and her mother departed without me. Each day that passed without an approval, my patience boiled to the edge of eruption. I needed to take control. Inspiration struck from the depths of my frustration. During one of his afternoon calls, Hauptmann von Lüben commented on my appearance.

"Josephine, I am most concerned. You're very pale. Your expression is as dour as your gray frock. Are my visits that dreadful for you?"

There he goes again, I think. Assuming he has any part in my despondency. Then again, maybe he could play a part in changing my attitude.

"It's not you, Gustav. But if I don't escape this sweltering city soon, I expect to fill a German grave. Will your government be pleased to see me gone, or irritated to have an American interred under German soil? Perhaps you can help me? A man of your standing must have some influence to help process my application to visit Hannah in Bad Elster."

A week later, he arrived with the coveted document. "Here you are, Josephine." He handed me the papers. "It took extra convincing and the promise of a night at the Prater biergarten with my wallet open, but it's done."

His lake-blue eyes widened with anticipation. My asking for help had placed me on a slippery slope. Now that he had delivered on my request, I must uphold my end of an unspoken bargain. I raised my heels off the floor to reach his face four inches above my head. My lips swiped across his cheek.

He placed his fingertips on the damp circle and grinned. "I shall try to visit you in Bad Elster too."

"I would look forward to it, Gustav," I said aloud, while praying to myself that I'd find another rescuer: limited train schedules and army orders to keep him in Berlin.

♪

Onkel Klaus purchased a ticket for me with the best accommodations. However, when I boarded, I found every first-class coupé packed beyond capacity. As the train lurched forward, I passed through each car. Soldiers, many of them wounded or ill, traveling to the baths for convalescence, crammed the seats and aisles.

Toward the rear of the train, I found one compartment occupied by seven people. My body, less the fifteen pounds I had lost since arriving in Germany, could squeeze in with the five women and two men. The men, clad in refined suits and polished boots, had secured the wooden bench seats and showed no gentlemanly inclination to give them up. I joined the women in taking turns sitting on the floor and standing up for the expected five-hour journey.

To distract myself, I struck up a conversation with the two younger women. Like me, a vacation in the countryside awaited them. When I shared my destination, they shrugged their shoulders in unison and prattled on about their plans, too focused on their holiday to care about someone else's.

The men seemed eager to impress me. Once they deduced my nationality—I couldn't disguise my accent, even after eight months—they invited me to squeeze onto the bench next to them. They launched into exaggerated tales of adventures in America. Yet, when they mentioned seeing the Statue of Liberty in the Boston harbor and enjoying a seaside inn in Chicago, I doubted either of them had ever set foot in America. I bit my tongue until I tasted the iron of blood droplets. No need to correct them. Their German arrogance and ungentlemanly ways could prompt them to report me for some imagined grievance and have me tossed off the train.

I turned my attention to the landscape whizzing by outside the grime-streaked window. The farther we traveled from Berlin, the brighter the picture became. Tree limbs, lush with leaf, drooped and reached their full complement to earth and sky. Among the soft green meadow grasses, swaying in a light breeze, wildflowers bloomed. Blue cornflower, white Queen Anne's Lace, yellow Black-Eyed Susan, and purple balls of thistle blurred into a giant artist palette. The metronome chug of the engine, *forward, forward, forward*, carried my body and mind to a restful doze.

I awoke with a shudder when the older woman standing next to me gasped. With an intake of breath as sharp as a sewing needle, the sound pierced my peaceful slumber. Opening my eyes, I saw her hand covering her mouth. She turned away from the window. The other occupants of our compartment stared out at the tracks running parallel to us. I followed their gaze. Someone had stuffed three English uniforms with straw and tied them to the tracks. To this day, I can't shake the image and nagging thought, wondering who had worn those uniforms and what had become of their bodies.

When the conductor announced Bad Elster, the train jerked to a stop. I grabbed the handles of my luggage and nudged my way ahead of my compartment companions. As I shifted from one foot to another, the closeness of the car collapsed around me. The stale air mixed with cigarette smoke choked me as tight as my growing anxiety.

Move it! I yelled in my head to the crowd before me, shuffling forward slower than the *drip, drip, drip* from a leaky water pipe. I rose on my toes to look over heads to check how much further to the doorway of my escape. Minutes that felt like hours later, I found Hannah waiting on the station platform. Her graceful figure, accentuated by the soft frame of her blond locks, always made her stand out in a crowd. A glow of warmth radiated from her sweet face. I didn't blame the men who stole admiring glances at her. If exhaustion hadn't laid claim to every bone in my body, I may have sent the dogs scurrying with tales of her army officer husband's bravery at the front.

"Josephine, you made it. I hope you didn't have too much trouble?" she asked.

"No more than usual. Although I wish someone would invent a portable gramophone. I'd record my answers to the same tiresome questions to play at every checkpoint."

We laughed together at the idea of an opera student wanting to record her voice with phrases like, "I am a student at the *Konservatiroum*" rather than a moving piece by Wagner.

On the two-hour journey by motorbus, we wound higher and higher into wooded hills. I inhaled the crisp, pine-scented air in great gulps through the open window. Vast forests, rolling fields, and glistening lakes encircled me like an embrace. The greens and blues of the pleasing portrait reminded me of childhood trips out to Milton, just beyond the edges of my home in Roxbury. At last, we reached our *pension,* the König Albert Hotel. While some buildings near Tiergarten in Berlin boasted majestic opulence, they didn't compare with the intricate detailing, ornate arched windows, and decorative balconies on either side of a grand entrance. Manicured gardens with elaborate flower beds, trimmed hedges, and elegant walking paths surrounded the building. Wealthy guests seeking a respite from the realities of wartime Europe could revel in rest and rejuvenation.

As we stepped inside, Hannah turned to me with a bright smile. "I hope you'll find our room to your liking. But first, hurry and wash up! We're having lunch—or is it supper?—out in the summerhouse. We'll get some fresh air into you right away."

Mention of food made my stomach growl with anticipation. The reminder of war, however, crept in like a slinking black cat when the proprietress asked for our food cards. Not until she tallied the points did the servers set down our plates of plenty. Asparagus soup, rich with the rare luxury of milk, crusty bread slices, tender rounds of roast with potatoes swimming in butter, and a delicate tart filled with jellied berries completed our feast.

After lunch, Hannah linked her arm in mine to lead me through the charming *Kurplatz* promenade. The lively little street, with its quaint shops, had the festive air of a miniature inland Nantasket Beach, the amusement spot south of Boston I had often visited with my family. When my legs felt as crumbly as the flakes from our lunch tart, I pointed to a bench nestled under the overhang of a hedge and next to a stone-rimmed pool. Spray from a fountain in the middle of the pool spurted from the mouth of a cherub, its chin lifted to the heavens.

"Can we sit for a moment?" I asked my friend, whose vim and vigor seemed boundless.

Hannah turned, placing her hand over her heart at the sight of me. My reflection in the pool warranted her concerned reaction. The dull eyes of an old hag gazed back at me. My hair had frizzled into a nest made of black cherry twigs. Slumped shoulders lacked the strength to hold my neck and head erect.

"Oh, *mein liebe freundin,* how thoughtless of me. Look at you. Seven hours on a train and bus and I drag you off on an afternoon sight-seeing excursion. I'm just so happy you're here."

She sat down beside me and took my hand. With a slight lowering of her head, she checked her delicate A. Lange & Söhne lapel watch. The golden slivers of clock hands against the white face pointed to the Roman numerals of three and six.

"Three-thirty. We need to hurry back to town," she said.

"It's so peaceful here. Supper isn't until much later. Can't we stay a bit?"

"My father reminded me that regulations demand that you report to the local police within six hours of your arrival. The station will close at five."

I heaved myself off the bench. Obedience to rules outweighed personal pleasures. We set off for the police station. Me with my plodding, dreading gait and Hannah at my side, urging me onward.

The flag of oppression waved over the building. As I walked beneath it, the familiar shadow of dread fell upon my spirits. With a huff, the officer in charge declared they would see Americans at ten o'clock in the morning. I apologized for my error, having arrived in Bad Elster in the early afternoon. "Please, Herr Kommandant, wouldn't it be easier to check my papers now so you can get home on time and not worry about opening up just for me tomorrow?"

Noticing the thin silver band on his third finger, I added, "Your wife must have a lovely meal ready for you. My friend here tells me you don't face the severity of the rations out here in the country."

His eyes seemed to roll back into his head as his tongue slipped over his lips. I envisioned an earthenware plate of Wiener schnitzel with a fried egg and potatoes laid in front of him by an equally rotund Frau Kommandant. The officer must have seen that plate in his mind too. My interview concluded in quick measure with an added surprise. Eager to escape from rigid rules and regulations sent down from the top, he allowed me to skip daily check-ins for the duration of my stay. One less task for him for the next five weeks.

We returned to the König Albert, where I turned the key of the bedroom door lock and hoisted my valise onto the bed. Hannah watched as I unpacked, chattering about tomorrow's planned activities. When I unfolded my beloved flag, which I had slid in between my chemises, she went quiet.

I raised my eyebrows in her direction. "Is it all right? I sleep better when I know it's close by. But if you prefer…"

She took the flag from my hands and spread it across the pastel-colored floral quilt on my bed. Its edges had frayed in a few spots. The vibrant red and blue had faded. The white had grayed. Without a word, my German friend smoothed the cloth against the wall.

"Did you bring tacks?" she asked.

I hunted through my valise for the small envelope containing the four straight pins.

Far from Berlin, in a fairy tale setting of peace and tranquility, a German girl, wife of a German officer, pushed pins through the four corners of an American flag, securing its display on the wall.

SCENE IV

Frivolity and Fight

July-August 1917
Bad Elster, Germany

In Bad Elster, everyone understood the grim realities belonged on the front lines, not shrouding expansive landscapes of nature's grandeur. Germany at play offered far more pleasantries than Germany at war.

Hannah and I spent our days reclining on chaises set out in the hotel gardens. With our faces turned skyward like dried up sponges, we'd soak in the sun. A stack of books on white-painted wrought-iron tables climbed and dwindled as we devoured pages with an insatiable hunger. We drifted away for hours into fantasy and fiction. A dog-eared copy of *Mein Herz* by Else Lasker-Schüler traded back and forth between us. The poetry's truth seared with the author's existential reflections on love and relationships.

One afternoon, as the sun disappeared behind a rare bank of clouds, I read aloud one of Lasker-Schuler's passages. "*I have fallen permanently in love with the Slav—why—only the stars know. I love him in an entirely different way from the Muslim, whose kiss still sits, a golden butterfly on my cheek.* Isn't that a perfect image, Hannah? A butterfly as a light kiss."

Hannah closed her eyes and stroked her cheek. I wondered if Friedrich's kisses brushed her face like a butterfly wing. Or did he maul her with coarse, cracked lips, insatiable for the taste of her?

"The image is pleasing, but I find her notion of loving many men disturbing. If you give your heart to love, as I have done with Friedrich, it should be in entirety. No others should elbow their way in. It's a dangerous game to play. What about you, Josephine? Would you give your heart to many, or are you saving it for that pianist?"

Quoting the book's subtitle, I said, "As of now, *My heart belongs to nobody*. I think the author means she can love many men because her heart belongs to her. She's in control, not bowing to the whims of any one lover."

I thought back to the butterfly kiss I had placed on Gustav's cheek when he produced my travel papers. I should heed my words and those of Else Lasker-Schüler. Stay in control. Possession of fate may be what would save me. Or free me.

After late suppers, we'd join other guests for boat rides across the lake. The moon guided rowboats across the rippling water. Overhead, stars added pricks of light and reflected off the water before plunging down to the depths of grass and sand. With a guitar strapped across her chest, a musician from Munich, Bertha Roth, would sit at the lake edge, where we'd gather to sing folk songs. Echoes of our young, carefree voices bounced to the other shore, hit the stone walls surrounding the hotel, and returned as we gathered the notes back into our souls. We'd finish with the gentle, childish "*Der Mond ist aufgegangen*". As Bertha strummed the last notes, we lifted our voices and sent the lyrics westward. If only the battling sides could hear our voices. If only they could find the peace that we clutched to our hearts. *Lie down, my friends, reposing, Your eyes in God's name closing. How cold the night-wind blew! Oh God, Thine anger keeping. Now grant us peaceful sleeping.*

One afternoon, Bertha joined Hannah and me at the *Damenbad* baths for women. We arrived at the entrance, where, after we handed over our precious marks, the attendant gave us each a black "swimsuit" and a white cotton robe. Sleeveless and form-fitting, our legs were exposed below mid-thigh. The neckline plunged to the top of the bosom. I dangled the piece by its straps in front of Bertha. "Where's the rest of it? I can hear my mother screaming from Boston about modesty and proper attire for nice girls."

"Don't be a prude, Josephine. Have some fun." She tossed her head like a fiery filly and trotted off to the changing rooms. I followed like a whipped puppy, eyes downcast and hands trembling.

When I emerged, with the robe clutched tight at my neck, Hannah called out to me from the pool. "It's lovely, Josephine. Honest. Take off those horrid sandals they call shoes and your stockings and come join me."

Women of all ages stood in the pool, chirping and bending down to splash water up to their faces like a brood of hens fluttering their wings in a fight for corn kernels strewn across a barnyard. I lowered myself into the warm, mineral-rich waters. Healing elixirs seeped through my skin on a path to soothe my nerves and stimulate my metabolism. Between the calming waters, restful nights, and full plates at every meal, my skin tone soon pinked and my dizzy spells disappeared.

♪

As the end of my five-week visit drew near, I succumbed to Bertha's pleas to accompany her to the open-air *Familienbad*, a spa for men and women. Bertha, like Hannah before her wedding, often prattled on and on about men. With a glint of mischief in her eye, she asserted, "You cannot leave Bad Elster without taking in all the sights. That includes the men in their bathing costumes at the *Familienbad* pool."

This spa offered the same one-piece suits as those at the *Damenbad* baths. I dared to wear one among a brood of women there. But, here? In front of the packs of men whom I saw strutting around the pool edges and floating on the water with hair sticking out from every imaginable crevice not covered by their one-piece suits? No. My rented robe, shoes, and stockings would not come off here.

Bertha and I emerged from the changing rooms looking more like Jane Eyre and Bertha Mason than Josephine Marzynski and Bertha Roth. She had loosened her hair from pinned-up braids to flow over her shoulders and down to the tops of her breasts, barely covered by the thin mohair wool of the navy-blue bathing suit. Her robe hung draped over the crook of her arm. She must have tossed the matching tights into the trash barrel. I had tied the robe's sash with a double knot at my waist. It fell mid-shin, covering the black stockings and lace-up ballet shoes whose ribbons criss-crossed over my calf and shin. My hair remained tucked up under a pleated pure gum rubber bathing cap trimmed with a ruffle.

The pool and its surrounding grounds teemed with men and women wearing revealing swimsuits. Splashes arced over the pool's surface. Shouts of *hallos* and *Wie geht es dir?* traveled from side to side, inviting newcomers in and asking about their health. Many of them seemed to know Bertha, calling her to join them in a circle standing at the shallow end. She dove in, Jezebel that she was, leaving me to sit in a corner.

I watched and waited. The stoic German men I knew from Berlin, with their crisp heel snaps and reverent bows, did not exist in Bad Elster. Frivolity reigned and romped.

After I had spent an idle hour sitting in a back corner, Bertha climbed out of the pool and strode over to me. Her left hand rested on the arm of a man whose bathing costume accentuated his broad shoulders and sculpted physique. He walked with purpose and knowing. The moment our eyes met, recognition jolted through me. I had seen his face in photographs. Herr Otto Feld, the celebrated Austrian opera singer.

"Herr Feld, may I present Fräulein Marzynski, a standout student at our *Klindworth-Scharwenka*? I've heard said that her voice descends from the heavens. An American who has found her place in Berlin's finest music academy."

Feld asked about my studies, his questions smooth and flattering. I didn't notice Bertha easing herself out of the conversation until I saw her re-entering the pool, splashing another man next to her like a playful otter. "I would like to hear you sing," he said. "Through your eyes, I see your passion. Does your golden throat truly speak from the place of angels?"

"Oh no, I couldn't." I hadn't exercised my voice for over a month. To perform in front of such an esteemed performer? I could not, lest he think me an American show-off of minor talent.

"Please, Fräulein. I've tired of listening to those who think they can sing. I'm sure Herr Direktor at the *Klindworth* would not have accepted you if he didn't think you, an American, worthy of our German instructors' time and energy."

As if he had waved a red flag in front of me like a toreador, the evil sin of pride rose up my back. I didn't snort at him, but motioned to the empty spot where I had sat alone. "Please sit, Herr Feld."

He looked at me with raised eyebrows. A slow smirk spread over his tanned face.

"Classes ended five weeks ago, and I haven't sung since then. I need to warm up a bit."

I hummed a few quiet scales. My head lolled as I closed my eyes. Agatha's soprano aria "Leise, leise, fromme Weise" in *Der Freischütz* came to me. In a public space, I knew I had to choose a German composition. Did I dare challenge myself beyond my mezzo soprano range? I relaxed my tongue into a neutral position.

My body swayed. I felt myself losing control. The natural feeling of the moment took hold. I opened my mouth to release the first lines.

"Leise, leise, Fromme Weise!" (Softly, softly, My pure song!)

A large paw grabbed my outstretched arm and caressed my skin where the robe's sleeve had fallen back. "Please, Fräulein, take off the robe. I want to see your throat."

Shock rippled through me. I couldn't finish my prayer about the halls of heaven. Jerking my arm from his grasp, I snapped, "I most certainly shall not."

He grinned. "Why not? Are you deformed? I don't think so, I am sure there is perfection beneath that cloak of shame you seem to have glued to your body. There is nothing to be ashamed of, *mein süßes junges Mädchen.*"

My cheeks burned as hot as the pavement of Berlin's streets, the tar bubbling and boiling from a relentless sun. "How dare you? I am not your sweet young thing," I said, releasing the steam from inside my burning cheeks. As precise as any German soldier, I turned on my heel, ready to stalk away. My heart pounded with anger and humiliation.

Laughter spilled from his deep-throated tenor. He leaped at me. His arm clamped around my waist as his other hand grabbed at my robe, trying to strip it from my body.

I struggled, flailing my arms in wild abandon. I stared in horror as the others nearby egged him on as though they sat watching a sporting match. "Kiss her, kiss her," they yelled. Clearly, he had championed over many other women. He would not claim me as another trophy.

I roared toward the others as much as to him. *"Widerlicher mensch!"* (Filthy swine!)

My fingers twisted in his long, wavy hair. I yanked with every ounce of my strength. He cried out and let go of my waist.

Breathless, trembling, but defiant, I faced him. "If there were an American man here, he'd smash your face, you beast!" I spat at his sandal-clad feet.

The surrounding laughter died down. I stood tall, chest heaving, eyes blazing. My robe sash loose at my waist. He slunk away; his bravado shattered. But I knew the fire in my cheeks would burn long after he had gone. Why did I choose an aria telling the story of a young woman praying for her beloved? *Foolish move, Fräulein Josephine.*

♫

With a heavy heart, I removed the pins from the corners of Old Glory and refolded it into its tight traveling square. The end of August arrived like the clang of a steel cover set upon a simmering pot. My escape to paradise during wartime ended in two hours. The gold filigree mirror over the chest of drawers reflected a different image of Josephine Therese than the one who had checked in five weeks ago. My cheeks had filled, no longer gaunt and gray. A honey-colored tone covered my face and neck from hours of soaking up sunshine. I slid my fingers into the waistband of my skirt. It fit snugly compared to when I had arrived.

I tucked my flag into my valise's inside pocket. Hannah and I had said our goodbyes earlier. I walked to the bus station alone, grateful for the time to gather my thoughts. Prior to my scuffle with Herr Feld, doubts about leaving the *Konservatorium* had stolen into my mind. Was I making a mistake? Could I tamp down my fears about what awaited me in Berlin? More interrogations. Groping soldiers. More hate. Suspicions. More desires to lock up an American. Could I muster past those fears fed only by a passion for music?

The bus from the hotel deposited me at the train station. Soldiers swarmed the platforms. Keeping my head down, I made my way past them. Many of the soldiers stretched out on the bare floor. Each one looked wan and battle-weary. Vile tobacco smoke and the odor of perspiring humanity plugged the atmosphere. After my time in cool, clean mountain air, five hours on a train would feel like an eternity.

Thankful for an empty seat in the middle car, I settled in and unpacked two egg sandwiches and a slice of bread with marmalade. I had depleted all my bread ration cards in Bad Elster, but with a dramatic flourish, Hannah's mother had produced the sandwiches wrapped in wax paper as a send-off gift. Kind and generous souls still walked the roads and hotel kitchens of Germany.

Occupied with the delicacy of my sandwiches and rereading a recent letter from Cousin Jack, I didn't notice the man striding toward me until he plopped himself down next to me. "Ah," he said, "so you are reading a love letter, *mein Fräulein*."

Herr Feld had again intruded into my space with contemptible words and actions. I folded the letter in half lest he catch sight of Jack's mundane sentences about the weather in Amsterdam and another request as to my status on the waiting lists for departure.

"Ahh, hiding those sweet sentiments from your lover. His words to his beautiful woman must be quite tantalizing. Does he write about your stormy blue eyes? How you must look at him with unabashed adoration. Or of your dark hair? How he wishes to run his fingers through those chestnut strands of silk, down your neck, further to another spot of softness?"

A vile, insidious man. The mere suggestion of such intimacy between a man and a woman would have shocked the Josephine who had boarded a ship in New York. But that Josephine had disappeared with every day that demanded resolve and courage in front of a police officer, investigator, and checkpoint.

I looked around. Injured, sleeping German soldiers appeared no different from the men who had laughed at Herr Feld's advances by the pool. No doorway to a ladies' changing room provided an escape this time from his paws and heavy breath. My words must outwit his actions.

"Herr Feld. You are correct about my letter, but please grant me some privacy. This is the first letter I've received from my lover in three months, what with him at the Western front, killing Germans and Austrians left and right. A man not afraid to pick up his rifle and bayonet for his country."

Let him think my lover was a man of honor and duty while Herr Feld traveled to spas and baths, acting like a boorish oaf and performing at theaters with half-filled seats.

"Bah. You are a tease, Fräulein Marzynski. And you sing too American."

He stumbled back down the aisle, stepping on a soldier's foot, who let out a yip. I watched as the soldier's compatriot stuck his boot out in Herr Feld's path. When he fell face down onto the floor, I laughed. So did the soldiers.

SCENE V

The Fate of the Understudy

September 1917
Berlin, Germany

Thoughts of Berlin loomed before me like the Queen of the Night's aria in *Die Zauberflöte*. Defiant, yet teetering on the edge of collapse. Like the Queen herself, driven by vengeance and consumed by control, Berlin had become a ruthless monster. A city I now despised. What awaited me when my train pulled into Berlin and without a ticket on a ship to take me away?

Der Hölle Rache kocht in meinem Herzen, Tod und Verzweiflung flammet um mich her! "Hell's vengeance boils in my heart, Death and despair blaze about me!"

In Bad Elster, fresh air, mineral springs, time spent with dear Hannah, and hearty meals nourished my body and my soul. During the precious moments at the lake, when music lingered in the cool night, my dreams of becoming a professional opera singer found their voice again. When I sang, I lived. I felt. I was. Without my music, who could I be? Who would I be? Berlin offered no answers, only more questions—with the daily check-ins I would endure beginning the next morning.

My nightmare returned on the Anhalter Bahnhof's dimly lit platform. One last breath of smoke and hiss escaped from the train's smokestack. Mechanical silence fell with a finality. During my time away in fairy-tale land, the nerve center of a mad nation seemed to have ratcheted its anxiety even higher. Those who waited at the station tonight painted a grim picture. Clothing hung slack against bodies more malnourished than when I had left five weeks ago. Empty eyes searched for any signs of food or coal arriving on the tracks. They would find none.

Only the thought of returning to the embrace of Onkel Klaus and Tante Helga propelled me to step off the train. I feared that if I didn't see their kind faces on the platform, I would reboard, eager to escape to anywhere but Berlin. After scanning the crowd, I saw them. They each stood rigid. Stoic even, like the typical German. Not at all the welcome I expected from my found family.

Tante Helga clutched a handkerchief, twisting it like a wringer on a washing machine. Onkel Klaus ran a finger around the brim of the hat in his hands. They didn't lift their eyes from the pockmarked pavement under their feet when I called to them, waving my hand like an untethered kite bobbing in wind gusts.

To Onkel Klaus' right, the glint of a tie clip at the throat of a man caught my eye. I slowed my pace and dropped my arm. The man wore a black, stiff-brimmed fedora and charcoal three-piece suit. His high-collared shirt, pressed and brilliant in its whiteness, meant soap and coal rations hadn't touched his home. Yet, there was something about him that told me he wasn't one of Onkel Klaus' business associates. A coldness enveloped him like an invisible ice cocoon. His black-gloved hand went to his hip, touching a bulky object under his suit coat.

He stepped forward. "Josephine Marzynski," he said. Not a question.

I froze. How did he know my name? My eyes begged the silent Müllers for an explanation.

"Onkel..."

The man who had stepped into my father's role for the past ten months, guiding me, helping me, shook his head.

"Under the demand of the Kaiser, for the protection of the German Empire. You will come with me," the unknown man said.

A hand seized my wrists while the other pulled a pair of iron handcuffs from his inside suit pocket. Shaped like a figure eight, the solid metal appeared dark with age and use. He snapped one loop around my left wrist with a practiced force. Then the right. The ends clanked closed together with a metallic bite. The cold, infinite loop of iron dug into my skin.

"I don't understand. What have I done? I've followed all the orders. Please, my papers. Let me get my papers." I nodded toward my handbag, which contained every possible stamped and approved document the German government had commanded I keep with me.

"Josephine," said Onkel Klaus, his voice halting yet firm. "Herr Detektiv Bauer needs to ask you some questions. He'll call us as soon as he's done."

While I lounged by pools, sang folk songs, and read novels, what more had changed in Berlin? New procedures? Did they haul in every American left in the city for questioning? In handcuffs?

Tante Helga's arms, which had embraced me time and time again, stretched wide. She moved to envelop me in that familiar feeling of motherly concern. With a swift step, Onkel Klaus blocked her gesture. Without a word, he gripped her elbow and steered her away. Like a ship's captain spinning a wooden wheel, hand over hand on the spokes, intent on navigating his charge out of the path of an impending storm, they left me. Alone in the eye of a hurricane. A porter followed them, carrying my luggage.

Herr Detektiv didn't take my elbow in the same kindhearted manner. He pushed the center of my back, compelling me to walk forward. Away from the platform and anything that could save me from uncertainty. As I walked ahead, I felt like I had stepped into the Torah's story from Genesis and read on Rosh Hashanah. God tests Abraham by telling him to bind his son, Isaac, and ready him for a sacrifice. Would my God spare me as he did Isaac as long as I obeyed?

Inside the police station, Herr Detektiv brought me to an unfamiliar room. Smaller than other processing rooms I'd been in. A straight-backed chair stood in the middle of the otherwise empty space. Without a word, he motioned for me to sit.

I watched as he pulled a cigarette from a scrunched pack and lit it. With one deep drag on the tobacco, he held the inhale before smoke spewed out of his thin, chapped lips. I shut my eyes to shield them from the acrid puffs wafting toward my face. A high-pitched *pop!* startled me when he snapped his fingers inches from my nose. My shoulders rose, and my eyes opened.

"Fräulein Marzynski. Brava!" He clapped his hands in a slow smack of palm to palm. "The performance in front of the Müllers was commendable. Acting as if you don't know why you're here. Hmmrpph."

"But I don't know…"

"Enough. I don't have time to waste on your play-acting." His body bent toward me. A sneer crawled across his face. "You are an American. Living here in Berlin. In a relationship with a German officer and an association with a Russian spy. Tell me now how you seduced von Lüben for information and gave it to Natalya Duysen."

My mind scurried back in time to seven months ago. One time. One casual remark about Frankfurt and my supposition it meant a build-up in troops in that area. And for that, I found myself in a room seeking to suffocate me? Alone with a man looking for any excuse to detain an American?

"Herr Detektiv, I have not seduced Hauptmann von Lüben. I am not in a relationship with him. He is a friend, yes, but nothing more." I squared my shoulders and glared into eyes as black and beady as a grackle pecking at dirt, searching for an elusive worm.

"As for Fräulein Duysen, I accompanied her on rounds to visit tenement families. If she got herself involved with Russian intelligence, I know nothing about that. I know her only as a Red Cross nurse, tending to injured and dying German soldiers. Caring for German children, whose lives were destroyed by the war. Neglect. Hunger. Dead fathers. Absent mothers who spend their days looking for work and food. Seeking compassion, which they find in Fräulein Duysen."

He pursed his lips tight. As his hand reached for the doorknob, he spoke over his shoulder, "I'll give you some time to reconsider your practiced lines and whether you want to accompany Fräulein Duysen on her new rounds. We've changed her nursing assignment. At the Eastern front, she can watch us kill Russians."

The door closed behind him, leaving me in silence. Like curtains dropping onto a stage at the dramatic finale, I wondered if Natalya's fate echoed that of so many opera heroines. A crumpled body at center stage. A white apron puddled around her like a voluminous robe. The spotlight faded to a pinprick. An audience awash in grief as the beautiful woman drew her last breath, singing of desires for peace.

Could the same fate await the understudy? Me?

♪

Concrete walls surrounded me with no windows, no clock, and no sound save for the gurgle of water rushing through a distant pipe. Two wall lamps on either side of the door shone with a slow ebb of light streaks onto the dusty wood-planked floor. I stood up from the chair and checked the door. *Of course it's locked, Josephine.* Did I think they would allow me to waltz out of the station, pick up a cherry strudel at the corner store, and return to the Müllers to share stories about communal pools and novel readings over a glass of Onkel's Asbach Uralt?

For thirty minutes, I paced. I think it was thirty minutes—it may have been longer, or shorter. There was no way of knowing. I returned to the chair and let my head droop, chin to chest. Whenever I sought to escape a situation or unpleasant thoughts, my mind rifled through the bundles of sheet music my mother kept in the bottom drawer of her ladies' dresser. Closing my eyes, I envisioned her bedroom. Blue chintz curtains tied back with grosgrain white ribbon at the window. A heavy patchwork quilt folded into thirds at the foot of her single bed. The pink milk glass lamp on her bedside table. My parents' wedding photo in a silver frame, angled just so on the table to catch the lamp's light.

From the tied-up stack, which sheets did she pull from the bundle when she learned of her family's emigration plans? On her wedding day, did she run her fingers over the sheets of *Romeo and Juliet*, unaware her marriage would also have a fateful end? Which ones did she caress and press to her chest when they took my father away? Did she find solace in reading her way through a composition when he died? I saw my mother's eyes following the notes up and down on the black bars. Her body swayed with the ascents and descents. A soft hum purred in the back of her throat. The text beneath the bars called forth the emotions of the composers and performers. Longing, love. Fear. Hatred, betrayal.

The sheets for Tosca's "Vissi d'Arte" floated into my imagined view. Did Detektiv Bauer intend to continue questioning me like Scarpia questioned Tosca? The libretto spoke to me in that moment of uncertainty.

I lived for my art, I lived for love, I never did harm to a living soul!...I gave my song to the stars, to heaven, which smiled with more beauty. In the hour of grief, why, why, o Lord, ah, why do you reward me thus?

Like Tosca, I sat in a chair, stripped of my voice and the snatches of freedom I had in Bad Elster. Each time I shifted my weight on the seat, the uneven legs forced a tiny seesaw motion. I gave up trying to get comfortable. With my legs extended before me, my head fell back as my body elongated. I entwined my fingers into a locked prayer clasp and let them lay still in my lap. Exhaustion took hold. Time ceased to have meaning. I slipped away into an abyss carved by fingers clawing, clinging to concrete walls.

SCENE VI

Darkening Shadows

I awoke when I could no longer suppress the urge to relieve myself. A small puddle in the farthest corner declared my humiliation. Footsteps neared. I dropped my skirt's hem to the floor. The click of metal sounded, and the door swung open.

"Come," said Herr Detektiv Bauer. He turned away, and I followed him like any good soldier would, unaware of what orders I'd receive next. Upstairs, morning light flooded the station's entryway. The brightness attacked my senses after an overnight in a room of nothingness. I cupped my hands over my eyes. When I removed them, I saw Onkel Klaus standing next to the check-in desk. I remembered how he had seized Tante Helga's reach for me last night. Best to wait. Not speak until I was spoken to. Be the good girl, as Jack had instructed all those months ago.

Herr Detektiv cleared his throat, as if the words he must say pained his very being. "Fräulein Marzynski, considering Herr Müller's work for Riedel and his son-in-law's service to the Kaiser, we will release you to his supervision. He understands the seriousness of the charges we could levy against you as an enemy of the Empire. We've agreed to his proposed conditions for your release."

Onkel Klaus nodded at his feet, still unable to look at me, hesitant to reveal his sense of failure in protecting me.

"You will have no further interaction with von Lüben, nor any other German officer," continued the Detektiv. "At no time will you be outside the Müller's home unless accompanied by Herr or Frau Müller or Frau Hauptmann Schmidt. The only reason for you to leave their house is to attend your classes at the *Konservatorium*."

Although I had developed softer feelings for him, I could abide by the directive to end any interaction with Gustav. I certainly wouldn't miss his lessons in propaganda. Permission to continue my studies would distract me. My remarkable good fortune buoyed my spirits. I resisted the temptation to curtsy, lest he find me mocking him and his golden words. "*Danke*. I understand."

I wanted to grab Onkel's hand and run. Run down the street, around the corner and into my Tante's arms. To my mother, an ocean and a lifetime away. Instead, Onkel picked up my hand, placed it in the crook of his arm and steered me toward the safe harbor of my German home.

The second the door closed behind us, I fell into Tante Helga's embrace and asked, "Why, why, why?"

Anna appeared with a plate of brown bread, a coveted soft-boiled egg, and a cup of weak tea. We settled at the dining table for Onkel to share the disturbing details of the past five weeks.

"Evelyn noticed Natalya's disappearance two weeks ago. When Bauer arrived at my office inquiring about you, he said they had seen you in her company many times. I told him I had no doubts your relationship with her was purely altruistic, that you enjoyed visiting the families and children and an occasional visit to the hospital wards."

"But me as an American and her as a Russian made our innocent friendship unbelievable."

"Yes, guilt by association."

I dotted my lips with the scrap of paper napkin, savoring the runny egg yolk trickling down my throat. "Herr Detektiv indicated they've sent her to the Eastern front, to tend to German soldiers. He implied they would make her watch them kill Russians. Do you believe that, Onkel? Do you think she's there?"

"Could be. Her nursing skills may be the only thing to save her."

I slumped in my chair. *Please, please let that be true. Let Natalya live to help keep others alive. And please, please let this war be over soon.*

"We didn't read the newspapers much in Bad Elster. And I don't trust what they say. How do you think the war's going? Could Natalya be home before winter? Ernst? All of them?"

"Josephine, you saw the people at the train station. They should be on their knees begging for retreat. Instead, they remain silent, driven by a spirit and a government that tell them to endure in the name of the Kaiser and the might of the German doctrine. I must be frank with you. This war may continue for another year, or more."

His informed opinion cut through the air with truth. Tante Helga choked back a sob. I turned to face him, looking for any other relevant commentary.

He continued, "We need to expedite your departure. You cannot be brought in again and suffer more indignities."

I thought back to the "welcome signs" I had seen when I first arrived. *Achtung! Spionen Gefahr!* With every inch gained by the Americans' march toward Germany, my presence here would only intensify any thoughts of suspicion. Onkel's words lingered, heavy with both love and fear. I couldn't live with myself if the ogres also rounded up the Müllers for suspected espionage.

"Tomorrow, you'll report for your check-in," he reminded me. "And Evelyn will escort you to school, showing that you've returned to your routine and you have nothing to hide."

Nothing to hide. Only an American flag waiting to be unpacked from my luggage. I would need a new hiding spot for it before I said my silent goodnights to my family in Boston.

♪

On my first day back at the *Konservatorium,* classes ended under a sky swollen with clouds; humidity hung like sheets from a clothesline. Evelyn waited outside for me. We fell into step to head home. I had a sense that if the heavens opened, we might have to tear home like Siegmund in the opening scene of *Die Walküre,* seeking shelter from a thunderstorm. The sound of low D-minor chords and strings swirling in a raging torrent filled my head and pushed us forward.

A man's brown derby glanced off my shoulder. Lost in my visions of the opera, I hadn't seen the commotion forming ahead of us. Hats flew upward like tossed bouquets, cheers burst like cymbal crashes, bodies swayed and collided in wild embraces. Doors and shutters flung open. People spilled into the street in tearful embraces. My heart quickened. This type of celebration meant one thing.

The war was over.

The crowd's elation surged around me. I added my mezzo-soprano voice to the cheers. "Hurrah! Hurrah!" A newsboy sliced through the press of bodies, waving an afternoon edition over his head like a conductor's baton.

"Peace! Peace at last!"

Peace.

The word snapped the music in half when the thought struck me. Peace for Germany meant defeat for America. Had my countrymen fallen? I stopped my *hurrahs*. Evelyn fumbled for a coin to give the boy. Together we read the headline: *The Reichstag Declares General Peace*. The air drained from my lungs. I longed to collapse onto the curb and weep.

Instead, we rushed home. Bursting through the front door, my eyes met a shadow in Onkel Klaus's eyes. "Peace?" I said, thrusting the paper toward him.

He stood there, his face pale and drawn. "A mistake," he said.

"No, you must be wrong. It's here, right here." I punched my finger against the newsprint.

"There is no peace. The Reichstag admitted its error."

♪

Like the boy who cried wolf in the famed Aesop fable, five weeks later, Germany again deceived its people. A new government in Russia, the Council of People's Commissars, or *Sovnarkom,* led by Vladimir Ulianov-Lenin, distributed booklets containing his "Decree on Peace." Within its text, Lenin appealed to all those "exhausted, tormented and tortured by the War" to enter an immediate truce.

Smiles returned to the crowd. And while I didn't notice any hats flung into the air, I heard whispers on every street corner: "Just a little longer. With our army from the East set free, we will swiftly conquer the West." In shops where lines snaked out the door, "Rationing will end. Many will come home." They had endured for so long, their hopes worn thin by endless hardship. Their hopes flickered anew. Most believed in the vision of triumph and plenty.

Beyond the whispers and wishful thinking, my thoughts strayed eastward. I searched for tents at the front lines with large red crosses sewn to the outer flaps. Was Natalya still there? Bending over cots lined with broken men, her apron stiff with dried blood? Had she read the decree? Would she be among those to return home to Berlin? Or did she no longer consider Berlin her home as I did?

Onkel Klaus, however, tempered our enthusiasm for Lenin's decree. My wise onkle saw beyond the weight of truth pressing against the fragile façade of dreams. With a translation of the Soviet Decree of Peace laid out on a table, he ran his fingers under one line and read it aloud to us. "*...an immediate peace without annexations (i.e., without the seizure of foreign land, without the* *forcible taking over of foreign nationalities) and without contributions.*"

He looked up from the page. "The common man does not understand. The Reichstag will never agree to these terms. It undermines the philosophy it has espoused for years. It would admit defeat."

I knew he was right. The teaching and adherence to militarism concepts coursed through the blood of nearly every German. Talk of peace, or defeat, would not staunch the bleeding of deep cut wounds. Like the Valkyries in the finale of *Die Walküre*, the Germans would charge forward once again.

SCENE VII

She Who Guards Her Tongue

November 1917
Berlin, Germany

By November, winter's weight in Berlin bore down. I'd turn twenty next month. Last year's birthday had brimmed with promise. After a celebration dinner with the Müllers, Hannah and Zara had swept me off to the Royal Opera House. We'd sat breathless under the glow of the chandeliers. Beloved soprano Clare Dux shimmered in her high notes. Lilli Lehman, though over seventy, wrung every drop of power from her voice. Joseph Swartz owned the stage with his commanding baritone. And Richard Strauss, conductor extraordinaire, baton in hand, pulled the audience into his grasp. They swooned and called out, "Encore, encore!"

This year, the stage lights dimmed and went out. I'd spend my birthday celebration on a hospital tour with other students. My gift? Written permission from Herr Detektiv Bauer to leave my house arrest.

When I visited the wards of silent men, my heart broke. Shattered like the bones of men lying on cots. Their immobile bodies lined up like coffins that hadn't closed yet, stretched end to end. Limbs gone, faces hollow. Some wept. Whether from pain or for lives stolen, I couldn't tell. I sang anyway, letting my voice search for them in the shadows, hoping it might give even one of them a flicker of solace.

You might call it giving aid and comfort to the enemy, but I have no shame in it. I didn't see enemies, nor soldiers killing Americans. I saw boys. Some barely past seventeen. Missing their mothers' gentle caress, pushing their hair off fevered foreheads. We did not wage war against the sick and wounded. We healed with the only treatment available. I could offer them music, which soothed and reminded them they weren't forgotten. I didn't sing for one country against another. For enemy versus enemy. I sang for the souls of those boys. Those notes may have been the last ones they ever heard.

In their pain and illnesses, I sympathized with the bleakness of their existence. Clad in prison-like striped pajamas, they seemed more like captives than patients. As I stood before them, wearing my favorite blue dress with the cluster of rosebuds at the waist, I, too, felt trapped. Like the sash tied tight with a knot, I was bound tight by regulations, bureaucracy, and the fear of an unknown future.

Upon returning home after another performance in front of men who couldn't clap with hands severed or mangled by the sword of my countrymen, Onkel Klaus called me into his study.

"Josephine, I have news."

My breath caught in my throat. Ever since my return from Bad Elster and release from Herr Detektiv, Onkel had without fail checked the waiting lists for departures. *Please, please.*

"A Norwegian-American line steamer, the *Bergensfjörd*, will sail from Christiania on December seventh."

"Yes? And? And will I be on it?" The excitement bubbled through my body, tingling every nerve into a sense of hope.

"With luck, and the extra insurance measures I took, yes. This afternoon, I submitted your application. It required my promising a substantial amount of chocolate to the girl who processes them to make sure she refuses any other applications."

I flung my arms around his neck and covered his face with kisses. "You can have all of my ration cards to find that chocolate for her! If you think it will help, I'll wrap it in tissue paper and add a bow from one of my dresses."

"Let me worry about finding the chocolate. Your job? Be more careful than ever. No more hospital visits. Not one word of English anywhere, even inside the house. Anna and Greta have been loyal staff, but there's no need to provoke them into accepting payments for any information while your application is under review."

"Done, done, and done." I would eagerly play the role he asked of me. That night, I took my flag from its new hiding spot, layered between letters from my mother and Jack, and smoothed it out on my bed. Tomorrow, I would reopen the hem of my gray suit and fold the red, white, and blue into its concealed travel spot. We'd both be ready to leave this loathsome land.

♪

With my application for the ship passage under review, I steeled myself with the proverb, "He who guards his tongue is greater than he who takes a city." Every day walking to and from school and during classes, I praised everything German. From famed composers, artists, and writers like Wagner, Winterhalter, and Goethe, to inventors like Braun and Benz.

Am I a hypocrite? Perhaps. But in harking back to all things German, I pointed to the philosophy I heard often from men like Hauptmann von Lüben: "War is war, and expediency excuses anything." I waged my war every day with the travel office and the Kommandants, who still suspected I might be a spy.

Excited to share my news and make travel plans, I asked Onkel Klaus to contact Jack in Amsterdam under the pretense of needing him for a business meeting. To our delight, he arrived at the Müllers three days later. When he stepped across the threshold, he brought more than his valise with him. Hope, strength, and family ties cut through the gloom and agitation that met me upon my return from Bad Elster. The twinkle in his deep-set blue eyes flamed my longing to see my brothers with the same blue eyes. His greeting of "Hello there, feisty Jo" made me think of the nights Lillian and I read to each other from *Little Women*. As he ran his fingers through the thick, dark waves that fell over his widow's peak, I'd recall the way my mother would do the same, brushing my father's hair back out of his eyes. I needed my family. I needed to go home.

The next day, Onkel Klaus laid out the next steps I'd need to undertake before I could claim the ship's ticket. "Don't let the amount of paperwork alarm you. We'll figure it all out," he said, opening a ledger from his briefcase. With his fountain pen, he listed dates, locations, and actions, beginning with December seventh on the bottom of the sheet. Working his way up the sheet, he added more details.

Date	Location	Needed
By November 20	German Kommandantur	Exit passport
By November 20	Spanish Embassy	Entry passport
By November 28		ALL DOCUMENTS & TICKETS
November 30	Depart Berlin to Warnemünde	Train ticket
	Ferry to Gedser, Denmark	Ferry ticket
December 1	Train to Copenhagen; overnight	Train ticket Lodgings
December 3	Ferry to Göteborg, Sweden	Ferry ticket Overnight lodgings
December 5	Train to Christiania; overnight	Train ticket Lodgings
December 6	Arrive in Christiania	Overnight lodging
December 6	Processing through American Embassy	
December 7	Departure from Christiania	Ship ticket
December 19	Arrival New York	Train ticket Train to Boston

The completed listing looked like a battle plan, with strategic cities marked as one step closer to freedom from tyranny. I had less than three weeks to secure every piece of ammunition needed: passports, travel documents, and tickets. Victory was within reach. In the days that followed, we adopted a morning mantra: "Respect the Schedule." For once, I appreciated the Germans' proclivity to organize their world into controllable units. Our master plan may have been one of the few nods to a German value Onkel Klaus showed during my thirteen months of living with him.

Jack accompanied me the afternoon I visited the *Kommandantur* to apply for my exit passport. The gravity of my mission weighed on me like a millstone around my neck. Checking my tongue at the door, the scene played out in a loop of my life for the past seven months. I sat down across the desk from a German official. Had there been a mold at birth that every German mother had pushed their sons' faces into at their first breaths? Or did those stern countenances and beady eyes develop as they trained under the empire's doctrines?

"Name."

"Josephine Therese Marzynski."

"Why are you in Germany?"

"I've studied opera at the *Klindworth-Scharwenka Konservatorium* since November 1916." Jack had primed me to comment that I had arrived before America had entered the war.

"And now you wish to leave your studies here in Germany? Why? Do you not like our country? We have afforded you, an American, one of our enemies, many privileges."

"Oh yes, I like it, of course. The country is so beautiful. And the schooling I've received is beyond compare with the most talented instructors. But I shall be glad to get out..."

Jack whacked his knee against mine under the table. I backpedaled as quickly as a pianist's fingers fly across the keys playing "Flight of the Bumblebee."

Continuing, I said, "I shall be glad to get out of the Müllers' home. They have been most gracious with their incredible generosity and hospitality, but I've overstayed my time. They shouldn't worry about securing ration cards for me as part of their household. I would prefer anything extra go to their grandson, Rupert, son of Herr Stabsoffiziere Schmidt."

I prayed my concern for Rupert, the next generation of the German empire, would correct my error. Still, my heart pounded.

"That is a noble gesture, Fräulein Marzynski. We will take it under advisement."

Even though the official gave no sign of when I should return, Jack nodded at him and took my elbow to rise from the chair. "We are most grateful for your assistance," he said. I almost smelled the syrup on his tongue.

♪

After Jack left to return to Amsterdam, Onkel Klaus set about assisting me with the next item on the plan of attack. With my application submitted for a passport to *leave* Germany, I would likewise need one to *enter* the United States.

Over breakfast, he said, "Josephine, bring me your old passport. I have time to drop by the Spanish Embassy today to file your application."

"Shouldn't we wait until Germany approves my exit passport? What if it's delayed? If I miss the December seventh sailing, we won't know what departure date to use," I said.

By now, I knew the workings of the Prussian bureaucracy. Delays could stretch on into eternity. "It might be for years, it might be forever," the oft-spoken saying went. I feared if we proceeded too quickly with positive hopes, a letdown would plummet me into an abyss of despair.

"It's better to err on the side of caution and optimism. The Spanish embassy needs time to contact Washington. You need their permission to re-enter the United States."

I'd never imagined my country refusing me entry. I also wondered, did *Beware of Spies* posters cover walls and train stations from Boston to Chicago, from Miami to Los Angeles? What about my German-born mother? I doubted any of my letters had reached her in the past six months. She had no proof I wasn't returning as a German sympathizer. Absurd? Maybe. But my mind spun worst-case scenarios until a picture formed: a woman draped in two flags, claimed by neither.

That afternoon, after a dreary morning lesson, I returned home to find Onkel Klaus waiting for me, my passport dangling from his hand. Usually unshaken by any crisis, he stood with his jaw locked as solid as the door closed by Herr Detektiv. White knuckles curled into a fist. His lips pressed thin. I wondered what type of indignity had befallen him at the Spanish Embassy to have cracked his composure?

I held out my hand. "Is that my passport? Did you need proof of the German exit one?"

"The state of affairs is worse than expected. I had to pass through an outer checkpoint manned by a German woman. When I explained the reason for my visit, she asked to see your passport. I handed it over."

"But it's in your hand? She didn't keep it?"

"She didn't. But maybe that would have been better than what she did."

He unclenched his fist and flattened the passport in his palm. I gasped, then choked back a gag. A jagged hole tore through the front cover where an embossed eagle had displayed my country's freedom. Its wings outstretched, clutching an olive branch and thirteen arrows, it once declared *E Pluribus Unum*. Now, gone. Someone had slashed the eagle away with a razor blade. The

American symbol of unity, now lay in the bottom of a wastebasket at the feet of a German official. Wingless, grounded. Trapped.

"I tried to stop her and asked to speak to her supervisor, but she denied me any admittance. I'm sorry, Josephine. We'll need another plan."

Like the German army's recent losses at the hands of British troops in Passchendaele, Belgium, during the Third Battle of Ypres, I retreated to my room, exhausted by the ongoing battle.

♫

I spent the rest of the afternoon on my bed, with Old Glory in my lap like a miniature, grandmother-knitted afghan. I poked my finger through the mocking hole in my passport. If I didn't secure my reentry passport, I would remain in Berlin, facing another winter of cold and rations. Newspapers that heralded German victories, real or imagined. Comments from Paulina that my American voice would never reach the exalted level of full soprano. Interrogations. Inspections. Check points.

Onkel Klaus, who secured eggs, milk, and butter, provided for his family, and paid for my travel and tuition, had failed me when I needed his help the most. The time had come for me to re-strategize. I could no longer ask nor expect him to lead this charge across the battlefield of paperwork. I needed a new ally for this battle. One with ammunition to fight to the end.

I folded Old Glory into its tight square and pushed it under my pillow. Downstairs, and against the conditions of my release, I called Gustav von Lüben. If he had time in his schedule, I wished to see him. He accepted without hesitation.

With a dash of eau de toilette splashed behind my ears and on my wrists, a blend of tuberose, jasmine, and orange blossom preceded me into the living room where "my" Prussian officer stood at attention.

"Gustav," I said, extending my hand for the kiss I knew he would press to its back. "I'm delighted you could drop by on such short notice. Please sit."

"Ah, Fräulein Josephine, it's been a long time. You should know by now that I welcome the chance to visit with you. I am sorry I wasn't in Berlin when you returned from your trip. An unexpected assignment detained me longer than I expected."

A stroke of luck for me, I thought. If Gustav hadn't been in Berlin, perhaps he remained unaware of the conditions of my house arrest

"I'm sorry too." I wouldn't tell him I missed him. "And I see congratulations are in order, *Major* von Lüben." When I opened the door, I had noticed an epaulette with a circle of fringe clipped to his shoulder. His promotion should bode well for my pursuit of government approvals.

"Yes, well, thank you. But please, you may always call me Gustav," he said. "You're back in class? I hope your studies continue to go well. Perhaps you have an upcoming performance I might attend?" Overeager as ever.

He offered no sign of knowing Herr Detektiv had forbidden my seeing him. Not wanting to prolong a charade, I diverted our small talk to my request.

"I hope you will come to the one I have next week. It may be my last one."

His eyebrows lifted. "Your last? Are you leaving the school?"

I placed my palms together and rubbed them as if I hoped to start a fire.

"I am. Leaving the *Konservatorium*. And Berlin. And Germany."

His head jerked around, his eyes narrowing into slits. Waiting for his reaction, I quieted myself before asking for his help.

He exploded with a sharp condemnation. "How foolish you are to leave us now. Russia can't hold on much longer. Italy is as good as out of it. The war will soon be over. Then we can be so much more."

Did I flutter my eyelashes? Did I purr to him in a pleading voice? Yes, I admit it all.

"Perhaps we can, Gustav, someday. But today, as a friend who finds herself in a most dire situation, I need your help. Herr Müller couldn't get past an outer checkpoint at the Spanish Embassy. A German woman denied him. I need my entry passport application processed by November twentieth."

I placed my hand over his and rubbed my thumb across his knuckles.

"Please, Gustav. You may think me foolish, but I am not. I am homesick and scared. I can't stop thinking about my mother's worry. When you were at the front, did you ever feel that way?"

His pursed lips softened. A slight nod of his head told me, "Yes."

With this part of my plan accomplished, now I needed one more piece to fall into place. How would I dare walk to the Embassy, unescorted by a member of the Müller family, with the forbidden Major von Lüben by my side?

♪

The next morning after Tante Helga left for the market with Anna, I dressed in one of Evelyn's left-behind suits. The simplest, most German-looking one I could find in her closet. A gray wool tweed, with buttons down the front and two large patch pockets on the skirt and matching jacket with black piping at the collar and cuffs, would work. The everyday style and drab coloring would mingle with other Berliners. I slipped into my German-made wooden sandals with leather straps, forgoing any stockings, despite the nip in the November air. The broad brim of my travel hat would conceal most of my face if I pulled it down low over my brow. With my chestnut hair tucked up tight under the hat, I whispered "*viel glück*" to the German image staring back at me in Tante Helga's cheval mirror.

Twenty minutes later, I strode past the German woman at the outer checkpoint on the arm of a tall, distinguished Prussian officer, a monocle at his eye. The gold ornamental buttons on his collar gleamed with a polished shine. No one at the Spanish Embassy would know that I shouldn't fraternize with Major von Lüben. It took one line from my major to grant us entry. "Who is in charge of American passports?" he barked.

Inside, we met Señor Huerta. Middle-aged, his face bore the marks of a hard-lived life: weathered by sun, thinned by wariness, tested by living as a foreigner in a hostile country. He had slicked back his dark hair with heavy dabs of pomade. His mustache was neatly trimmed in precise lines above his lip. I prayed this Spaniard was also a noble-hearted man, like the lead from *Don Carlos*, intent on railing against tyranny with his own kind gestures to help.

His gracious and warm welcome put me at ease. I finished recounting my story. When I mentioned I held a reservation on a December seventh departure from Norway, he assured me he would contact Washington without delay and do everything in his power to secure permission for my return entry into the United States.

SCENE VIII

Passports, Papers, and Parcels

November 1917
Berlin, Germany

The last week of November stole in like a soldier crawling under barbed wire, wary and tense. Every morning, I awoke with my heart choked in my throat. Onkel Klaus' master schedule spread across the dining table. We hadn't drawn a line through one action item. The *Bergensfjörd* would sail in two weeks. The coveted documents that would allow me to walk up a gangplank and wave goodbye remained elusive. A blessed morning greeted me on November 25 just as I teetered on the verge of surrendering to despair.

I held a long, official envelope, bearing the seal of the Spanish Embassy. I steadied my hands and tore it open. Inside, I found a sliver of hope in the form of my reentry passport back into the United States. Someday, I might behold something more precious, perhaps a child of my own. But today, that piece of paper breathed life into my world. Onkel Klaus shared in my joy, his laughter blending with mine as I danced around the room, waving the passport above my head like a victory flag.

I ran my index finger over the words that proclaimed my OATH OF ALLEGIANCE. *Further, I do solemnly swear that I will support and defend the Constitution of the United States against all enemies, foreign and domestic; that I will bear true faith and allegiance to the same, and that I take this obligation freely, without any mental reservation or purpose of evasion: So help me God.*

My flowing signature as "Applicant" anchored the words. No one had forced me to swear allegiance. No German had ripped the page in half in front of me, broken the words or my spirit. *Freely.* Soon I would live free.

"It is fine to celebrate this first step, Josephine. But remember, you face other formalities before you can pack your bags," said Onkel Klaus.

Tante Helga rushed to the entryway when she heard the rare sound of laughter. "We will pray for a speedy decision from the *Kommandantur*," she said upon eyeing my envelope. "Surely that's all she needs now?"

"An exit passport to leave comes from them, but Josephine also needs visas to pass through Sweden, Denmark, and Norway. They document anyone who may eat food."

My waving arm dropped to my side. "A visa just to eat? Why, I don't eat more than a lapdog."

"Those countries face the same problem as Germany. There is not enough food for their people. Any foreigner who passes through could take food from the mouths of Swedish, Danish, Norwegian children. They must tend to their own, which is why they're reluctant to award visas and will fix a strict time limit. You must agree not to stay longer."

"I have no intention of staying one minute longer than I need to. What's next?"

"After the travel visas, you'll also need formal papers which attest to German sympathies, regardless of what your United States passport's Oath of Allegiance says. They will serve as official protection in your travels to Warnemünde and will allow you to skip the usual questioning at checkpoints. I'll try to make an appointment later today."

Another unsettling scene entered my thoughts. Onkel Klaus could not leave Berlin, and Jack could not re-enter Germany on short notice. I would have to navigate the journey on my own. Those additional formal papers would ensure easier passage.

When I had told Onkel of my successful trip to the Spanish Embassy and Gustav's help, he had been furious. "That was a risky move, Josephine," he had said. "If the police had picked you up, they would have come for me and your tante as well. You put us all in a precarious situation. I'm disappointed with your rash decision."

My profuse apologizing had done little to temper his anger. Although Tante Helga had told me later, "Sometimes, Josephine, we must do what we must. Klaus knows that too. The important thing to focus on is your success."

While I was reluctant to disappoint my dear Onkel again, I knew that with the clock ticking, I needed some insurance. There was only one way to secure those papers by November 28.

"Onkel, there are only a few days before the train to Warnemünde. I appreciate all you've done for me, I do. But I think the only way I'll get those papers and all the visas is to ask again for Gustav's help."

My suggestion landed on the table between us like one of the mortar shells flying through France. I waited for an explosion. He jerked his head up and opened his mouth, ready to spew another round of admonishments. The fear in my dull, tired eyes must have stopped him.

"I would never want any harm to come to you and Tante Helga. I'll be careful. It's been almost three months since my questioning. They must be surveilling others who are more dangerous than me."

He sat in his chair—rigid, arms folded tight across his chest. "Do what you must" is all he said. It wasn't support. It was surrender.

♪

"What do you need now, Josephine?" Gustav said at the Müllers' door when he arrived at my request.

His voice cut sharp, laced with disappointment. My major had grown weary of me. I'd hinted on the phone that it might be the last time we saw each other. He'd agreed to an after-dinner drink when I mentioned the Müllers would be at Evelyn's with Rupert and Anna and Greta in their quarters. We'd have privacy.

I swung my hips as I opened the door. The skirt of my favorite performance dress rustled against my leg. Two steps and I stood before him, eyes meeting his. My hand landed on his shoulder, fingers trembling.

"What I need, Gustav, is this..."

I cupped the back of his head, tilted up, and drew his lips to mine. Soft, damp, as if he'd been licking them before he came in. I had kissed fumbling boys at school. This was different. A delicate friction filled the space between us. His arm slid around my waist, pulling me close. The tang of cigarette smoke clung to his breath. His heartbeat thudded quick against my chest. Heat coiled deep inside me. My shoulders loosened, lips parting to his probing tongue. This moment felt right; not merely a ploy. Under different circumstances, maybe I would have fallen in love with him.

With a jerk, he broke from our embrace as if caught stealing from his father's flask behind a hay bale. His gray eyes, wide as an owl's, lost their haze of passion. Wisdom and wariness edged out passion and regret.

"Josephine, I think there is something else you need. Out with it before you make fools of both of us."

"I wanted to say goodbye to you, Gustav. But you're right; there's another request. Can you find a corner in your heart to escort me to the Scandinavian consulates for my visas and the Foreign Service office for travel papers? And I'm still waiting for the exit passport from Germany."

An irritated huff escaped his lips as his shoulders dropped. "You ask much of me."

I nodded, leaving my head staring down at my American boots. Shame and anxiety vied for a spot in my thoughts. "Gustav, I'm running out of time. Please, I need your help."

After another long moment of contemplation, he said, "If I comply, you must do something for me."

"Yes?" I inched nearer, my fingers fumbling with the pearl button at the base of my throat.

"*Das reicht*. Stop. I will not sully your reputation, nor mine. I would only ask that when the war ends, will you return to Germany?"

All he said was to return to Germany, not to *him*, not to a formal proposal. I replied forthright without hesitation, "I would like that." No need to add that I wanted to finish my studies at the *Konservatorium* when Berlin returned to a country at peace. When opera students sang in any language and every language. When I could pull from the recesses of my feelings and speak the language of love. When we'd speak of appreciation and affirmation of our affection for one another. A time when I could touch Gustav on the shoulder and know that I wanted to spend time with him, give myself to him.

♪

With Major von Lüben by my side, my exit passport met a speedy approval. It didn't hurt that I also handed over seventeen marks. Thank you, Cousin Jack. When the officiant muttered under his breath, "Another damned American going back home to knock us," I endured the caustic departing remark by guarding my tongue. Biting it until I drew blood.

When I asked Gustav to elaborate on the officiant's remarks, he explained and extracted another promise from me.

"You've seen the hardships here in Berlin. You've lived them."

I watched his bright eyes deaden. A strain of pain and sorrow settled around the corners of his mouth.

"I think you understand by now the power of German pride, of the people who have condemned weakness since their birth. Strength and commitment to the cause win wars. If our enemies should learn about the truth of the situation here in Germany, it will embolden them."

He picked up my hand again. His usual gruff baritone voice softened into an octave just above a whisper. "I ask you, Josephine, do not tell our stories. Share only your experience of studying music with the exceptional talent at *Klindworth-Scharwenka*. Tell them about your visit to Bad Elster and the beauty you saw there. Expound on the majesty of places like Tiergarten. Let them know about the goodness in a German heart. The hospitality of Herr and Frau Müller. Friendships you've made with Evelyn, Hannah, and Zara. The kindness that a German officer of the Prussian army provided. That is what I ask of you."

This time, my confidence that I could answer him honestly faltered. I could not utter such an agreement. Instead, I responded with a vague answer: "I understand, Gustav."

The next afternoon, we walked into the Foreign Office, a fortress of power into which no foreign adversary stepped. Major von Lüben had, true to his promise, secured special clearance for me to enter the hallowed halls. That morning, he had presented my case to Herr Doktor Roddiger, emphasizing my pro-German sympathies. I knew I had to impress. More likely, I'd have to comply with whatever he directed if I wanted to walk out of the meeting with my final papers.

Upon presenting my card of introduction, another cardboard cutout of a German aide ushered me through a grand reception room filled with luxurious furnishings in rich garnet hues. Walls adorned with portraits of royalty and distinguished members of the diplomatic service stared down at me with severe, chiseled faces. The opulence overwhelmed me. When I thought back to Gustav's warnings, not to mention hardships and rations, I shook my head at the incongruity inside these walls with what lay outside.

Beyond the reception room, the aide pointed me to a single chair in a small anteroom. The minutes dragged with each tick of the clock. I clutched my hands in my lap, tightening the squeeze on my fingers until they went numb. After thirty minutes of clenching and unclenching to force feeling back into my fingertips, the door to an office opened.

"Fräulein Josephine Marzynski," said a voice from behind the door.

Bag clamped in the crook of my arm, I stepped into the office ready for a stern-faced statesman, hard eyes, decades etched in his face.

Instead, I found a tall, well-groomed young man with striking blue eyes and blond hair. Not yet thirty. A remarkable feat for someone with the title Herr Doktor.

The way he extended his hand in a warm and courteous greeting further surprised me. For a few minutes, we traded pleasantries, his voice smooth, almost coaxing. Would I clear my last hurdle with relative ease? Then he asked about my studies at the *Konservatorium*. I felt like he evaluated each answer, turning my words over in his mind for what I hadn't said.

When I thought we'd continue our discussion about my living arrangements with the Müllers, instead, his tone shifted. "Fräulein Marzynski, Major von Lüben has informed us that your sympathies lie with Germany. I trust he would not tell us a falsehood?"

"Yes, absolutely, Herr Doktor. Major von Lüben is one of the most honest men I've met. He is a dedicated and loyal officer."

"And yet, you have been here for..." He shuffled through my documents. "...since October of last year. For over a year, you experienced our hospitality and witnessed our realities." He paused. It served no purpose for me to lie. No one who had lived in Germany for the past thirteen months could close their eyes to the tragedies that tore apart its people.

"Herr Doktor, I have had the incredible good fortune of living with the Müllers, whose hospitality and kindness are unparalleled. I made close friendships with German students in my classes. One of them, whose husband serves in France, asked me to witness her wedding. Yes, we have all eaten meager meals in accordance with our ration cards, and yes, some nights were colder in the house because of coal shortages. But I don't think we've suffered any more than our neighbors. I understand the sacrifices required in the name of Germany's fight in this war."

He steepled his index fingers together and nodded at my answer.

"You are very observant, Fräulein. However, I have one request before I can process your papers today."

I looked over my shoulder at the closed door. No one else sat in the empty waiting room. The aide who escorted me stood at attention on the other side of the grand reception room. What exactly would a charming, handsome Doktor request of a young woman? One who needed his approval stamp on the papers to allow her to leave Germany in three days? I swallowed the bile that had swum up into my mouth.

"Yes?" My voice wavered as I waited for him to rise from his chair and unbuckle his belt.

"Have your music sheets and any personal letters that you wish to carry out of Germany delivered to me by tomorrow morning. I will officially seal them to ensure they pass through inspection without being opened."

My mind raced through the few letters I had received from home before April and from Jack. I couldn't recall immediately whether any of them contained any subversive commentary. Then again, how would he know if I simply turned over only the ones I considered safe?

"I can bring them to you within an hour, Herr Doktor."

"Fine." He leaned over his desk. The intensity built in his eyes. "In return, I am confident that, given the circumstances, you will be glad to oblige another request."

He gestured to a stack of ten or so typewritten pages on his desk. "I have prepared a factual account of the situation in Germany. It proves beyond a doubt that our cause is just. You will take this to America and deliver it to the editor at a New York newspaper. The United States shall know our truth. I must rely on von Lüben's judgment that we can trust you to do this for Germany."

I sat up straighter. This simple request surpassed any I could have imagined. Playing courier may be one of the least challenging roles I would ever undertake. I would defer to the recipients of the document to decide how the Germans defined truth. I quickly replied, "Yes, indeed."

Our interview concluded with no grand gestures or dramatic farewells. Yet, as I stepped out into the bustling streets, I knew this meeting—this rare favor—would serve me well in the days to come.

When I returned to the Müllers, I rushed upstairs to my room. I pulled my sheet music from my valise and read a few of my notations in the margins. Underlined words. Punctuated notes. A swirled line where to soften and extend a breath. As I turned the sheets over in my hand, I realized the themes and spirit of an opera held the power to set me free, this time as camouflage for German propaganda.

Next, I pulled loose the ribbon around my packet of letters. A quick scan of each found no traitorous comments. I placed them in a neat stack, tapping the pages of sheet music to align the edges. I laid half of the sheets atop the letters.

On my bedside table, the esteemed pages of *Faust* by the German great, Johann Wolfgang von Goethe, sat closed. A small triangle of red satin marked the last page I had read the previous evening. The pages and lines of Goethe had become Old Glory's new hiding place. I feared I wouldn't remember to remove it from my pillowcase on laundry days, lest Anna should find it.

As I pulled my flag from between the pages, it occurred to me this was the time to seize upon Goethe's words. *As soon as you trust yourself, you will know how to live.* Now more than ever, to exit Germany emboldened with clarity and purpose, I needed the heart of my country with me. My strength. My compass. Pointed toward home. I had planned to sew the flag back into the hem of my traveling suit, returning it to its safe haven during my trip over. Could I take another chance at the same spot? I definitely couldn't place it in my luggage where the inevitable and multiple searches would discover and confiscate it. I smoothed it out and placed it atop one half of the sheet music and pressed the other half of the sheets on top, ensuring no corners peeked out.

I called out to Anna that I had to return to the Foreign Service office with another set of documents. As I set one foot down in front of the other, I straightened my back to the ramrod posture of a German soldier and marched forward. I would hand deliver my papers to Herr Doktor Roddiger and leave with a silent triumph. The flag of my homeland would sail home under the protection of the German imperial seal.

SCENE IX

Swan Song

November 1917
Berlin, Germany

My last three days in Berlin mixed joy and sorrow into a bittersweet blend of emotions. I dreaded saying goodbye to Klaus and Helga Müller, the people who had become like parents to me and had saved me from the tedium of being a file clerk in Boston. Thanks to them, I swapped shoe factory orders for sheet music of the finest operas. They supported me in every sense of the word. From opening their hearts to me, to upholding my desires and protecting me from the grips of the German police.

Now, leaving them behind, I would worry endlessly about their safety. How much longer could they endure rationed food? Would Onkel's business continue to protect and sustain them? Would the Americans break through the Western front and march into Germany? I hoped Evelyn's husband and Major von Lüben would watch over them through whatever they faced in the days and months to come. Yet, at the same time, I rejoiced, thinking of my reunion with my mother, sister, and brothers. As Emily Dickinson had said, *they both belong to me*. The Müllers and the Marzynskis. I would hold them all tight in my arms and in my heart.

A whirlwind of last-minute farewells left me with scarcely a minute to gather my thoughts. Evelyn set the tone with a warm, intimate gathering at her home. Hannah and Zara joined us, filling the house with melodies of friendship. When we moved to the dining room, our eyes lit up. Evelyn had decorated the table with red, white, and blue ribbons. Streams of my country's colors swirled between plates and serving platters. It may sound modest, but we oohed and aahed, and may have drooled, at the small dishes of pudding drizzled with vanilla sauce. Above each dinner plate, tucked into a nut cup, stood a small, tissue-paper American flag on a spindly toothpick pole. I doubted even the black market would dare sell such traitorous items. Evelyn must have made them herself. Not only was she a gracious hostess, she was bold and creative too. I hastened to brush away the tears forming in the corners of my eyes. Evelyn's thoughtfulness showed that for a fleeting moment, we were young women, not citizens of opposing nations. We chatted late into the night, celebrating each other and the joy of one of us.

The next day, Frau Trebicz invited me and ten other students into her lovely home. The high-ceilinged foyer boasted stucco moldings around the edges. Crisp, elaborate floral scrolls and geometric flourishes stated a restrained elegance. A tall mirror, framed in dark walnut, hung opposite the door. As I passed by, reflections of German women bounced back at me. Smiles and laughter crinkles spread across their faces. Today, they gathered for a peaceful afternoon. A time to say goodbye to me, their friend.

We spent the afternoon singing, our voices weaving through the room. Each sweet note echoed against the wood-paneled drawing room. Before lunch was served, Frau Trebicz asked me to sing. "Your choice, Josephine. Today is not bound by rules. We are celebrating you and the music that you carry in your heart."

"I'd be honored, Frau Trebicz. You know my favorite is 'Je suis heureuse.' The words convey how I feel today. But may I have your permission to sing the original French version?"

Frau Trebicz looked around the room. Hannah and Zara nodded in rapid unison, knowing how much I loved Philine's aria from *Mignon*. Its libretto represented the pure joy I felt. An audible *tsk* came from Paulina at my request. I hoped she wouldn't report me and Frau Trebicz to Herr Robitschek.

After several long moments of consideration, Frau Trebicz stepped to the bench before her piano, shuffled through her pile of sheet music and said, *"Mademoiselle Josephine, commencez lorsque vous êtes prêt."*

I beamed as bright as a spotlight directed at a soloist on stage. Her reply in French instructed me to begin when I was ready. I abbreviated my warm-up routine. Just a few neck circles—over, back, over, down. Shoulder shrugs up, down. Inhale and hold. Trills over my lips. I clasped my hands in front of me and looked out to the girls who had welcomed an American, then the enemy, into their circle.

My voice lifted as the words poured like bubbling champagne over my tongue and lips:

"Je suis heureuse, l'air m'enivre…" (I am happy, the air intoxicates me.)

Like a carefree nymph from the gardens of Bad Elster, I flitted over to Hannah, placing my finger under her chin. *"Nous reverrons la douce fleur."* (We will see again the gentle flower.)

I sashayed over to Zara, picking up her hands in mine. *"Et les beaux jours et le beau ciel!"* (And the beautiful days and the beautiful sky!) I reveled in the moment's beauty.

"Le rossignol chante aux échos! Ah! quel plaisir! ah! quel bonheur!" (The nightingale sings to the echoes! Ah! What pleasure! Ah! What happiness!)

Paulina, who hadn't heard me sing in some time, rose to her feet as the finale spilled from my heart. "Josephine, your improvement is remarkable. You hit the soprano notes as well as Clare Dux," she said, swiping at a trickle from her eye.

Her comments lifted me to the pinnacle of my brief musical journey in Berlin. Paulina, in comparing me to the German diva of the day, was as rare as seeing a German parade without red, white, and black bunting hanging from every building along the route.

When the maid entered the living room carrying platters of food, our celebration turned from glorifying art to something more primal. Real bologna sandwiches on crusty light bread, cups of black tea (no one expected sugar or cream), and cake topped with a marshmallow-like frosting. We gasped with delight. The spread seemed fit for royalty. I felt like a princess surrounded by my ladies-in-waiting. We devoured every morsel like revelers at an imperial feast. Smacking of lips and groans of delight filled the air with a different type of musical note, but no less appreciated. When I recounted the meal to my mother, I would omit the bologna sandwiches. Without having lived through the experience of rations, she might never understand that you ate what was available, whether or not it was kosher.

After each girl left, with our shared tears and promises to write, unsure if the mail would get through, Frau Trebicz motioned for me to wait.

"Josephine, I have made an appointment for this afternoon with Herr Direktor Salter. He would like you to sing for him before you leave."

Herr Direktor Hans Julius Salter's name alone as a renowned conductor and a formidable critic commanded respect and a touch of fear.

"Me? But I haven't completed even one full year of study, Frau Trebicz. I couldn't. In the eyes of a man like Herr Direktor Salter, I'm a mere novice. I've barely mastered any of the works he would expect to hear."

"He expects us at three o'clock. I wouldn't dare cancel the meeting after he agreed to it. Get your coat."

Not wanting to disappoint the teacher who had trained me to levels I hadn't dreamed of reaching, I buttoned up my coat and slid my arm through hers to link us like a duet—teacher and student.

My heart pounded as we entered a studio room at the *Konservatorium*, nerves threatening to overtake me. Herr Salter remained seated in an oxblood-red, leather-studded Chesterfield chair. His bald head shone from the gooseneck lamp positioned next to him on a tall shelf. Through his wire-rimmed glasses, his eyes held a stern and confident gaze.

Frau Trebicz introduced me. "Herr Direktor, I am pleased to present my student, Fräulein Josephine Marzynski, the one I told you about last week."

"*Ja*. The *Amerikaner*. Well, let's have a listen, Fräulein. Do you need to warm up?"

"Thank you, Herr Direktor. I've just had a practice session at Frau Trebicz's. With your permission, I'd like to sing the same selection from *Mignon*. In French?"

"It does not bother me what language you use. I've always believed a composer would want his music played or sung as he intended to capture his true feelings. Proceed."

I closed my eyes. This would be the finale of my Berlin chapter. Once again, I placed myself in the scene. *Je suis heureuse, l'air m'enivre.* I allowed the air to intoxicate me. To find my soul filled with musical notes as I wondered, was this the end of my time in Berlin? Would I board a train in less than thirty-six hours and reach the port of Warnemünde? Or would other tests try to thwart me? A change of mind by Herr Doktor Roddiger. A canceled ferry to Denmark. Missed connections along the five hundred kilometers between Copenhagen and Christiania. A stamp of DENIED on any of my documents. Or worse, DETAINED.

With a shake of my head, I banished those troubling thoughts from my mind. *This is a happy moment, Josephine. Embrace it.*

Live it. Believe in it. I opened my mouth and poured golden sounds from my throat.

When I finished, I looked at Frau Trebicz. She nodded with a smile as wide as the collar on her dress. I exhaled with a soft *whoosh* escaping through my parted lips. Searching Herr Direktor's face, I found no evidence of an opinion until he spoke.

"Fräulein, you have a fine voice." He rose and extended his hand. "I believe I can guarantee you a career here in Berlin after you finish your studies."

One of Berlin's most revered conductors wanted me! Josephine Therese, from the back streets of Boston. Like a peony whose petals waited packed tight like a clenched fist, nourishing sunlight and water had found me in the bleak days of wartime Berlin. My study with Frau Trebicz had pried at my petals, revealing the many layers of my hidden talent. With Herr Direktor Salter's affirmation, his studio could become my greenhouse, forcing me into full bloom.

Maybe I should stay in Berlin? Continue my studies and training. Reaching for the spotlight on a stage surrounded by other performers. Together we would delight audiences like an entire garden of peonies, each petal spreading cascades of color.

Then, a slashing torrent of rain beat down upon the idyllic scene in my head. The peonies flattened into dark, squishy mud. Broken stalks and strewn petals fluttered in the gusts. Away, away. I reached out my hand to grasp at the nothingness. It fell limp at my side.

No, I had decided. The risks were too great. All the work to gain my papers had been done. I'd made promises. Most of all, the relentless war and my desire to go home had dampened my dreams.

"Thank you, sir. That is a most generous offer," I replied, "but I'm going home."

"To America?"

"Yes. Even if I only find a spot in a chorus, I need to return to my family."

His expression darkened for a moment, then softened. "I wish you all the best. If you can, please keep Frau Trebicz abreast of your plans. I will want to know which American company bested the Germans in capturing Fräulein Marzynski for their stage."

The smile that spread across my face went past my cheeks as if it would touch my ears.

♪

My grand finale arrived on my last night in Germany. The Müllers planned a farewell soirée. I hold that night tight in my memory like a hazy dream, clouded by tears when I thought of the dear friends I would leave behind. Many of the guests marveled aloud at my success in securing permission to leave Germany. They thought it an impossible task. I did not share all the details behind those approvals, including the stamped and sealed papers now tucked into my hand satchel.

As if my heart weren't heavy enough, my friends overwhelmed me with gifts. From Onkel Klaus: an envelope filled with one hundred marks and the assurance it would cover the rest of my travel expenses. Tante Helga: a sleek alligator-hide suitcase with green sides, black handles, and my initials JTM embossed in gold. Evelyn: an elegant stationery travel set and armfuls of flowers. Gustav presented me with a silver cigarette case, monogrammed with my initials and trimmed with a band of tiny ruby beads. A thoughtful gift, although I did not smoke, and he knew that, but he had tried. I feigned my gratitude with promises I would cherish it and place it in my keepsake box at home. Then came Hannah, who undid me by slipping a ring onto my finger, with JTM and HVS intertwined in a delicate engraving.

Major von Lüben was the last to leave. I had done everything in my power to avoid being alone with him throughout the evening. But I couldn't turn from him taking my hand nor from leaning in to whisper, "Are you truly glad to be leaving me?"

I met his gaze and replied, "I've told you. I am glad to go home." The truth and a careful deflection bounced between us. I didn't dare speak about the stirrings in my heart.

"Berlin won't be the same without your voice." He kissed the back of my hand, slower than at our first meeting in the Tiergarten.

Reverting to his erect posture and firm speech, he said, "Don't forget what I said. What Herr Doktor Roddiger has told you. Our cause is just. We are going to win, Fräulein."

With the final unshaken creed of a Prussian officer, he turned and walked away. My heart knotted like the intricate lines of a ship's rigging. Each tugged me in a different direction, waiting for the sails to fill and my emotions to set upon a clear course.

I rose the next morning by five. After a breakfast eaten in silence, the Müllers and I stepped out their front door together for the last time. Onkel Klaus, Tante Helga, and Nichte Josephine headed down the shrouded streets in near darkness to the Bahnhof. There, I stowed my new alligator-hide suitcase and flowers in my train compartment before returning to the platform. I held my precious papers and passports in my hand baggage.

Tante Helga, between sniffles of her own, kept repeating, "Now, don't you cry. Don't you cry."

As the final five minutes ticked away, the emotions I had held in check gathered in my throat. How could I convey what these people meant to me? What type of farewell does a girl utter to the city of her enemies, from which she's barely escaping? My gratitude, my sorrow, my affection. What does she say to the family she'd leave behind—perhaps never to see them again? It should be fashioned with philosophical intent. Something charged with emotion.

"*Auf Wiedersehen*" was all I managed. A simple goodbye for a complicated situation. Real life doesn't write perfect endings.

As the train pulled away, the dam broke, and I wept for several minutes. I finally wiped my eyes and stared at the morning fields. The landscape receded. And then it hit me. I was not heading out on holiday to Bad Elster.

I was leaving Germany.

Overwhelming relief surged through me, drowning out my sorrow. The train click-clacked down the tracks, carrying me farther and farther from the city I had longed to escape. My heart lifted. In my mind, I composed a folksy melody for a silent arrangement of Walt Whitman's poem, "I Hear America Singing." Guitar strums. No banjo picks. Percussive undertones to celebrate the dignity of work and the beauty of everyday life, far from a dramatic operatic production.

I hummed the lines.

…Each singing what belongs to him or her and to none else,

The day what belongs to the day—at night the party of young fellows, robust, friendly,

Singing with open mouths their strong melodious songs.

I couldn't wait to sing of the day that belonged to me. At home, in America.

SCENE X

One Goal. Five Fingers.

November 30, 1917
En route to Denmark

Throughout the five-hour trip to Warnemünde, my mind whirled with what might await me. Fourteen months ago, with Jack by my side, I had talked and sung my way into Germany. Now, I had but one goal. I needed to talk my way out alone, with only a packet of papers bearing the imperial seal. Going home meant getting home.

Halfway into the trip, a man and his wife sat down next to me after boarding at Neustrelitz. They both wore the same beaten expressions I'd seen too many times. A populace tired from war. Tried by war. Their coats, once plush with heavy wool and a fur at the collar of her coat—fox I supposed, like the coats my father once sold in his store—appeared matted and thin. The man stared straight ahead in silence, ignoring his wife. She didn't speak either. With her voice, that is. In a fluid motion, she touched her right index finger to each of the five on her left hand, folding down the finger upon her touch. After the close of the pinkie, the five fingers sprung open again. She repeated her five-finger touch. Over and over and over. An indistinguishable murmur accompanied each fold as tears welled in her eyes.

Across the aisle from us, a pair of soldiers laughed. I heard one say to the other, "What child's game is she playing? Maybe she can teach us. A good way to pass the time in the trenches, eh?"

Hearing their laughter and comments, the husband waved his hand at them. "Please. Do not laugh at my wife. Take pity. She has lost her mind. I am taking her to the asylum. She counts and repeats the names of our five sons. Soldiers for the Kaiser. Killed. One after another, after another, we received the notifications. All we have are five slips of paper. No bodies, no gravestones."

As if a cannonball volleyed through the train car, the reality of what awaited the jovial infantrymen shot down their levity. Their idea of a children's game had transformed into a mother's nightmare, one from which she could never awaken. Trapped inside her overwhelming loss, soon she'd be locked behind the walls of an asylum.

I turned away from the couple, my back blocking the view of five fingers up…five fingers down. The war's tragedies seemed like they meant to usher me out of the country. Rather than being seated in a grand music hall to watch human artistry perform, I had to endure another two hours of watching a human's descent into madness.

The train jerked to a slower *chug, chug, chug* for its last stop. The steel wheels ground against the rails. My stomach matched the revolutions with an adagio of tumbles. Out the window, the same barnlike building of my first inspection over a year ago in October came into view. The building had sagged further into its foundation. I imagined the extra baggage that other departing enemies had carried through its doorways. Jammed-packed valises and crates containing not only clothing and household belongings, but unfathomable weights of disquieting fear and dread.

I gathered my bags and joined the crowd in the queue at the entrance. Demands of *"Öffnen, öffnen"* echoed through the inspection room. Each person in line opened their bags. The entire room inhaled a collective breath and held it until the person ahead of them closed their bags and walked out. As my turn neared, trembles in my toes inched upward along my legs, clenching my stomach, until they reached my fingertips. Quaking like a reverberating drumbeat could arouse suspicion. I pursed my lips into a thin line, determined to take control of my body.

The inspector extended a gloved hand. I spread my papers on the table. Exit passport, entry passport, three visas, one sealed packet. His gaze fixed on the packet, its emblem matching the embroidered crest on his shoulder strap. Without a word, he flipped open my bags, poked through, and snapped them shut.

"*Gebilligt.*" Approved. The word landed with the same weight as the day Herr Doktor Salter told me my voice could earn me a spot in a Berlin opera company. I nearly floated into the next room. There, a stone-faced woman commanded, "Take off all your clothes. Let down your hair."

I obeyed. No invisible ink marked my back. My brassiere hid no secret notes tucked into the cups. No carvings on my toenails. Let her study my gaunt, pale frame, pry my mouth open, prod my tongue with a wooden depressor. I didn't care. I could endure the indignity, knowing that within minutes I would take my last steps on German land. Another clipped "*Gebilligt*" and I dressed quickly.

Outside, I drew in a deep breath of salty air. Gulls swooped low with the misguided thought any of us had spare food. Dockworkers unloaded crates of canned meat from the ferry into army trucks. More food for soldiers while civilians counted ration cards for a scrap of sausage.

The gangplank dropped. I gripped my bags until my knuckles whitened. My scuffed American boots hit the rough wood. At the stern, Denmark's red flag with the Nordic white cross snapped in the wind. Ropes thudded to the deck. We pulled away from the German shore and headed north across the Bay of Mecklenburg toward Gedser, Denmark. A widening expanse of wintry gray water foamed in our wake—and with it, my captivity.

Twenty minutes out, fog swallowed the boat. Bells clanged to warn other nearby ships of our position. Spotlights stabbed the dark and failed. A wind gust tore off my hat, pins scattering into the black water. The ship pitched and dropped, waves slamming hard enough to rattle the deck beneath my feet. Ships must travel through fog all the time, I thought. The captain must know the way. Other passengers along the rail abandoned me, seeking shelter inside from the ominous barrier. I heard a crew member call out, "Come about, we're heading back." Bile filled my mouth. I spewed the vile vomit overboard.

I grabbed at the man's navy peacoat sleeve as he passed me. "No. We can't turn back," I said, while inside I screamed, *NO! NO! I won't go back.*

"It's up to the captain, Fräulein."

A raw mist mixed with tears streamed down my cheeks. I braced myself for a turn. I contemplated hurling myself over the rail. Reckless ideas of swimming to Gedser filled my head. Yet, I felt no slowing of the boat's travel. A sliver of light peeked over the port side of the boat. To the west, where the sun set. The fog lifted its pleated folds. We still pointed north toward Denmark. A coastline emerged. New tears of relief trickled past and covered the ones of torment only minutes ago.

When the boat bumped against the Danish dock, my spirits soared. If propriety had allowed, I would have hugged the official inspecting my passport and baggage, rather than silently cursing him as I had done so often at all the German offices.

The train station was a short walk from the docks. I set my bags down and exhaled a gush of anxious breath. For all I knew, I had been holding it since leaving Berlin.

Another train trip beneath a spread of glimmering stars until we pulled into Copenhagen. Like tiny spotlight beams, the stars lit my path to the platform where Jack paced up and down in front of the station house. I ran to him. "Jack! I'm here," I said, collapsing into his arms like a lost child returned home.

He wrapped his arms around me and soothed as a father would a babe. "You're safe now, Josephine."

"We almost turned back because of the fog. I thought I'd have to swim to Denmark."

"Feisty Jo, I have no doubt you would have." He stepped back from our embrace. "But while you might have the determination, I'm not sure you'd have the strength. You're skin and bones. Let's get you something to eat."

"Real food?"

"How do a thick, juicy steak and decadent cream cakes sound to you?"

"Don't tease me, cousin."

"I wouldn't dare. C'mon, there's a restaurant down the street that stays open late. You'll be moaning from a full stomach in no time."

Jack was right. Once the waiter set a plate before me, I wolfed down every morsel like a ravenous animal. With a slice of thick black bread, I sopped up melted butter pools with unrestrained hunger. I savored every bite and asked for seconds, then thirds. For the first time in what felt like forever, I was free. And I was full.

SCENE XI

Lost in Scandinavia

December 1917
En route to Sweden

My visa allowed me two days in Denmark before I had to cross the Swedish border. Settled into comfortable lodgings after our decadent dinner, the next morning I awoke to the sound of a hard knock.

"Josephine, are you up?" asked Jack. Oh, how the boom of his voice lifted me. I threw off the covers in a defiant statement of *I'm ready for anything that brings me one step closer to home.* No worry a police officer would grab my arm and yank me toward a basement room. Door closed. Lights dimmed. Fear and anxiety on overload.

Here in Denmark, an American walked with her head held high. The red, white, and blue colors could emerge from hiding behind an imperial seal.

"I'll be down soon."

"Well, shake a leg. We can wire Aunt Ricka your travel plans from the telegraph office."

Mother! As close as the other end of a telegram station. I imagined her standing at our front door as the delivery boy placed the envelope in her hands. She would press on her apron, drying them of any dishwater droplets, not wanting to sully the paper.

Would she cry out for my sister and brothers, or would she keep the news to herself? A private elation connecting mother to daughter. I would have cried out to the entire street, the whole neighborhood, and the city of Boston.

Before I dressed, I slid a fingernail under the seal of Herr Doktor Roddiger's packet of lies. A slight crinkling of the tear sounded like gunfire in my mind. As if I had shot and killed the very idea of his request. To serve Germany. Without a clear plan yet of what to do with the papers, I freed Old Glory from my tied-up bundle of music sheets and placed it inside my new valise. The rest of the papers? I scanned the falsehoods that filled the pages and stuffed them into my hand satchel.

Before we could depart for Sweden, we faced yet another inspection aimed at preventing the smuggling of gold or silver out of the country. I pulled the ring Hannah had given me off my finger and placed the cigarette case from Gustav on the table. The woman inspector acknowledged both items were German-made and she wouldn't confiscate them.

After the inspection, we moved into a line to have our bags checked for foodstuffs. As we waited, I watched a young Danish boy arrive with a lunch basket brimming with treats. One by one, the officials confiscated each tempting parcel without mercy. The boy's face contorted with surprise and dismay. My heart ached for him when I thought of how hungry he might be.

We boarded the train, and in under an hour, we reached the northeast tip of Denmark, where a ferry would take us over the Øresund Strait, the entrance to the Baltic Sea, to Helsingborg, Sweden. From the deck of the ferry, I saw Kronborg Castle rising into view. Its spires and copper-roofed towers pierced the Scandinavian sky, green with age and history. The ghosts of Hamlet's world stirred through the mist. It's a fitting inspiration for Elsinore, Shakespeare's setting for his tortured tale. With a slight shake of my shoulders, I shrugged away the haunted tragedy and banished the thoughts of Gertrude's aria from the opera. A mother's torment in "Dans son regard plus sombre" captures Gertrude's fears and desperation as Hamlet's madness consumes him. I wondered if my mother had descended to the same depths of distress, imagining what had become of me while she waited for news of my departure.

Sweden's expansive land stretched ahead of us like a long finger, extending north to the far reaches of Scandinavia. After yet another border inspection, we caught our train to Göteborg and settled in for the twelve-hour trip. Eager for another full meal, I delighted to find the dining car served *raggmunk* for lunch. With a tin fork in my hand, I speared the potato pancakes with as much vengeance as Hamlet stabbed at Polonius with blind abandon. Swishing the chunk through the lingonberry sauce, I let my tongue savor the crispy fried potatoes and tart sauce.

At Göteborg, we would change trains again. As I heard the officials call out for our luggage, I searched for my suitcase in our compartment. I had my hand baggage containing my papers and passport. But where was my alligator-hide suitcase?

"You had it at the station in Helsingborg," said Jack. "Remember? I told you to put your flag in the back pocket so no one would see it upon opening the bag."

"And I did as you instructed. Then, I watched the porter take it with your suitcase. Yours is here. Where's mine?" Panic gnawed at me. I could wear the same plum velvet dress all the way to Boston. But to lose my flag, which had comforted me during the darkest days in Berlin, would be my final undoing.

After scouring the crowd for anyone carrying an unblemished green leather suitcase with black handles, we lined up for inspection. Beaten, ripped, and worn brown valises and various sizes of carpet bags covered the waiting area's floor. Stacks of black steamer trunks teetered in piles over Jack's head.

"It's not here. We'll have to go back," I said, with a catch in my throat.

"That's impossible, Josephine. There's not enough time. I'll buy you some new clothes before your ship leaves."

I rubbed the throbbing, which had started at my temples. My beloved flag might end up in the hands of a Swedish inspector. I hoped the finder would rescue it by turning it over to the American embassy, not burn it in a trash heap. With one more sweep of the waiting room, I relented and climbed on the train without Old Glory.

With the scarcity of coal, wood fueled the train, which meant our journey dragged on at an unbearable pace. By this point, I tired of train travel, wanting this leg of the journey to end. I counted the hours before I would board the ship in Christiania and leave all of Europe behind.

When we stopped at Trollhättan Falls, I stepped off the train, grateful for the chance to stretch my legs and breathe the sharp, icy air. The falls cascading through a world of snow and stone offered a breathtaking glimpse of a Scandinavian winter landscape. We ate lunch at a humble boarding house perched high in the mountains. I sat close to the window, taking in a sweeping panorama of valleys and forests blanketed in snow. We dug into an unexpected feast served family-style with soup, potatoes, an open-faced sandwich on dark rye bread, a *smörbrod* topped with meat and cheese, dessert, and coffee. While we appreciated the laden plates, I silently cursed the landlady for capitalizing on weary travelers like us. The prices she charged guaranteed she'd be a millionaire before long.

Back in the cramped coupé, other passengers settled in next to us. From the next compartment, I heard a woman speaking German. With my keen ear and full comprehension now of the language, my pulse quickened. According to her description of life in Berlin, citizens found plenty of food and managed well. I had traveled hundreds of miles and traversed two countries, only to have another German propaganda spreader within earshot. Bitter anger stirred within me as she continued to paint false pictures of the reality I knew existed. I had seen the truth: the hunger, the suffering, the desperation. Her words distorted and dismissed the agony countless Berliners endured every day.

Jack watched the ire rise in my face. He shook his head and muttered, "Leave it, Jo. No good will come from any commentary or rebuttals from you."

I huffed at his directive and sank deeper into the traveling rug the trainman had given us to ward off the cold. The cozy cocoon lulled me into a deep sleep. I woke to the chatter of a conversation. Jack's German-tinged English mingled with that of a definite British accent.

"Josephine, this is Mr. Woodleigh. Mr. Woodleigh, my cousin Josephine Marzynski."

Roused from my slumber, I slipped back into German. I answered, "*Guten nachmittag.*" Jack's face paled. I watched him flail his hand out of Mr. Woodleigh's line of sight in frantic warning.

"Mr. Meyers said you were American, and yet you speak our enemy's language like a proper *fräulein*." He spit his mangled use of *fräulein* as his beady eyes narrowed in on me.

"I am American and proud to say so," I said.

"Ah, is that so? Proud to be an American?" he said, gesturing with a dismissive wave. "What have you done besides talk? A nation of blowhards, if you ask me."

My anger flared hot and my heart hammered, but I forced words out through clenched teeth.

"Is that so? Blowhards? All talk, no action? Have you forgotten 1775? Or 1812? And what about the ammunition, food, and money we've sent to Britain for years? Without it, Germany would have crushed you long ago. And now, our troops are shoulder to shoulder with yours in trenches across France. They are dying too."

My accusations and questions lingered in the air between us. He shot to his feet and stormed out. As he disappeared down the aisle, I couldn't resist one final barb.

"What if the situation were reversed? Do you suppose England would send troops across a sea to lend us a helping hand?"

My silent cousin picked up my hand. His eyes pleaded for me to calm myself.

"It's unfortunate that men like him exist, Josephine. But try to forget his bitterness and remember what that nation has endured and the extraordinary strength it has shown for three years."

I understood Britain's struggles. They mirrored what I witnessed in Berlin. Lives lost. Families torn apart. Rations. Uncertainty about when and how the war would end. While I took comfort in knowing my journey did not include a stop in England, I feared whether I should expect the same struggles in Boston. If so, at least I could burrow myself into my mother's embrace.

SCENE XII

Despair and Delay

December 5, 1917
En route to Norway

Inside the Strömstad station, our destination in Sweden, we breezed through the checkpoint. The Swedish inspector seemed bored with his job. Review, stamp. Review, stamp. Ask a single question. Review, stamp. Perhaps they were eager to move foreigners through and out of their country as quickly as possible.

Tucking my papers into my hand baggage, I thought again of my missing suitcase. I could shop for at least a couple of dresses in Christiania. Out of the corner of my eye, I noticed a block of green. In a nook at the back of the depot, thick loops of roping around stanchions created a designated area of some sort. I peered harder at the spot. There, set off to the side of stacks of suitcases, trunks and valises, I saw an alligator-hide suitcase.

I tugged at Jack's sleeve and pointed. "There's my suitcase!" I ran over to the spot and ducked under the roping. Between the handles, a gold *JTM* declared its rightful owner. I picked it up and hugged it to my chest, laughing and crying and cooing to my precious one. "I can't believe it," I called to Jack. "It's a miracle. God has watched over me."

A sharp tweet pierced the air. "*Stopp,*" commanded an official striding in my direction, a silver whistle on a thin cord bumping against his chest.

"These unclaimed items belong to the Swedish government. You cannot waltz in here and take any you please."

In short order, I pointed to the initials, showed papers for Josephine Therese Marzynski, and opened it to reveal Old Glory. "Do you think anyone but a foolish American would travel from Berlin, through Denmark and Sweden, on her way to Norway with an American flag?" I asked.

He checked my papers. "All is in order, *Frøken*. I hope you'll be home soon."

In a wash of emotions, I felt as if I had turned a corner, not only in finding my suitcase, but in realizing good, kind people in foreign lands still walked the earth.

With a firm grip on my suitcase's handles, we boarded the last train on our long journey. Christiania was less than a hundred and fifty kilometers away. As we approached the port city, I gasped at the sight in the streets. Everywhere I looked, flashes of red, white, and blue streamers, buntings, and flags waved as if the colors of my country welcomed me to a grand sendoff.

"Look, Jack. Streets decked out in the most glorious colors. It's as if they planned a parade for me!" A laugh escaped from my throat for the first time since my farewell parties in Berlin a week ago.

"That's our Josephine, always looking for the spotlight. I hope you continue your studies back in America. The performance stage calls your name."

He joined me in laughing at the size of my ego.

Upon drawing closer to the station, however, I also noticed bands of yellow on the colorful, celebratory display. With soft glows from the streetlights, now I saw the flags did not belong to me; they belonged to the Scandinavian countries. Red and white for Denmark, red, white and blue for Norway, and blue and yellow for Sweden.

Jack continued, "The flags aren't for you. The kings of the three nations visited Christiania last week. I heard they convened for a conference on the state of the war and the dire economic situation they all face. I hope they found some success in their talks. Everyone needs hope that resolutions are on the horizon."

♪

Jack, ever prepared, had wired ahead for rooms at the Missions Hotel. It proved a blessing, for the city swarmed with foreigners. I soon learned many were Americans, stranded for months, trying to find passage home.

My small room cost nine krona a day while every extra, even a requested hand towel, added to the bill. The equivalent of two dollars and fifty cents a day would quickly deplete my remaining funds. Thankfully, I needed only two nights in Christiania, which had become the most expensive city in the world. Greed bloomed in every shop, restaurant, and lodging. Proprietors who once scraped by now flaunted by with a showy false flair in furs and gaudy jewels.

After breakfast, we visited the police station to have my passport reviewed. By now, the ritual felt mechanical, etched into muscle memory. On this day, the sixth of December, however, the weariness of the chore disappeared. Outside the American Embassy, I paused, saluting the flag that rose like a sentry over the street—a grand, steadfast guardian to the small one folded in my case. A spacious, sunlit room adorned with more American flags and the familiar faces of George Washington and President Wilson greeted me on the inside. The stone floor under my feet might have been the brick walkways of Boston. I joined the line of travelers. How were so many Americans still here? Their drawn faces told the same story. Inspections, delays, and interrogations. Yet we had endured them all for the same reason: a desire to go home.

I shifted from one leg to the other. The wait dragged on until the woman in front of me watched a firm thwack of an American seal stamp her papers. The consulate assistant beckoned me forward as next in line. I handed my papers to Mr. Lane—as the tag on his chest read—eager to speak with a young man whose open face radiated warmth and intelligence, the very essence of the American spirit.

His eyes lit up with curiosity when I mentioned my recent escape from Berlin. I ended my account with a relieved sigh. "All's well that ends well, and it'll be Westward, Ho! for home tomorrow, thank goodness."

"Tomorrow?" he repeated. "The *Bergensfjörd* sails on the fourteenth."

My mind struggled to process his words as if he had spoken in Chinese.

"My reservation says the seventh," I stammered, my heart pounding.

"Yes, but an unforeseen incident delayed their departure from New York," he said, lowering his eyes to the stack of newspapers on the corner of his desk. I presumed he couldn't discuss "the incident," but the U.S. papers didn't censor their headlines. An inked oval encircled an article on the front page of the *New York Tribune*.

"May I?" I asked. He shrugged as I reached for the paper headlined with a line of intrigue: *Suspected Spy Taken on Liner; Had Aero Plans*. I scanned the article with a growing sense of unease.

Flier Thought to be in Kaiser's Navy Arrested Here.

A few hours before the Norwegian-American liner Bergensfjörd *sailed for Norway yesterday...arrested Kasper Wrede, an aviator...believed to be employed by the German imperial navy...described him as a "walking arsenal"...in his possession a large quantity of plans and specifications and fifty parts of an aeroplane...590 rounds of Colt cartridges, a Savage automatic pistol of .38 caliber in his overcoat pocket. A walking stick showed it was part of the motor shaft of an aeroplane.*

Now I understood the need for the exhaustive inspections Germany conducted. They knew what enemies might attempt.

"They caught the spy before leaving New York. How could that have caused a week's delay?" I asked.

"The Department of Justice had ticketed nearly seventy German and Austrian diplomats and their families for the sailing, sending them back to Germany. Due to an abundance of caution, they made the passengers disembark, and all persons and luggage went through a second, more comprehensive inspection. They also stopped in Halifax for a British inspection."

His words crashed over me like a wave of icy water and spilled through my veins. My chest tightened. Like the blockades in the Atlantic shipping lanes, my obstacles seemed to multiply as well. Jack's permission to stay in Norway expired on the seventh. He'd have to return to Amsterdam. Based on the price gouging costs of my hotel room and meals, I would need ten dollars a day to remain there. I'd need a much larger miracle than finding a suitcase.

Mr. Lane listened to me explain my predicament. Genuine sympathy etched across his face. "Miss Marzynski, I'm sorry. The ship won't arrive until the twelfth. All other ships are sold out."

"What am I supposed to do here, all alone?" I asked, my voice trembling. "Can you at least recommend less expensive lodgings? Outside the city?"

He shook his head. "I advise you to keep your current room where you're guaranteed a bed," he said, his tone kind but firm.

Before I could plead for more ideas, an aide appeared from the inner office. "Mr. Toth, the American consul, would like to meet the young woman who has arrived from Berlin," he announced.

I followed the aide, my heart beating a little faster. When I stepped into the inner room, I found a bearded man with gentle eyes and a welcoming smile. He reminded me of our family doctor, a kind, older gentleman who always took the time to listen to our complaints and carried candy suckers in his pocket for my brothers.

He gestured to a worn side chair next to his desk in the small office. "Miss Marzynski, a pleasure to meet you. As your consul, it is my business to know as much as possible about every American who has lived in enemy territory. We have had no one through here in weeks from Germany. I believe you may be one of the last Americans to get out."

I lowered myself into the chair. His statement hung in the air like the final note of a dirge. *One of the last Americans to get out.*

"I—" My voice faltered. I swallowed, forcing steadiness. "It... wasn't easy."

He nodded. "I'm sure it wasn't. We're looking to learn more about how people treated you and any other information you deem important."

After recounting my study at the *Konservatorium* and living with the Müllers, I launched into the five-month trial of securing my passports and visas.

He leaned forward over his desk, his voice laced with concern. "I have a daughter about your age," he said. "I want you to know that you're not alone here. Once you had your passports and visas, did you encounter any other difficulties? The Germans denied many Americans passage with one flimsy excuse after another."

My toe tapped against the carpeted floor. My bottom lip curled in as I bit against the chapped skin. Would my possession of blatant German propaganda cast me as a spy or an enemy sympathizer? Should I mention them? The pages were hardly aeroplane parts or rounds of ammunition, like those that Kasper Wrede had attempted to smuggle aboard the *Bergensfjörd*. Would Mr. Toth consider the pamphlet equally dangerous? Couldn't words inflict a different type of terror?

Lifting my eyes to meet his, I tried to assess the authenticity of his kindly family doctor persona. "Yes, Miss Marzynski. Is there something else?"

I reminded myself that Mr. Toth, despite living and working in Norway, was an American official. He spent his day protecting American citizens. Yet, I had made a promise to a German official to bring his typewritten pages to America. He had trusted me. I would not have been sitting there without his pages. Whose trust mattered more to me at that moment? Maybe the truest form of trust didn't exist in the external world. Perhaps Goethe had written the truest words. *As soon as you trust yourself, you will know how to live.* I needed faith in the decision to act in the best interests of myself and my country.

Over Mr. Toth's shoulder, furls of red, white, and blue folded in on themselves on a standing pole. Even in a limp state, it summoned feelings of its purpose: to convey freedom, justice and loyalty.

"Upon the advice of, and with the help from a major in the Prussian army, a German official in the Foreign Service guaranteed easy passage through Germany, if I carried this packet back to New York and turn it over to a newspaper editor."

I pulled the envelope with the imperial seal from my bag and handed it across the desk to Mr. Toth.

"Good heavens!" he exclaimed, his brow furrowing deeper with every line he read. "You agreed to serve as a courier for the Germans? Do you know what this means? You avowed an allegiance to them."

The bright and soft expression he wore when I walked into his office minutes ago cracked like a lightning strike of an approaching storm.

"No, no. I am not a spy!" I shrieked the word that had screamed at me when I entered Germany. *Spion.*

The word that had permeated everyday life in Berlin. The construct snatched people out of restaurants, off of streets, and from hospital wards, whether they wore a basic cotton dirndl, a pair of traditional Lederhosen, or a Red Cross uniform.

SCENE XIII

Use Your Words

December 6, 1917
Christiania, Norway

"Miss Marzynski. You need to explain yourself. What is your intention with these papers?" The storm in Mr. Toth's eyes swelled as a jolt of electricity passed between us. How would I diffuse his suspicion?

I began with the truth. "I do not believe the words written on those pages, Mr. Toth. The people suffer more than you can imagine. The food shortages weaken the children and adults alike. I've suffered from anemia for the past year. The lack of other daily necessities plagues the city, keeping buildings cold, transportation unreliable, and new clothing difficult to find. The relentless bombardment from the government demands that citizens remain committed to the cause. To sacrifice and stay quiet."

He nodded, indicating I should continue. I squared my shoulders and looked again at the flag hanging behind his desk.

"I reconciled myself to the fact that I could no longer live in those conditions. That, to live, I needed to leave. But I couldn't without all the necessary travel documents. The last one I secured came with the directive to carry this packet. I had no choice."

"And now? You made it out of Germany. Perhaps the sealed packet helped, maybe not. We cannot know. But I ask you again, what will you do with the papers?"

Right then and there, I took the pages from Mr. Toth and tore them to shreds. *Rip, rip, rip, rip, rip.* Five cuts. *Five fingers.*

"Mr. Toth, I'd like to tell you about a couple I sat across from on the last train I took in Germany. They were headed to an asylum. The husband couldn't care for his wife any longer. She'd gone mad. They'd lost all five of their sons in the war. The German people, the ones living through that hell, are devastated. It's a desperate situation. They've suffered enough. They're ready to see this war end. But the regime dictates that they cannot use their voices. To speak would mean internment or worse."

"Then, those are the words that need to be told, Miss Marzynski," he said. "Be their voice to America. The mothers there fear the same fate for their sons. But they don't understand why we have sent our troops and gotten involved in a European matter."

I thought of my brothers and how desperate my mother would become should they appear on her doorstep dressed in khaki uniforms. Ready to say goodbye. Possibly forever.

"I don't believe you are a spy. But you are very observant. I think there's a way you can serve your country. A young woman outside of governmental circles can explain the vulnerability you witnessed in Germany. Your story can help end this war."

I had lived for so long under two flags that the smothering shadow of black and red had eclipsed my life for too long. It was time to claim the glory of the red, white, and blue.

"How can I make a difference?"

"We need more than an article in your hometown newspaper. Your experiences ought to extend beyond Boston and New York. Mothers in Iowa and young men in Oregon need to know victory is within reach at the hands of a downbeaten German psyche." As he stroked his graying beard, the gears in his mind seemed to shift into overdrive. He pulled a folder from under a stack of papers on his desk. As he opened the front cover, I saw a small pile of newspaper clippings, several with *The Boston Post* and *The Boston Globe* mastheads.

"Miss Marzynski, before you left Boston, had you heard of William Wellman?"

The name sounded familiar as I thumbed through the corners of my mind. Not a name from my Jewish neighborhood. It sounded too Boston Brahmin. I narrowed my focus, staring at the clipping in Mr. Toth's hand. In a grainy photograph, a man wore an aviator's helmet, its straps loosened under his chin, his grin confident on the verge of smug.

"Is that him?" I pointed to the photo. "Yes, I recall a lot of ballyhoo about his return from France. I think he was injured, but well enough to speak at rallies, encouraging other men to volunteer."

"Yes, Captain Wellman flew with the Lafayette Escadrille. He became a flying ace of great renown."

"Mr. Toth, I am an opera singer, which is about as far afield as possible from a fighter pilot. I cannot rally crowds, waving a white-fringed scarf and pulling earflaps down on a fur-lined helmet."

A chuckle escaped from both of us.

"While I appreciate the amusing picture you've painted, no, I don't intend to put you on a speaking tour. Rather, I want your story published as a book. A memoir, if you will. And before you tell me an opera singer is not a writer either, I have a solution."

A memoir? Of my time in Berlin? I had shared minimal details, yet this American consulate official thought I had enough material for a book? I leaned in closer to hear his plan.

"Before I took this position, I taught at Harvard. I have stayed in close contact with one of my students. A bright young man. Studied at the Law School as well. Knows how to listen and to analyze. He has ghost-written Captain Wellman's memoirs, telling of his adventures with the Flying Corps."

Taking a blank sheet from a notepad, he wrote a name and Page Publishing and handed it to me.

"After you've recovered from your travels, contact Page Publishing and ask for Eliot Robinson. Explain that I've sent you to him and what I want him to do."

"Write my memoirs?"

"Yes. Between the two of you, I know you'll do a fine job."

"Should I show him this?" My fingers fluttered over the slips of German papers still on the edge of his desk.

"No. You will use your words. The true words of life in Berlin."

I brushed the pieces of German propaganda into a pile. Mr. Toth held out his hands. Whether he intended to glue the shredded strips back together and file them away or dispose of them into the wastebasket at his feet, I didn't care. I was free. That's all that mattered to me.

SCENE XIV

Westward Bound

December 14, 1917
En route to New York

When one scene ends and the next begins, the spotlight fades and then glows again to create seamless stories of trials and triumphs. While each may warrant a discussion or revelation, I do not wish to bore you with details of each scene when my story is so close to the end. My week in Christiania, waiting for the *Bergensfjörd,* felt like life suspended. I spent my days counting the minutes until the great ship would pull away from the dock and I would wave to a mass of anonymous Norwegians.

Kind Mr. Toth, upon hearing of my money dilemma, invited me to stay with him and his family, for which I was most grateful. I also partook of an offer from Mr. Lane to show me around the city. We took countless walks—once even wandering into a fort until a soldier stopped us with a bayonet. We visited the theaters that promised American films. One night, we watched *Joan the Woman,* a storybook gorgeous film starring Geraldine Farrar. I swooned, watching the operatic soprano transform her talent onto the silver screen as an actress. She gave hope to every singer that the end of one's singing days didn't mean a career in the performing arts was over. Watching the story of Joan of Arc unfold before me inspired thoughts of the battles I had endured to find myself sitting in a seat of a Norwegian cinema. I may not have led troops into battle and on to victory, but I had fought. And I had won.

Eager to slip back into speaking English at every chance, I chatted with several of the other theatergoers. Many had arrived in Christiania from Copenhagen in late October. They had pinned their hopes on securing passage on a November ship, only to face disappointment again and again. Also among the stranded were weary, desperate seafarers, who lingered on the docks. Mr. Lane had mentioned that penniless sailors approached him on a weekly basis. Too often, however, consulate investigations revealed that the hundreds who claimed American citizenship belonged to other nationalities. Their pleas for aid came from despair rather than truth.

My defining milestone arrived at noon on December the fourteenth. I climbed the steep gangway of the *Bergensfjörd*. The instant I stepped onto the deck, the invisible chains that bound me to Germany fell away as I watched the massive ropes tethering the ship drop to the waves. Countless miles of ocean still separated me from home, yet a quiet, undeniable calmness enveloped me. I looked over the bow toward where America lay across the sea.

A wave of loneliness, however, crested and crashed to smother my overwhelming joy of freedom and anticipation. As I wandered the deck, threading through a throng of unfamiliar faces, a heavy weight of solitude settled upon my shoulders. Without Jack at my side, like for my first voyage, I would travel thousands of miles and twelve days alone.

I found my small, windowless cabin in second class. My cabin mate had arrived, and we made quick introductions. Mrs. Stephen Browning, a petite woman from Milwaukee, was returning home with her two children, who were somewhere out on deck. Her gentle demeanor reminded me of my mother, whose arms I had longed to hold me many times in these last trying months. With four berths, two washstands, and our collective baggage, I joked I might need to step outside to find room to gather my thoughts. Yet, in that chaotic little room, a comforting glow of companionship rose as bright as the evening stars to light our way home.

"How long is the trip to Wisconsin from New York?" I asked her, sure that it would be much longer than my seven-hour train trip to Boston.

"Close to three days with stops in Philadelphia, Pittsburgh, and then on to Chicago. My parents will meet us there to take us to Milwaukee," she said as she unlocked the smallest of the three suitcases and shook out one of her daughter's dresses.

"That's a long time to travel with children. You've got your hands full."

"Oh, they love the adventure and are clever at entertaining themselves. Just don't get underfoot of the crew, I tell them, or they may be told to walk the plank like the pirates in *Treasure Island*."

I smiled at her reference to Robert Louis Stevenson's classic favorite, which my brothers loved as well. Hanukkah would start in two days. I wondered if Mother had bought a new book as one of their gifts. I realized then that I didn't know what books had been released in the past year. Did they center on the start of the war? Even for the children?

Turning back to Mrs. Browning, I noted, "We'll be at sea for the holidays." I assumed Browning was an English name, and the Brownings were Christian.

Mrs. Browning sighed, her shoulders dropping. "We had to grab the tickets when they became available. I hadn't shopped for any presents. Perhaps the crew can plan a few activities at least."

I expected that might be possible, with a small Christmas tree to gather around for a group sing-along of carols. But I doubted anyone had a menorah to light each night in their cabin for any Jewish passengers.

♫

On our first day out of Norway, a brilliant blue painted the sky like the background of an artist's canvas. The sea stretched before us as we steamed past a fortress, its battlements lined with soldiers standing at silent attention. Several enchanting little islands dotted the water, their beauty accentuated by a serene calm. When we arrived in Bergen the next morning, the tranquility persisted, and my heart swelled with awe as the ship approached the picturesque harbor.

The calm disappeared when we left Bergen and headed out further into open waters. Restless waves rose with a vengeance, eager to toss us about like a child's toy ship. A plague of seasickness gripped me with unrelenting intensity. Throughout the day, I held a basin beneath my chin, poised for the inevitable. After each heave, I wiped my mouth and beads of sweat, which covered my forehead despite the frigid December air blowing across the North Sea. I forced myself out of my cabin each day, my legs trembling with weakness. A rotund, good-natured waiter took pity on me and served my meals on deck, the only way I could keep a few bites down.

On the third day, the ship's officers called for a lifeboat drill. With our life preservers tied around our torsos, we waited for the signal bell, and then filed to our assigned boat numbers with careful precision. When the order came to "Man the boats," a sharp chill raced through me. My chest tightened with the realization that exploding shells from a submarine would drown out the clangs of signal bells and shouts to lower the boats. Practiced rehearsals would prevent chaos should those explosions become real. When the exercise concluded, I fumbled to unfasten my life belt. Behind me, a warm, steady voice asked, "You seem to be in trouble. May I help you?"

I turned to find a tall, distinguished-looking man with graying hair and a trimmed mustache. He wore the crisp, commanding uniform of a Red Cross captain. With practiced ease, he freed me from the mass of straps.

"Captain Williams of Baltimore, at your service, Miss..." he said.

"Josephine Marzynski of Boston. Thank you, Captain. These straps are as tangled as a spider's web," I said.

"Well, we can't have that, especially if we need to use them."

"I hope we don't!" I lowered my voice and asked, "Do you think we will? You're far closer to knowing what we might face."

"I won't sugar-coat the situation, Miss Marzynski, but I have faith the *Bergensfjörd's* captain has mapped the safest route for us."

During the rest of the voyage, we became fast friends. Captain Williams spoke with an unassuming pride about building hospitals from France to Romania to Russia. His story of escaping from Russia, however, lodged in my mind. A band of brigands halted his train, rifles gleaming in dim lamplight, all barrels pointed his way. "I am unarmed on a mission of mercy," he told them. "But if you choose violence, know that armed soldiers, ready to defend us, fill that car."

The bluff worked. The train rolled on. His courage and steady presence helped to assure me we would cross the vast, unpredictable ocean safely and on time.

The passenger list also included an entertaining assortment of people and personalities. The American consul's wife from Petrograd spoke of the frightful conditions in that city, from frostbite to famine. A Russian nobleman, rumored to have connections to the Czar, glided through the corridors as if he walked through the grand foyers of the Winter Palace in St.

Petersburg. The vice-consul from Stockholm strolled with his Polish wife, a lit cigarette dangling from an elegant holder every time I saw her. Even as she cradled her infant, a haze of smoke curled above his head and fine ash drifted toward his bib.

Rumors swirled, too, of Max Rosen, the eighteen-year-old violin prodigy bound for his American debut at Carnegie Hall with the New York Philharmonic Orchestra in early January. One afternoon, after my seasickness eased, I ventured into the stateroom. He stood beside the grand piano, his open case resting on the black lacquer lid. His fingers skimmed the chestnut-red rosewood, like a lover stroking his paramour's cheek. As I watched him slide his fingers up and down the violin's taut catgut strings, my elbow caught a tray of empty teacups. The bone china rattled together as if Rosen's fingers tapped strident, high-pitched piano keys.

Sharp eyes flicked toward me.

"They'll charge you if you break any of those cups," he said in a deep voice, traces of his Slavic birth in Romania barely perceptible.

I pivoted to make sure none were broken. "Ah, well, today Lady Luck has accompanied me on my afternoon sojourn. Not even a Humpty Dumpty crack. And I presume I have the further good fortune of meeting Mr. Max Rosen?"

He left the piano and walked toward me. "You know me?"

I introduced myself and told him how the mention of his talent arose in many conversations at the *Konservatorium*. A student of the famed Leopold Auer in Dresden, he had played in Berlin many times before the war. Our teachers often pointed to his musical gift as an example of the results of hard work. In awe of his success at such a young age, I continued to quake in his presence.

"You're trembling," he observed, his voice carrying the slightest hint of amusement. "An artist has no business with nerves, you know."

With a thin smile, I replied, "I expect that is easy for you to say, Mr. Rosen. I've read you never break a sweat, regardless if it's ten people at a private recital or a packed theater of thousands."

"That's because I learned early on that the audience doesn't care if you're nervous or confident. They care how you play. A brilliant performance will allow your feelings to come through the music."

"Would you consider playing for us one evening?"

He shook his head and sighed. "I wish I could. But my contract with the Philharmonic forbids me from giving unscheduled performances. Even on a ship in the middle of the Atlantic."

"Not even a single song? For me?" I pressed, the words escaping before I could consider my inappropriate forwardness. "I won't tell anyone," I added.

"I gave my word and must honor a promise. But perhaps I can arrange tickets for you and your young man to attend opening night. A woman as lovely as yourself...there must be a young man waiting for you in New York."

A burning warmth spread across my cheeks. My mind leaped at the thought of attending his debut. With equal measure, my heart lifted, thinking of the possibility I could manage somehow to ask Josef Bonime to accompany me. Before I tumbled too deep into a reverie of romance, Rosen took my hand and brushed his lips over the back of it.

"You can let me know." He snapped his violin case closed and strode out of the room. Watching him leave and thinking of what awaited him in New York, I felt a pang of envy. How I hoped I would still find a life in music. The war may have ripped me from my studies, but I refused to allow it to silence my passions.

Even without a performance by the virtuoso, other social activities kept us entertained throughout the voyage. Daily dancing on the deck brought couples out for energetic waltzes, warming bodies in the face of the brisk cold. I joined in with a group of other young women when a Polish man planted himself next to the dance floor area and revealed a well-worn accordion. We clutched the sides of our skirts and kicked into a quick polka, our feet quick-stepping to the upbeat, lively tempo set by the musician.

Hilarity consumed us when Mrs. Browning taught me the mitten game. She tossed me a pair of bright red, chunky-knit mittens. With her son and daughter as my competitors, we raced against each other to accomplish silly yet difficult tasks. Davey could button a jacket in less than a minute; Elise plucked up trinkets, including her mother's small earbobs, with the precision of a pickpocket. I fumbled through every round until I called for a new challenge: turn the pages of a book. Years of flipping sheet music paid off. A strip of blue ribbon landed in my lap. We laughed until tears ran down our cheeks, our American voices pooling into a warm pocket of comfort.

As no appearance at Carnegie Hall restricted Josephine Therese Marzynski from performing, I accepted the invitation to sing from *Carmen* as part of one of the evening's musical revues. Pulling my music from the envelope emptied of Herr Roddiger's lies, I sifted through the pages, looking for my familiar favorite. *Come, little bird, let us charm the crowd. Let us dare them to love with wild abandon.*

I hummed the lines from "Habanera" in my seat at the dinner table before my turn for the musical revue. The boiled halibut had sunk in my stomach like a lead weight on a fishing line. I suppose I hadn't done myself any favors by finishing the last drop of the giblet soup. The rich buttery broth, intensified by generous splashes of Madeira wine, a dash of lemon juice and the yolks of hard-cooked eggs, mingled with the hollandaise sauce that topped the fish. When the waiter set down a dish of plum pudding swimming in brandy, I didn't need the roll of the ocean to place my queasiness in motion.

"Next, we have Miss Marzynski. She is returning to the United States after studying opera in Berlin. Please join me in welcoming her to our humble stage aboard the *Bergensfjörd*." I saw the emcee for the night holding out his hand toward me, summoning me to a spot I adored.

I smoothed down the pleats of my green and gray plaid dress and, tightening the cinch of my belt, I walked up the steps to the stage. A large red rose attached to my hip bloomed like a flare. Rather than a simple decorative adornment, it looked like a bullseye drawing every gaze to me, amplifying my quaking nerves and rumbling stomach. My heart pounded, and my temples throbbed.

I hadn't sung in front of anyone, let alone a room full of strangers, since my fated session with Herr Direktor Salter. It felt like a lifetime ago. I nodded to the piano player and began the aria from *Carmen*.

"*L'amour est un oiseau rebelle...*"

The ship lurched, and the world tilted. Overhead, the lights flickered. Faces in the crowd swayed like flimsy shadows. Dizziness surged through me, but I clung to the melody, forcing each note out with sheer willpower, desperate to finish what I'd started.

By the time the last note faded, I could barely stand. The applause rose around me like a distant roar, but I didn't wait to acknowledge it. I fled the room, my vision blurred with tears and nausea, and collapsed onto my berth. My chest heaved—not just from my rich dinner menu, but from the overwhelming release of fear, relief, and vulnerability.

And from the thoughts of love, in its purest form, waiting for me. My family. A fluttering Old Glory hung over them. Tight embraces. Never letting me go.

SCENE XV

Sweet Land of Liberty

December 19, 1917
En route to New York

Our route from Norway veered in a wide arc toward Greenland before bending south. Lookouts, with binoculars glued to their eyes, scanned for U-boats below and icebergs above. I joined other passengers at the rail when one of the ice-blue giants drifted into view. Sunlight scattered across its crystal surface like a mosaic of gemstones. Five and a half years earlier, an ocean liner much larger than the *Bergensfjörd* sank in the frigid North Atlantic waters. Fifteen hundred souls floated forever in the murky depths of the Atlantic. My voyage had taken me too far, through too many checkpoints and delays, to imagine my journey at the mercy of an oversized ice cube.

Five days from New York, the captain announced we'd bypass Halifax. Cheers broke out to know we'd skip the customary and often grueling British inspection and save a day in our travel. Then we learned the truth. Halifax's dock no longer existed. A deckhand shared the details of an explosion that had gutted the city two weeks before. Seventeen hundred dead. His cousin among them, a crewman on the SS *Imo*, a Norwegian war-relief ship. The *Imo* had collided with the *Mont-Blanc*, loaded with picric acid, TNT, guncotton, and benzol. The blast erupted, hurling flames, smoke, vaporized fuel, clouds of hot gas, and metal through the sky. Buildings and people alike fell as if a giant had swiped a fiery hand across the waterfront.

We listened in stunned silence. The weight of the tragedy pressed into our hearts.

As we stood on deck, the cold sea wind bit at our cheeks. We stared out at the horizon, lost in our own thoughts—mourning for Halifax and praying for a safe, speedy passage for our last hours on board. Before our group retreated to our cabins, the Norwegian shared one more piece of information. "While I grieve for my cousin and the hundreds of others, we should also recognize the heroic work of rescuers who saved many lives, including my other countrymen on the *Imo*. If there is anyone here from Boston, you should know medical personnel from your city responded and traveled north, through a blizzard, to assist with treating the survivors. They were the first Americans to arrive on the scene."

My chest swelled and lifted. In a world overwhelmed by the chaos of conflict, tragedy and division, this Norwegian man reminded me quiet triumphs still occurred. By sharing the news about the Boston medical team, he showed us that kindness, resilience, and concern for others existed. Like an understudy of a performance, it waits in the wings, patient and steady, ready to step in when called upon to act.

The sweetest words sang from the captain three nights later at dinner, when he announced, "We have entered American waters." All the next day, we gazed toward the western horizon, where the Land of the Free stretched out before us. I gulped great breaths of air. Clear, sweet, American air. Throughout the day, I asked crew members to point out the land we passed. The rocky coastline of Maine filled my heart with overwhelming, inexpressible joy. When the crew called out, "There's New Hampshire," I rushed to the railing. Massachusetts would follow. I didn't want to miss the direction whence the gleaming white spire of the Old North Church, Faneuil Hall's golden grasshopper weathervane, and the new, gray granite Custom House Tower silhouetted the land of my city. Would the hands on the marble-and-bronze clocks on each of the Tower's sides mark the minute I passed by? I glanced at my watch to note the time myself. Eleven-eighteen. For the second time on my journey, I wanted to hurl myself overboard. The loved ones I ached for were so close. With long, even strokes, I imagined swimming my way to the piers of South Boston.

Mile after mile, we chugged forward. Past the outer edges and dunes of Cape Cod. Skirted the summer playground and former whaling center of Nantucket Island. As the afternoon sun dipped, the ship glided into the outer harbor of the great metropolis. One by one, the city lights flickered to life. Then, like the beacon of hope she had bestowed upon millions, she appeared. In the twilight, she radiated strength and grace. A cry of pure elation erupted from the ship's rail. She lifted her torch beside the golden door, welcoming us, one and all. Returning citizens and immigrants alike. We all yearned to breathe under the protection of the *Mother of Exiles*. Lady Liberty.

My throat tightened. Mrs. Browning squeezed my hand. Turning to her, I opened my heart and let the overwhelming sense of relief and gratitude spill out in the only way I knew how. *"My country, 'tis of thee, sweet land of liberty..."*

Around me, others reached for the hand next to them. Family, friends, foreigner. A sense of tiredness and wretchedness united us. A swell of voices sang out, loud, confident. *"Land of the noble free, Thy name I love..."*

I swiped tears away with the back of my hand. With our arms lifted high, we stretched them toward our Lady. *"Long may our land be bright, With freedom's holy light..."*

America. Home. After thirteen long months in the heart of Germany, I was home.

♪

Have no doubt; I meant to be first off that ship. My day dress waited on its hanger, bags packed. I smoothed Old Glory out for one last look. The red, white, and blue silk had carried me through

Berlin as a precious reminder of home and fading memories of my father.

Tomorrow, I would walk into Ellis Island's great hall, following his footsteps from twenty-five years before as a twenty-nine-year-old Pole stepping onto American soil with nothing but a suitcase and dreams. Freedom. A business of his own. A good Jewish wife. Children who would grow up respecting the values of loyalty to one's family, faith, and country. To hold those promises deep in one's heart, meant to last for generations born American.

Papa, I thought, *you believed in my music. Thank you for teaching me how to be brave and follow my passion. And to know when it was time for me to come home.*

The next morning, with a heart pounding faster than I thought possible and still live to see another day, the other passengers and I gathered in the stateroom. An American official handed me a numbered red card. I clutched it tight as I waited for my turn. When they called my number, I stepped forward, passport in hand, to face the representative of my homeland's authority. He examined my document. "Miss Josephine Marzynski," he called to a colleague who checked my record. Then, turning back to me, he smiled and said, "You may pass right along, Miss Marzynski. Welcome home." Relief washed over me like an incoming tide. I could have kissed him, bushy beard and all.

The next inspection officer examined my belongings and added another checkmark to my documents after I explained I carried only music, souvenirs, and personal letters. The first wave of panic left me, taking with it the last pinch of anxiety. As an American, my processing took less than twenty minutes. Most of the other eight hundred passengers from steerage would disembark only to face days of lingering at Ellis Island for medical examinations, confirmations of their destinations, and waiting for translators for the variety of Slavic and Scandinavian tongues aboard the *Bergensfjörd*. Although I felt for them and the added delays they might face, I couldn't dwell on their situation. I was home. I picked up my bags and, without a glance back, I marched down the gangplank, off to search for a telegram office to send my mother my expected arrival time at South Station, Boston.

Towering buildings, adorned with countless flags, offered a heartening contrast to the oppressive red, white, and black banners I had grown to despise. The streets bustled with life, crowded with people and dotted with khaki-clad soldiers. The sight of uniforms startled me—a jarring reminder of my country's involvement. Yet, these soldiers didn't sport upturned mustaches or monocles. No air of supercilious arrogance that marked the cold, rigid products of Prussian militarism. Instead, their uniforms, without dramatic flair, carried a quiet strength. A reflection of democracy itself. And the young men who wore them, with their bright eyes and confident strides, exuded a spirit of determination and promise that filled me with hope.

At three minutes past eleven on December 27th, a Boston-bound train lurched forward, beginning the last two-hundred fifty miles of my four-thousand-mile journey. The landscape blurred past like vaporous images floating in a dreamlike state. In a matter of a few scant hours, I would sniff my mother's musky eau de toilette when I pulled her into a close embrace. Touch my sister's cheek, kept soft with her nightly dabs of Pond's face cream. Gaze into my brothers' blue eyes, which always sparkled with mischief. Request a plate of scrambled eggs and a banana to satisfy my longings for a basic meal. And a strong cup of coffee that would burn my throat and awaken all my senses to the reality that I lived again in the United States.

As the train approached Boston and the brakes screeched, my knees jittered. Tingling chills danced up and down my spine. I gathered my belongings and followed the other passengers off the car. No familiar faces stood among the crowd on the dim-lit platforms and toward the entryways to South Station terminal. I dropped my bags onto the pavement. Utter desolation wracked my body, matched by sobs that I had tamped down for months and miles. Alone, again. Like the granite columns that supported the great beams inside the station, I froze. Until I cracked and crumbled as if a piece of dynamite exploded inside my core. I sank to the ground into a puddle around my bags.

Shoes and boots passed by me, hurrying on to loved ones. Over the din of the trains exhaling steam hisses and calls of "hellos" and "over heres," I heard a voice. The sweetest voice with a German accent she had tried to bury for twenty-three years. It repeated words meant for me. "Is it you? I can't believe it! My child."

Tears welled in my mother's eyes, her disbelief mixing with elated joy. She scooped me up like a rag doll. "My dear. Josephine. You're home."

"Mama, oh Mama. I'm home." My arms encircled her slight frame with a desire to melt into her, to become part of her body as I had at the beginning of my life.

The last minutes of traveling on the Atlantic Avenue El streetcar delivered us to Sunderland Street. Mother pointed to the second-floor windows of our apartment. Two faces pressed against the fogged-up glass, their cheeks streaked with wet tracks. My tears gushed again when I spotted the little imps, waiting for their big sister.

After a round of hugs and pets from little Julian, stroking my cheek like a lost kitten, at last, the house quieted. We stumbled upstairs to our bedrooms. With my mother's goodnight kiss still warm on my lips, I found myself in the bedroom I shared with Lillian.

Between our twin beds stood a small wooden nightstand with a white milk glass lamp, its base painted with faded violets. Our well-worn copy of *Little Women* rested there, along with a wrinkled handkerchief, a small notepad, and a pencil, used down to a nub. I noticed Lillian's careful cursive covered the top sheet of the notepad with two dates:

October 5, 1916
April 6, 1917

"Lillian," I said as she pulled her flannel nightgown down over her head and body. "What is this?"

With her soft hazel eyes, she looked at the pad in my hand. "Surely, Jo, you know the dates you left us."

"Well, yes, of course I remember the date of my departure last year from New York in October. But it's only possible to leave once."

"Not if you lived under the same roof with Ricka Marzynski. On April sixth, when we declared war against Germany, Mother screamed until Mrs. Hoffman downstairs knocked on our door, demanding she quiet down for the sake of her son's napping time."

"She thought she had lost me for good," I said. I closed my eyes, thinking of my mother in the kitchen. David standing in the doorway with his stack of morning newspapers to deliver. The headlines blazing with reports of the House of Representatives voting for war after seventeen hours of debate. President Wilson asking for three billion dollars to support the effort. My mother stirring oatmeal in a pan at the stove, dropping the spoon when she heard Lillian read aloud the headlines, watching the spoon sink and disappear into the gray mush.

A drip slid down my cheek. I left it there. The moistness seeped into my skin, marking me. Marring my heart. I wished it would burn a scar to remind me of this moment when I learned how my mother must have suffered for so many months. How she must have woken every day, not knowing my fate. Gone, like my father, in his spirit and body, but not from her mind and heart.

I whispered to her, "Do you hate me, Lillian? For my selfishness in going to Berlin? Leaving you with Mother and the boys? For causing you all so much worry?"

Lillian came to me and took my hands. She drew them to her lips and kissed them. She answered with one word. "Yes."

I shuddered into her embrace, sobbing on her shoulder until her nightgown felt as if it had come through the wringer of a clothes washer. "I'm sorry. So sorry."

She placed her hands on my cheeks and lifted my head. "Shhh, I did hate you. Then, the holidays came. When we sat in temple on Yom Kippur and recited the *Yizkor* for Papa, I realized my atonement would be incomplete without asking for forgiveness for hating you. Hate cannot sustain a life. It destroys it. Only love can nourish a soul. And I needed to live. For Mother, for David and Julian. For you and the hope that you'd return and that I could embrace you like I am at this moment."

I kissed her on both sides of her face, brushing a lock of her dark brown hair from her forehead. "I am blessed, my sister. Thank you."

Lillian crawled under her coverlet, and before I unbuttoned my dress, soft snores told me her atonement was complete. After stepping out of my dress, I stood next to my bed and muffled the snapping of the clips on my suitcase. Inside, Old Glory lay on top. Its stars and stripes glowed, a sacred symbol that had watched over me through every danger and hardship. The Pledge of Allegiance rose in my mind as a truth carved into my soul.

I pledge allegiance to my flag and to the republic for which it stands, one nation, free and indivisible.

One Nation—at one with my country and my family.

Free—from the dark empire's shadow of autocracy, desperate to crush the spirit of liberty.

Indivisible—despite the insidious German propaganda that tried to fracture the united countries fighting against its maniacal militarism.

♫

The next evening, thirty close friends poured into our home. The room buzzed with excited chatter and rapid-fire questions. I barely strung together coherent answers as I reached for another kosher dill pickle from my mother's favorite blue and white pottery plate with the swirl of blueberries at the rim. Over and over, I heard teasing remarks, like: "Why didn't you kill the Kaiser when you were in Berlin? You were closer to him than we ever were!"

I laughed with them over the idea of me, Josephine Marzynski, a young opera student from Boston, waving music sheets in the Kaiser's face. Tugging on the upturned ends of his ridiculous mustache, while demanding he end the war. The room settled from our frivolous conversations when my mother asked if I would sing.

"Oh yes, Jo. Please, you must," begged Lillian, her eyes pleading for the notes which had soothed our souls through trying times.

I hesitated, unsure whether I could share my raw vulnerability at that moment. My performance on the *Bergensfjörd* had come close to a disaster. I needed time to consider whether I could sing, would sing, on American soil. Or should I close the door on my thirteen months in Berlin as if locking my time in a memory box, only to be opened in private moments of reflection?

I looked at my mother. She sat as erect as a bantam rooster, chest out and expectant, ready to strut across a barnyard. Her hands clasped in a tight weave and placed in her lap; her pale skin even whiter against the black of her dress. On her face, lines of worry and fear etched deep into the furrow of her brow. One line for each month of my absence. Yet, she held her chin high and smiled at me, nodding for me to take the stage. Or rather, the center of the living room, where a bouquet of deep red roses swirled in a concentric circle of the faded Persian rug.

With one finger raised, I asked for a moment to find the perfect piece to mark my homecoming. I sifted through the sheets until I found the pages of Rossini's *Tancredi*. I knew the lead required a contralto, but it wasn't far off my mezzo-soprano range. Its lower register would provide the range of my emotions for this moment. I would sing my story. My heart would come alive again, home in Boston, when my voice lifted the libretto of *Tancredi* into a place of transformation. A young, eager woman, blinded by passion and adventure, had returned home, reverent, aware, and ready to surrender to dreams of happiness and victory.

Planted in the middle of the room, my body swayed. The opening lines pulled me inward as my eyes closed. The words belonged to me first as I hummed them inside my head. *Oh patria! dolce, e ingrata patria! alfine a te ritorno!* (Oh homeland! Sweet and ungrateful homeland! At last, I return to you!)

I pressed the pages to my breast and sighed. Music was as much a part of me as the blood that coursed through my veins. Life reached the far edges of my being. I would sing that night for my mother, siblings, and friends. And I would sing tomorrow and forevermore for myself.

FINALE

February 1918
Boston, Massachusetts

A serpent rules Germany—a creature of gleaming scales, lightning-fast strikes, and crushing power. It has coiled itself around the nation, hypnotizing the people until they worship its strength and submit to its will. But sever the serpent's head, crush its body under the weight of liberty's blade, and the German people will finally see its true form: a monstrous thing that has defiled their land and dragged them into darkness.

I read the closing paragraph again, and then once more. "Too dark," I say, shaking my head.

I recall *The Song of Deborah*. A prophetess. The only female judge of the Old Testament. Deborah, a woman who united the tribes of Israel against their oppressors. *But may those who love you be like the sun when it rises in its strength.*

"The rest of the book captures my experiences with honesty and integrity. But with this ending, you lose my voice and slip into the same tone of propaganda found in Germany."

Reaching for the pad, which accompanied Mr. Robinson at every meeting for his note taking and to jot down ideas, I ask, "May I?"

I travel back to my first days in Berlin, guided by a stream of consciousness. As Deborah had said, *The stars fought from heaven; from their courses they fought against Sisera.* Those who live through war, they endure. They defy. Some shine. I think of living with the kind and generous Müllers. Cementing friendships with Evelyn, Hannah, and Zara. Even Natalya. Under Frau Trebicz's tutelage, my dreams sparked. Major von Lüben, saying yes whenever I asked for help. I cherish the Germans I met, for I know that beneath the shadows formed by militarism, the country's beauty and humanity still exist.

I pick up Mr. Robinson's pen and cross out *A serpent rules Germany.* My words will recast perceptions.

Golden musical hours and the brilliance of the German people, heightened by the shadowy backdrop of war, filled my time in Berlin. Those moments of beauty brought light in the darkness. They are reminders of the enduring power of art and humanity. We, America and its allies, must free Germany from false rulers and entrenched obsessions. Peace will bring glory. Democracy and decency will prevail.

"Maybe something like this?" I turn the notepad toward him.

"Perfect, Josephine. Just perfect," he says.

A plate of butter cookies sits on the table between us. Crumbs fall to my lap as I nibble one more, savoring the creamy soft texture of the daisy-shaped sweet. I check my watch. Class starts at four o'clock. My students at the New England Conservatory expect to start on time. In three short weeks, I've taught them the importance of punctuality.

"What's next?" I ask.

"To save time, the editor at Page has worked chapter by chapter as I've submitted them. They didn't want to wait for the full manuscript. I'll review the edits, make any last corrections and send a proof to you at home for a last look through. We should hit the April sixth date for publication. The advertising company is keen to play up the one-year anniversary of America entering the war."

Like the libretto and notes of a musical piece, writing and publishing a book mesh together to create a work of art. I can only hope that this composition, my memoir, *Under Two Flags*, will serve its purpose in moving people to act. Purchasing war bonds. Accepting rationing into their daily lives. Deploying more American men to the trenches of France.

"And for you, Mr. Robinson? What's next for you? Helping another American returning from Europe with a story to tell?"

"Could be." He removes his wire-rimmed glasses and pinches the top of his nose where they've left an indentation. "But the next story may be mine. I've enlisted in the American Expeditionary Forces. The Army needs more troops. I intend to serve."

My hand shakes as I lower the teacup from my lips. The last drops slosh against the sides. "Oh no, but your boys. They're so young. Three and a half and nearly five? Aren't the conscription ages twenty-one to thirty?"

"Thinking I'm an old man, eh?" His chuckle eases the dread in my throat. A tad.

Stuttering, I try to catch my faux pas. "Well, it's just that you're so accomplished, and I recall Mr. Wellman's age and had read you were in school with him?"

"Josephine, our—your—book has wielded its power on its first target. As you said, we must ensure that democracy and decency prevail. For the people of Germany, and for the children, like mine, here in America, who need to believe in the freedom of liberty."

At my feet, I had crammed sheet music, my wallet, and a handful of wrapped menthol throat lozenges into my cloth handbag. A tote for many purposes. I had tucked one special item into the inside pocket to always keep it close. I reach in and pull it out.

"Mr. Robinson, would you do me the honor of taking Old Glory with you? I believe it has the power to keep you safe and bring you comfort, just as it did for me when I lived under two flags."

THE END

AUTHOR'S NOTES

Would you rather read a book that begins…

I Enter the Heart of Prussia
"Look, Josephine! There is Berlin!" The voice of my cousin and traveling companion aroused me from my conflicting thoughts. It was evening, a chilly winter's evening, and the darkness through which the train was moving seemed to hold a threat of something unseen, but real. If I could have looked into the future I might have understood; but, lacking the power of clairvoyancy, I felt it, and would have been glad to turn back had it been possible. It was not. I had definitely committed myself a month before, when Opportunity knocked unexpectedly. Now, on the very threshhold of my adventure, I faced it uncertainly. I had all ready had a taste of what Germany held in store for strangers, and the taste was bitter. Two hours before, I had crawled off the little boat which had borne us to the German frontier at Warnemunde, weak from seasickness, and with little enthusiasm for the "Fatherland."

Or, a book that begins…

Achtung! Spionen Gefahr
Tacked to a pier piling, a sign screamed in black capital letters: ACHTUNG! SPIONEN GEFAHR. At this point in my journey, after speaking German nonstop with Jack Meyers, my cousin and travel chaperone, I could decipher Spionen (spies) and Gefahr (Beware). Germany greeted us with suspicion, its teeth bared, poised to bite.

Jack and I staggered off the small boat at Warnemünde, Germany, the port city and entry point for those disembarking from Gjedser Odde, Denmark. My boots hit the splintered planks of the wharf. A tide of bodies from the boat swallowed us into a *swarm. Before we could board the train to Berlin, we needed to pass through Germany's entrance inspection. Pale faces tightened with tension as we shuffled forward. A suffocating wave of air buzzed with anxious whispers. Ahead, a barnlike building loomed, reminiscent of an American frontier fort, its wooden beams rough-hewn and imposing. This time and place, however, were no more like an outpost on the Oregon Trail than the ruins of ancient Rome.*

When I read the first version, I found the prose dense and laborious. Yet, I continued on and finished *With Old Glory in Berlin* by Josephine Therese. While my grandfather, Eliot H. Robinson, penned the foreword to the book, the writing style found in his nine other books permeated every page. Hence, I believe he collaborated with Josephine and ghost-wrote most of her memoir. Despite the style, I'm glad I persevered through the slow pace and overabundant use of "telling" a story. Within those pages, I learned about the extraordinary experiences of Josephine Therese Marzynski.

Inspired by my commitment to celebrate women in history, I felt Josephine's story needed to be pulled from the shadows. Rather than republish *With Old Glory in Berlin*, I believed a retelling of her story with added fictionalized elements of emotional depth, intrigue, historical connections, and more "showing" would appeal to a broader audience. Buoyed by the recent success Ariel Lawhon has achieved in retelling Martha Ballard's story, transforming *A Midwife's Tale: The Life of Martha Ballard, Based on Her Diary* into the NYT Bestseller, *The Frozen River*, I began.

Line by line, I rewrote the prose. I reordered scenes and deleted meaningless ones as well as extraneous characters that didn't move the story forward. With a new skeleton on the table, I donned my researcher hat to seek answers about Josephine to more fully develop her character. Why did she want to live in a country at war? What drove her passion for opera? Who influenced her?

I unearthed a few details in Boston newspaper articles from January 1918 when she returned from Germany and reiterations of the same information when the book published in December 1918. I also discovered a mention of her singing at Jordan Hall in 1908 under the tutelage of a Miss Kendall, her father's death certificate in 1914 issued by the Boston State Hospital with cause of death listed as "general paresis," her passport applications including a wonderful photograph of a beautiful, confident-looking young woman with upswept dark hair, her name on the passenger list of the *Bergensfjörd*, her 1919 wedding announcement to Josef Bonime in *The Jewish Advocate,* and her burial in Sleepy Hollow, New York in 1983. As you can see, scant information meant I had to imagine many of her motivations and influences.

The original book lacked two key themes which I felt would add to a retelling. First, she mentioned nowhere that she was Jewish. But her wedding announcement, naturalization papers from 1936 with her race listed as "Hebrew" and her parents' burial at Mishkan Tefina, a Jewish cemetery in Boston, indicated she must have been Jewish. I surmised that her faith, even if she kept a low profile about it, would have been a source of comfort and a connection to her family during her frequent periods of homesickness. I also wanted to balance her identity with a resolute sense of American patriotism and Old Glory's presence throughout the book. Through research into the experiences of immigrants in the late 1880s, like Leopold Marzynski and Ricka Meyers, I learned that most of them were eager to assimilate and embrace the ways of a new land of opportunity. Although Josephine said she received the small flag from a girl at the docks in New York upon her departure in October 1916, I created the connection to her immigrant father and that she received the flag from him. By the way, it's not a typo on Page 20. The original form of the Pledge of Allegiance, written in August 1892, read: "I pledge allegiance to my Flag and the Republic for which it stands, one nation, indivisible, with liberty and justice for all." In 1923, the words changed to: "the Flag of the United States of America." And, in 1954, in response to the Communist threat of the times, President Eisenhower encouraged Congress to add the words "under God," creating the 31-word pledge we say today: "I pledge allegiance to the flag of the United States of America, and to the republic for which it stands, one nation under God, indivisible, with liberty and justice for all."

The second element I wanted to expound upon was Josephine's opera singing. Only an overwhelming passion could have driven her to bravely travel to a war-torn country to study. She mentions a few pieces by title in the original book. But I wanted to place her in situations where a composition would enter her psyche and shape a scene with either the emotional drive of the piece or the context of its libretto. A copy of *100 Great Operas and Their Stories: Act-By-Act Synopses* by Henry W. Simon sat on my writing desk for frequent reference to find the right piece for a scene.

Further, where did her passion begin? While I have zero ability or background in music, I know a thing or two about parents guiding (forcing?) their kids to pursue the same interests they had as a child. I grew up watching my brothers play hockey. When my first son was born, I couldn't wait to get him into skates and onto the ice. Perhaps Josephine's mother loved opera, and someone thwarted her dreams to study and perform? Perhaps Josephine traveled to Berlin, and stayed there in honor of her mother's dreams?

One major addition in this fictionalized version is Josephine's association with Natalya Duysen. She became friendly with a Red Cross nurse of Russian background (named Olga Duysen, which I changed to Natalya to avoid any confusion to Olga Povitsky in my other books, *The Unlocked Path* and *The Path Beneath Her*

Feet). To add intrigue to the story and as many of my beta readers insisted, I inferred Natalya was a Russian spy and Josephine assisted her, leading to her detainment after her time in Bad Elster.

A few other clarifications to keep you out of the rabbit hole of Google research. Christiania, Norway, became Oslo in 1925. The 1917 explosion in Halifax happened, and Boston medical personnel were the first from the United States to arrive and provide aid. Civilian travel during World War I was difficult, especially into and out of Germany. All the documents, inspections, and processes Josephine went through were typical of the times. There's no mention of their checking her body for invisible ink, but she mentioned it was done to others. The train scene with the man who was taking his wife to the asylum came from an account detailed in *An English Wife in Berlin* by Evelyn, Princess Blücher. She also lived in Berlin during World War I, English by birth and married to Prussian nobility. Her memoir echoes many of the same sentiments and observations as Josephine's about the German people, the overbearing adherence to militarism, and the unwavering use of propaganda. Josephine's delayed departure was real. I found newspaper articles about the *Bergensfjörd* and the capture of a German who had boarded with ammunition and instructions of how to build an airplane.

The Overture, Intermission, and Finale are one hundred percent my additions, as is the introduction made by Mr. Toth, the American consulate officer in Norway. I don't know how my grandfather came to write Josephine's story, except he had ghostwritten William Wellman's memoir through Page Publishing in early 1918. Perhaps Page assigned him the project.

I know what became of Eliot Robinson. He went to France with the American Expeditionary Forces. He returned, separated from my grandmother and left my father and uncle at the ages of five and seven, wrote seven novels (sappy romances, in my opinion), served as a secretary to a Massachusetts congressman in Washington, divorced my grandmother in 1936, married his longtime paramour, a lawyer, Helen Bradlee, and died of cirrhosis of the liver in 1942 at fifty-eight. From this information, those of you who have read *The Unlocked Path* or *The Path Beneath Her Feet* may recognize the inspiration for Harrison Shaw.

But what about Josephine? Beyond marrying the accomplished pianist, Josef Bonime, in 1919, I found no further information about continuing with her opera instruction or performance. Her 1936 naturalization application lists "Housewife" as her occupation with two children, Leopold and Elaine, living at home on West End Avenue in New York City. Perhaps her thirteen months in Germany and her trials to get home changed her. Today, we'd wonder if she suffered from PTSD. It wouldn't surprise me if she did. Yet, I applaud her for telling her story in 1918 and revealing the widespread use of German propaganda to manipulate its people and the conditions they endured in the name of the Fatherland. One hundred and eight years later, I hope this retelling of her story reaches more people to honor the extraordinary experiences of a young woman from Boston living under two flags during World War I.

If you have a specific question about what was fact and what is fiction, which I haven't addressed, drop me a note. You can contact me through my website, www.janisrdaly.com/contact/.

ACKNOWLEDGMENTS

I have gone by the name Janis R. Daly for nearly forty years. However, I knew I would use my full name, Janis Robinson Daly, when I embarked on writing historical fiction with my debut novel, *The Unlocked Path*. Just as I assumed Josephine's interest and vocal talents as an opera singer originated from her mother, maybe I inherited my passion and abilities in creative writing from my grandfather, Eliot H. Robinson, Sr. As my mother used to say, one of her greatest disappointments was that she never met him—a modern-day Renaissance man. He passed away months before my parents met in 1943. Shortly after publishing his first novel, *Man Proposes*, in 1916 at the age of thirty-one, a profile in *The Boston Sunday Post* described him as, "He does a little of everything and does everything well. He's a jack of all trades and master of most of them...a contagious smile, talks straight from the shoulder and generally has something to say worth listening to...most likable fellow, more than ordinarily hospitable. Most of his literary work is done at home, in front of the big open fireplace, flanked by row upon row of his favorite authors." I wish I had met him too. At the very least, I would honor this man for passing on some of those genes by including Robinson in my author byline. Thank you as well to the rest of my Robinson and Daly families, who have supported me from day one, when I opened a blank document and began writing about the Woman's Medical College of Pennsylvania. All of those men—my brothers, my husband, and my sons—encourage me to keep looking for and finding the women in history whose stories need to be pulled from the shadows.

To learn and write about opera, an art form of which I had zero knowledge, and to present those scenes with authenticity, thank you to Jessica Bloch-Moisand, who answered my inquiry requesting help with research. Jessica is the Interim Artistic

Director of MassOpera and a member of the Voice Faculty at the New England Conservatory. Beyond my interview with Jessica, she also invited me to meet one of her students, fourteen-year-old Madison. What a treat to watch the instruction and guidance of a beautiful talent as she practiced an aria by the Dew Fairy in *Hansel and Gretel*. I played and replayed my video of Madison as I wrote Josephine's scene at her first class at the *Konservatorium*. Special thanks goes out to Harlie Sponaugle, a member of my Women's Fiction Writers Association's Historical Fiction group, for beta reading. Harlie is not only a published historical fiction author (*The Pharaoh's Dark Garden*), but is also a classically trained soprano. Harlie corrected many of my opera piece references, indicating they would not be appropriate or attainable for Josephine as a young mezzo-soprano. Also from my WFWA Hist Fic group, thank you to Colleen Adair Fliedner, who wrote about World War I in her novel, *In the Shadow of War: Spies, Love & the Lusitania*. Colleen provided many notes on spots where I could expand on a few of the historical events and their impact on Josephine.

As I don't speak German, who better to read my manuscript than Christina Malter McComiskie, whose email address includes "berlinerchick"? Yes, Christina grew up in Berlin. She made corrections on my Google translations and will join the blog tour for *Under Two Flags*. Don't always take Google's word for anything! My good friend and fellow Black Rose Writing author, Linda Rosen (*Abandoning the Script*) was instrumental in double-checking my inclusion of Jewish practices and prayers. I learned from Linda that whether the character speaks Yiddish or Hebrew determines the spelling of certain words. With German and Polish heritage, Josephine's family would have used the Yiddish forms. Thank you to Linda Kirwin for taking me on as a new client to help me edit and polish the retelling of Josephine's story. I think the polish shines. A heartfelt thank you to reader Deb Kiley, who researched my historical facts and assisted with asking the questions that I need to answer in my Author's Notes. I cannot express how thankful I am for the assistance I received from fellow Black Rose Writing author Pamela Taylor who allowed me to enjoy my trip to France while she navigated the dreaded proofreading stage. I promise, Pam, I will learn the correct usage of that vs. which before my next book.

To beta readers extraordinaire, who have read all three of my books and each time identified where I need to probe deeper and write with more passion: Ashley E. Sweeney and Dennis Blackmon, you are my heroes, writing champions, and friends. Thank you for the time you take away from your own writing to help me continue to learn and develop as a writer. I think the three of us need to meet up someday over a glass of Writer's Tears whisky. Where's a central point for Massachusetts, Washington state and Georgia?

Thank you again to Black Rose Writing, led by Reagan Rothe. They have built an incredible community for their authors. I am grateful for their professionalism and belief in my stories. The concept of literary citizenship is alive and kicking within our BRW family to support one another.

Finally, to the other historical fiction authors who so kindly took time out of their busy schedules to read my novel and provide words of encouragement and endorsement—thank you Kate Quinn, Penny Haw, Eliza Knight, and Martha Hall Kelly. And thank you for all that you have written to elevate and celebrate the stories of women in history.

READING GROUP DISCUSSION QUESTIONS

On the author's website (www.janisrdaly.com/book-clubs) you can find the following questions plus a more complete book club kit, including recipes for dishes and a playlist of operatic pieces mentioned in the book. Daly is also available to join book clubs for an author chat, in person or over Zoom. Contact her through her website.

1. Over the past 10 to 15 years, much has been written in historical fiction about World War II. *Under Two Flags* occurs during World War I. How much did you know about the war that was known as the Great War? Had you ever heard about the origins of the association between poppies and WWI, the *Lusitania's* sinking, the explosion in Halifax, or Black Tom Island among other historical events referenced in the book? Why do you think there have been more WWII novels released compared to WWI?
2. The author credits her grandfather for an interest in novel writing and a creative writing "gene." In the book, she presents Josephine's passion for opera singing as influenced by her mother, Ricka Meyers Marzynski. Do you think that presentation is plausible? Do you have a passion or interest that you think was "passed down" from an ancestor?
3. *Under Two Flags* is a retelling of the memoir, *With Old Glory in Berlin*. Other recent popular novels have also used this strategy.
    - *The Frozen River / A Midwife's Tale: The Life of Martha Ballard, Based on Her Diary*
    - *James / The Adventures of Huckleberry Finn*
    - *Demon Copperhead / David Copperfield*

- *Hello Beautiful / Little Women*
What responsibilities should an author take with the original story when they rewrite or retell it?
4. In the original book, Josephine Marzynski never mentions she is Jewish. Why do you think she omitted any reference to Judaism? Do you think its inclusion in the retelling enhanced Josephine's character?
5. Have you ever attended an opera performance? What is your favorite opera or aria?
6. Did you trust Josephine as a narrator, or did you consider her unreliable at any point?
7. If you had seen only the two titles presented as book options, which one would have enticed you to pick up the book? *With Old Glory in Berlin* or *Under Two Flags*? Which one better reflects the book's content?
8. After reading the Author's Notes, are you curious to learn more about Josephine's life after she returns home? Would you read a sequel, even if it was highly fictionalized?
9. What do you think happens or would want to happen to other characters—Herr and Frau Müller, Cousin Jack, Gustav von Lüben, or any of Josephine's friends—after the story ends?

ABOUT THE AUTHOR

Janis Robinson Daly. Reading, Discussing, Researching, Writing Books. Splitting her time between Cape Cod, New Hampshire, and snowbird destinations, Daly finds a spot for reading and writing wherever she might land. Inspired by the discovery that an ancestor founded the Woman's Medical College of PA, Daly's first two books honor the work of pioneering women in medicine. Her third book, *Under Two Flags* is a retelling of a memoir from World War I originally ghostwritten by Daly's grandfather, Eliot H. Robinson, Sr.

Daly graduated from Wheaton College, Norton, MA, at the time a women's college, where she developed a keen appreciation of female-centric issues. Her annual literary citizenship program, #31titleswomeninhistory, has gained recognition from historical fiction authors and avid readers as an innovative way to celebrate Women's History Month in March. She is an active member and moderator for four book clubs and offers author chats to clubs that read her books. Daly has become a sought-after speaker for women's groups, local libraries, and national associations.

To learn more, connect with author Janis Robinson Daly at:
- www.janisrdaly.com
- www.janisrdaly.com/newsletter/
- @JanisRobinsonDalyAuthor on Facebook
- @janisrdaly_writer on Instagram
- Subscribe to her monthly newsletter for other timely information, book giveaways, book reviews, forthcoming novels, and upcoming events: www.janisrdaly.com/newsletter/.

OTHER TITLES BY JANIS ROBINSON DALY

THE UNLOCKED PATH

#1 New Release for US History on Amazon, Finalist, 2023 Goethe Awards, Late Historical Fiction: Chanticleer International Book Awards, Honorable Mention for General Fiction from the New England Book Festival Awards

THE PATH BENEATH HER FEET

#1 New Release for US History on Amazon, First Place Winner, 2025 Goethe Awards, Late Historical Fiction: Chanticleer International, Honorable Mention for General Fiction from the New England Book Festival Awards

Note from Janis Robinson Daly

Word-of-mouth is crucial for any author to succeed. If you enjoyed *Under Two Flags*, please leave a review online—anywhere you are able. Even if it's just a sentence or two. It would make all the difference and would be very much appreciated.

Thanks!
Janis Robinson Daly

We hope you enjoyed reading this title from:

www.blackrosewriting.com

Subscribe to our mailing list – *The Rosevine* – and receive **FREE** books, daily deals, and stay current with news about upcoming releases and our hottest authors.
Scan the QR code below to sign up.

Already a subscriber? Please accept a sincere thank you for being a fan of Black Rose Writing authors.

View other Black Rose Writing titles at www.blackrosewriting.com/books and use promo code **PRINT** to receive a **20% discount** when purchasing.

www.ingramcontent.com/pod-product-compliance
Lightning Source LLC
LaVergne TN
LVHW041623060526
838200LV00040B/1406